BACKWATER, FLORIDA

KAY DEW SHOSTAK

Kay Dew Shostak

To Becky~
Go Dawgs~!
Kay

August South
PUBLISHING

ISBN: 978-0-9962430-8-7

Library of Congress Control Number: 2017901099

FICTION: Women's Fiction / Small Town / Florida / Beach / Contemporary Women / Georgia

Text Layout and Cover Design by Roseanna White Designs
Cover Images from www.Shutterstock.com

Published by August South Publishing. You may contact the publisher at:
AugustSouthPublisher@gmail.com

To Louisa May Alcott

1

Strips of sunlight try to pierce the darkness, but the little damage they do isn't what stirred me awake. Voices. Men's voices right outside the window. Pulling the covers around me to make sure I'm covered doesn't help me figure out where I am. I never sleep with my room this dark. My room at Momma's and Daddy's doesn't even have curtains, and Caleb hates a dark room so we—

And it all comes back. There in the strip of sunlight are puddles of black clothes. A pair of hose, scuffed black heels, the stiff blazer I had dry cleaned just last week, and my borrowed black dress. Through scrunched, puffy eyes, I look around to make sure no one can see me. I drop the covers and pick up the dress from the floor. My underwear and bra are here somewhere, but for now this is good enough, and I tiptoe into the bathroom to get dressed, or at least covered.

The voices aren't clear enough for me to hear what they are saying, but they don't seem to mind me knowing they are right there. Right outside the window. Intense Florida sunshine shocks me when I open the bathroom blinds. It's like a spotlight trained on the window, so I quickly turn away and make my way to the bedroom door.

"Oh my word, this place is huge!" rings in my head, and out my mouth. In last night's dark at 3 a.m., I just stumbled from the car after my five-hour drive and, without turning on a light, found the bathroom and a bed. Now I see that I own a mansion. More of that sunshine floods the living room, and the glossy expanse of—*is that marble?*—spreads out, reflecting the light around the empty room.

"Hey, there she is!" a woman yells as she begins to bang on the glass doors to my right. My cousin's dress isn't thin, but I hold it close to my body so the woman, and now her crowd of friends, can't see I'm naked underneath it.

"I'm coming." Dirty glass doors are hung with cobwebs, which I brush away before I unlock and then turn the door knob. Four women with visors or hats pulled low against the sunlight wait on the outside, and all of them have their arms crossed. My head is the only part of me I allow to cross the threshold.

"Yes?"

"Who are you? How did you get in there?" a lady wearing turquoise Capri pants and holding a little dog demands. Her visor is white and has gold writing on it I can't make out. Too sparkly.

Ms. Orange Floppy Hat steps closer to me and pushes on the door. "Come out here, right now, young lady."

So, I step out. Some because she called me a "young" lady, but mostly because somehow a clone of my fifth grade teacher, Mrs. Montgomery, is wearing an orange hat and standing at my door. A clone in both looks and bossy attitude.

Barefooted and arms clasped around me, I stand in the middle of the hat-wearing ladies and see where the men's voices were coming from. Gathered around a table between the house and the pool (*oh my lord, I have a pool*) are six old men playing cards.

One of the men unfolds himself from his chair and shields his eyes with his hand. "Your car tags are from Georgia. Are you from Georgia?"

"What's your name?" demands the lady in the orange hat, which flops dramatically as she practically shouts at me.

Again, conditioned to respond to teachers, I answer. "Rebecca Sue Mason."

Another man rears back from the table to look at me. "Like Caleb Mason? Are you saying you are related to Caleb Mason?"

Groans, mumbled curse words, and maybe even some spitting from the one dark-haired lady, accompanies Caleb's name.

Stubbornness I get from Daddy's side makes me stick out my chin. "I might be. Why?"

The tall man walks toward me and then holds out his hand. "Dr. Eason King. Rebecca, are you here to help us?"

Quickly I shake his hand, and then tuck my hand back where it came from. "Help you do what? And, can I ask why y'all are here?"

"It's our club house," another man at the table answers. "Mason Developments promised us a club house, and now that you're here with a key, we can use the house and not just the pool."

"This pool? This house?" My head begins to throb a bit. I shake it to loosen the throbs and summon up some of that disappearing stubbornness. "But this is my house."

The short, dark-haired lady pushes in front of her friends. Her hair is black and in a long braid. She has on all white, bright red lipstick, a small straw hat, and big sunglasses. "So you *are* related to Caleb Mason." She grabs her sunglasses and points them at me. "Is he in there? Right now, is that rat in there?" She reaches for the door, but Dr. King stops her.

"Esmerelda, stop right there. Let's let Rebecca tell us what she's doing here and why she thinks this is her house."

"I think it's my house because I signed papers on it before the funeral yesterday. Because I have a key to it and because, well, that's what the lawyer said."

"Funeral? Who died?" the Mrs. Montgomery clone asks through clenched teeth.

My hands drop to my side, and my head lifts. "The rat."

"Caleb is dead?" Now all the men are standing, and the women have taken a step back from me. The lady with the dog shifts her arms to place a hand on my shoulder. "Did he commit suicide?"

I jerk away from her hand. "Suicide? No! It was a car wreck. Why do you think he'd commit suicide?" Looking at them, I see sideways looks and shifting eyes that tell me some of them want to ask if his car ran into a bridge embankment. "A car ran into him. It wasn't suicide." No one apologizes; there's just a shrug or two and a lowering of defenses.

The bald man lifts a hat off the table and jams it onto his head. "Well, folks, we are totally and royally screwed now. I'm going home for a drink."

The tall Mrs. Montgomery clone is sniffling, and one of the men comes up and pats her arm as they head off to the side of the house. Soon there's only three of us left: Dr. King, the lady in turquoise holding the little dog, and me.

The woman holds her hand out to me. "Ruth King." I touch her fingers with mine, but quickly so she can't feel how cold my hands are. The sunlight I'm standing in must be warm, but it doesn't feel warm. I'm freezing.

"Ladies, let's sit down. Rebecca, here, sit in the sun and relax. It's all going to be fine."

I can see from the way the doctor keeps looking at his wife he knows I'm not doing so good, and they just sit quietly for a minute and wait for me to stop shaking. Mrs. King gets up and goes into the house. When she comes back, she has a paper cup of water.

"No dishes, but I did find a stack of these cups in the kitchen. Must've been for the sales staff. I guess there's no need for dishes in a model home."

After a sip of water and another deep breath, I feel better. "Model home?"

Dr. King shakes his head. "You don't know anything about this situation, do you?"

My tiny head shake causes him to sigh. "Okay. How are you related to Caleb?"

"We were married." A part of me wants to close my eyes, so I don't see what I've watched happen for the past ten years. First a smile, not an "Oh, that's nice" smile, but a "You're joking, right?" smile. Then a shake of the head followed by a shot of sympathy for the poor delusional girl. And finally, as the person truly remembers what they know about Caleb, a look of "Wait, really?"

"The rat," slips out of Mrs. King's mouth, and the doctor gets those thin lips good men get when they can't say what they want to say.

Now, my part, rehearsed for a decade. "It's not like that. We really are in love. He is, I mean..." Tears choke me for a minute. "He *was* the love of my life. I don't care what you say or what you think or..." anger and grief raise my voice "...or what he did."

Dr. King leans forward on the table. "So you know what he did?"

"Of course I know. She's having his baby, for crying out loud."

Both of them sit back at that, and after a moment, Mrs. King reaches out to touch my arm. "Rebecca. What do you know about this house?" She lifts her hand off my arm to wave at our surroundings.

"Only that the lawyer said I could have it if I signed over the house in Piney and everything else. I couldn't take the house in Piney away from Audrey and the kids and the baby, and besides, there's nothing left for me in Piney. I'm going to start over here."

Mrs. King looks at the doctor, but he just closes his eyes and speaks quietly. "So you're the owner now. Let me guess, the lawyer is Jameson Mason."

His presumption startles me. "Yep, Jameson took care of everything."

2

"That poor girl." Ruth King pushes open the white gate. "Now, Ruth, don't get all emotional about this. She's not exactly a girl, you know."

"How old do you think she is?"

Making sure the gate is latched behind them, he turns and shrugs. "Thirty?"

"Yes, that's what I was thinking. Younger than our boys and definitely without the benefit of any real education. Poor thing."

Dr. King touches his wife's back. "Okay, here they all come. What should we tell them?"

The group from the pool had grown by a few, and they all now came straggling off the shaded front porch of Esmeralda's home.

The short, fiery woman with the dark braid and red lips waves at the couple from her front steps. "Ruth, Eason. I've made some lemonade. Come have a glass."

Anticipation hangs around the small crowd, but it leaks away as the Kings ease down in the just-vacated rocking chairs. When they sigh, the sigh echoes around the room, person to person, as the last dregs of hope fade away.

"She as simple as she seemed?" the bald man asks, his hat wadded up in his hand.

"John," Dr. King admonishes. "You practiced psychiatry for forty years. You know people are rarely 'simple.'" A long pause goes uninterrupted until Dr. King finally nods. "But yes, she's rather, uh, she seems rather uncomplicated."

"And she really is the sole owner now?"

"Appears so. We got a look at the papers she signed, and they look tight. Magnus, you'll want to look them over and see if your legal eyes can spot anything fishy. However, as we've discovered, Jameson Mason doesn't leave a lot of loopholes."

"Can we sue her?" Magnus asks.

"For what? According to her, this is all she owns."

"But what about the rest of Mason's estate? He's worth millions, right?" Esmerelda declares with a flourish of the glass in her hand.

Eason King reaches for his wife's hand. "You tell them, honey."

"From what we can tell it's tied up now in a trust. He has two children from a previous marriage, and his girlfriend is pregnant. Rebecca, or Becca Sue, as we've been told to call her, signed over everything to the children. She just wanted to get out of town. She has no idea of all the holdings and doesn't even care. She just wanted the house in Florida. Which she didn't even know existed until Jameson told her right before the funeral."

"Are we sure he's dead?" pipes a voice from the other end of the porch. "Maybe he read my third book and faked his death to get out from under everything." Heads swivel from the small, neat author sitting in his wheelchair deep in the shade, to the Kings in their rocking chairs. A faint bit of hope circles, then dies with the words, "Open casket funeral."

"What did she say when you told her the situation here?" Magnus rumbles, "Did she understand?"

The Kings look at each other and then at their neighbors. Eason answers for them both, "No. She doesn't understand."

3

They don't think I understand. Hot water from the faucet drips on my toes, so I submerge them under the silvery water. This tub may just ruin me for plain ol' tubs. Especially ones with rust stains and mold in the corners, like in Momma and Daddy's trailer. I hated to take a shower there, much less even think about taking a bath.

The back of the huge tub slants perfectly for laying my head back, and I can stretch my feet all the way out. No knees sticking up or getting a crick in my neck when I try to read. And there's a whole deep shelf, for candles and stuff I reckon, where I could lay my book.

When I close my eyes, I can pretend there are lit candles, music, and big, fluffy towels. With my eyes open I see un-curtained windows, bare floors, and walls, and my old faded beach towel waded up on the toilet seat. Next to the toilet is a stack of McDonald's napkins I found in the glove compart-ment of my car. Guess toilet paper should be the first item on my grocery list.

Imagine Caleb owning this beautiful house down here and never even telling me about it. Of course, he didn't tell me a lot of stuff. Most of it I knew, like him and Audrey. Him and Kimmy. Him and Janet. But it was a surprise when Audrey turned up pregnant, even bigger of a surprise when her daddy offered Caleb his farm to divorce me and marry his little girl. Oh, well, Caleb always knew a good deal, and besides, what was he going to get out of my daddy? A case of beer? Shoot, like my daddy would give up a case of beer to help me. And my babysitting job was about to end with Cab and Maggie grown up now.

Poor babies. The funeral was hard on them, what with Audrey being the center of attention now. Her and her big old belly full of Caleb's baby. Audrey's momma causing such a scene, and her brother sitting right up there on the front row.

No wonder Caleb's first wife Margaret didn't show up for the funeral, although she would have had her kids to sit with. I drag my hand through the water and mentally add bubble bath to my grocery list. Margaret had a business meeting in Hong Kong or somewhere else important, and as she was only the first ex-wife, she didn't feel she had to attend. That might've been smart; all being an ex-wife got me was a seat on the third row, where I had to watch Audrey squirm, rub her belly, and flip her blond hair around. At least Cab and Maggie were in front of me, and I could pat them on their backs. They seemed mad at me, though. Guess I did something to piss them off, too. Why not?

Momma said she wasn't coming to the funeral to witness once again what a failure I had turned my life into. Funny, for someone in whom no one placed any expectation, I sure have disappointed a lot of folks.

And now I've disappointed all these folks here. Well, they all look like they've got enough money to take care of themselves. So, Caleb left them high and dry with their big old mansions. So, they don't have no clubhouse or pool. So, they've got to deal with weeds and no landscaped entrance. So, they can't sell their houses. I look around the high-ceilinged bathroom with the tall, frosted window and the chandelier hanging above the round tub. Why would you sell a house like this anyway?

Holding my breath, I sink below the water.

I've never been happier in my life.

4

"We've put together some things to help you get settled in," Ruth King says as she holds out the bags in her hands.

"Wow! Thanks. Here, come on in." Becca Sue holds open the door, and Ruth enters followed by two other women. Country music blares from the boom box sitting in the middle of the bare living room.

The tall woman takes off her orange, floppy hat and places it on the kitchen counter next to the box she'd carried in. She raises her voice. "I don't think we exchanged names this morning." She holds her hand out. "I'm Pearl. Pearl Manningham."

"Hey, Miss Pearl. I said I was Rebecca Sue this morning, but please call me Becca Sue. You know, you remind me of my fifth grade teacher, Mrs. Montgomery. She sure scared me to death."

Becca Sue turns to the third woman and sticks out her hand. "Hi, I'm Becca Sue. You weren't here this morning, were you?"

The small, white-haired lady takes Becca Sue's thin, hand into both of hers and looks up into Becca Sue's dark brown eyes. Her words can't be heard over the music, but Becca Sue listens anyway, and tears come to her eyes as she nods. "You don't look nothing like my Granny, but you sure do make me think of her. Let me turn that music down. The only chairs are those outside," she yells over the music as she leaves the foyer and walks into the big living area with its wall of windows and doors. When the music dies down, Becca yells again, "I'll bring in some of the chairs. C'mon in here."

Pearl offers to help, but Becca turns her down. "Naw, I ain't always been this scrawny. I'm real strong. Something about finding out Caleb was having a baby with that Audrey just made me stop eating. Now none of my clothes fit. Had to borrow a dress from my cousin to wear to my own husband's funeral. Can you beat that?"

Sitting down, Ruth laughs a bit at Pearl's horrified expression. "No, Becca Sue, I don't believe I can."

With the four patio chairs facing each other in a square, Becca Sue finally sits down and crosses her bare feet and legs up in the chair. "Didn't see no sense in going out and buying a dress to wear for a couple hours. As long as I got shorts and tank tops, I'm set for living in Florida, right?"

Pearl jumps for the opening. "So you plan on living here? For good?"

Pale shoulders, with only a small strap of a lime green tank top crossing them, shrug. "I guess. Nowhere else to go."

"Sweetheart," the white haired woman whispers, "what about your family?"

"Oh, well, I've got lots of that. Piney is full of people related to me, but most of them don't really... well. It's hard to explain. You know how family can be, right? Aren't there parts of your family you can't make sense of?" She looks in each woman's face, and they find themselves nodding. "Now, ma'am, what is your name? I missed it earlier with the music and all."

"Mrs. Bell," the older woman says. "I live on the other side of the empty lot next to your home here." Her soft voice matches a softness in her face. "My husband and I were the first to buy from your Caleb, but Mr. Bell never made it here to live. It's just me in that big old house."

Ruth reached out to pat the older woman's arm. "Mrs. Bell welcomed us all here, and when we realized we were all that would be living here, she helped us get to know each other."

"Shoot, these houses are beautiful. Why wouldn't folks build more here? I bet everyone would want to live here."

Pearl tsks and shakes her short, grayish-brown hair. "No. Amenities are all the rage for people living on Oyster Break. Plus, not knowing where one stands legally with your home is not attractive."

When Becca Sue leans forward, her damp hair falls into her eyes. As she pushes her brown curls back, she asks, "On? Do you mean *in* Oyster Break? Is that the name of the town here?"

"We live *on* Oyster Break. It's an island." Pearl can't keep her eyebrows from reaching for the sky, or the bite out of her words. "Didn't you know you were on an island?"

This time, as her head drops and her hair falls over her face, she leaves it there. "No."

Ruth cuts Pearl a look. "That's okay. How would you know? You crossed several bridges getting here. Anyway, we just wanted to welcome you to Oyster Break and to our little sub-division, such as it is. We put together some staples so you don't have to rush out to the store."

"Staples? Why would I need staples?" Becca Sue asks with another brush back of her hair.

A wheezy laugh comes from Mrs. Bell. "My dear, Mr. Bell would've loved you. You are such a breath of fresh air, sweetheart. By 'staples,' Mrs. King meant things you need every day."

"Oh, like toilet paper. I sure do hope there's toilet paper in there. Y'all are so sweet," Becca Sue shouts over her shoulder on her way to the kitchen.

By time the ladies join her, she's going through the box and bags, and spreading things all over the granite counter and huge kitchen island. "Oh my gosh! There's food in here. Milk, some eggs, and even toilet paper. Why would you do all this for me?" Holding a small frying pan up to her chest, she turns to stare at the ladies. "I just can't believe all this."

Embarrassment at the young woman's emotions steals Ruth's and Pearl's words from their lips. They watch as Becca

Sue yanks open the huge steel refrigerator and puts the milk and eggs on the bare shelves. "Back in Piney, no one liked me going into the kitchen. Caleb said that was what the help was for. And at Momma and Daddy's I wasn't allowed to fill up their fridge with my junk. But this is all mine." Closing the door, she leans against the big cold slab of gray metal. "All mine. Right?"

Ruth and Pearl look to each other because they don't know how Becca Sue can possibly think she can keep the huge house, but Mrs. Bell shuffles up to her. "Of course it is, sweetheart. Of course it is."

They wait on the steps outside until the heavy wood door inlaid with beveled glass shuts behind them, and then Pearl and Ruth both admonish Mrs. Bell.

"She can't possibly afford to maintain that house."

"Can she even buy groceries?"

"Mrs. Bell, you shouldn't have encouraged her like that."

In the hot mid-morning sun, they slowly walk past the vacant, weed-filled lot between Mrs. Bell's house and Becca Sue's. They walk in the street because the sidewalk wasn't completed on the lots not yet sold. Across the street is a barbed wire fence where the land was leased to a local farmer. Land set aside for development is taxed at a much higher rate than farmland, so acres of undeveloped land across Florida were turned back into cattle pasture when the housing boom went bust. Cows now claimed some of the most exclusive property in the Sunshine State, and there was nothing their unhappy neighbors could do about it.

Ignoring the wafting fragrance of the cow pasture, the ladies turn up Mrs. Bell's concrete drive. When she pushes the front door, much like the heavy glass and oak one they just left, a shot of air conditioning greets the ladies. "Thanks for coming to get me to go visit Becca Sue." Mrs. Bell holds onto the front doorway for support. "You know my biggest concern when Mr. Bell wanted to buy in this neighborhood was it being just for people over fifty-five. I like young people, and I think I'm going to like her. Now, I'm worn out and need to sit down. You ladies have a nice afternoon." Mrs. Bell closes the door, and they listen to make sure she locked it behind her. Everyone worried about her being so near the neighborhood entrance, especially since the idea of it being a guarded community was long gone with the wind.

Back at the street the women walk and try to not feel down. Weed-filled lots, barbed wire, mosquito-breeding puddles, unfinished roads, and decorative light posts with no lights on top greet their every step.

Pearl sighs. "It's like we're on an island on an island. Kind of like the 'Island of Misfit Toys from *Rudolph.*'"

Ruth joins with her own sigh. "And Becca Sue Mason sure isn't Santa Claus."

5

With a heave, the black suitcase I took from Caleb's attic lands on the bare mattress of my new bedroom. Being so tired last night, I didn't even realize there weren't sheets on the bed, just a bedspread and some decorative pillows. Guess that's what Miss Ruth meant by it being a 'model' home. Just has to look good. Jameson did tell me there wasn't any furniture but the bed.

"And I can't keep dragging the outside chairs inside. Hope there's a Goodwill store around here," I say as I look around the room for somewhere to put my underwear. Then I just drop them back into the suitcase and pull the suitcase off the bed to sit, propped open between the windows. Even looking out the dirty window, the pool looks good. Wonder if Caleb thought we might move down here?

Just thinking something good about Caleb causes Momma's voice to ring in my head. "Of course he wasn't going to move down here with you! Look at you!"

"Yeah, Momma, look at me." I step to the bathroom door and the wide mirror shows the skinny girl Caleb deserved. But he's not here and what's the use in looking good if Caleb ain't here to see it?

My cutoff shorts and tank top look tiny to me. It's the first time since I was fourteen I haven't worn a bra. Funny, when you're fat and your boobs bounce, no one thinks it looks good. If you're skinny, bouncing boobs are just fine. Caleb loved all my bouncy parts that summer back so long ago when we fell in love.

He didn't look twice at me when I waited on him at the Short Stop. He'd just bought a case of cold beer and was leaving when the back dumpster caught on fire. He jumped out of his truck, grabbed the water hose, and shot water on it, while I called the fire department. Once the firemen got the fire out, they shut down the store and told me to go home since no one could get hold of the owner. When I started off walking home, Caleb offered me a ride. He'd had quite a few beers while he watched the firemen, so I thought I should go along to make sure he was okay to drive. Besides, sitting in the truck next to Caleb Mason was the closest I was ever going to get to being somebody.

"Your truck is really nice."

"Thanks. Figured if I was coming back to live here, I'd need a truck."

"So you're back for good?" This was a question everyone in Piney had been asking since the spring, when suddenly Caleb Mason was spotted back in town. He hadn't been home for more than a night since he left for Georgia Tech ten years before.

"Looks like it. You want a beer?"

I pulled on the front of my tee shirt and sat up taller to hold my stomach in. If only someone could see me riding around with Caleb Mason. We were only going to be on back roads and nowhere near town. Course, I can tell people, but who's going to believe it? "Sure."

The beer might've been cold a half hour ago, but now it was kinda warm. The first sip reminded me of the sips Daddy would give me on Saturday afternoons sitting out on the front steps of the trailer. Momma would be at work and Daddy would be all easy to sit with, until it was time for him to go to the bar and meet up with his friends. Then Momma would come home and be mad because Daddy had left me alone. I never told her he only left when his buddy that worked with Momma at the Burger Shack called to say Momma had left. Daddy would say, "Becca Sue, you'll be fine here for a few minutes, but you know, if I stay until your Momma gets here, we'll have a big row and none of us want that, huh?"

I always wished he would take me with him.

The can in my hand is empty, and I'm not sure how that happened, but I toss it through the sliding window behind me and it smacks the truck bed and rattles around until it finds a place to rest.

"Girl, you sure drank that fast! I forgot that about country girls. Shoot, Margaret, was always so worried about gaining weight she quit drinking altogether."

Tugging again on my shirt, I turn some in the seat. "You know, we passed my road back a ways."

"You don't like riding around with me?" He looks over, and I expect to see that look boys and men get when they want you to do something you don't want to do, but instead he looks kinda sad. And he may be near thirty, but he's still so good-looking, it makes my stomach flop.

"Beats going home," I admit and take another can from the box on the seat between us. "So, Margaret. That your wife?"

"Not anymore. Got the papers today." He flicks his hand at the very papers laying across the dashboard. "That's why I'm not going home. Mother is going to be fit to be tied."

"Your mother?" I take a sip as I think of what to say. "She's so beautiful and classy."

"My mother is hell on wheels when she doesn't get her way. She would trade me for Margaret in a heartbeat." He finishes his beer and tosses the can over his shoulder into the truck bed to join mine.

"Well, maybe she's just thinking about the kids. Don't you have two little ones?"

He snorts a laugh. "Mother does not do children. Especially now that it's been proven they aren't tying us to the Worth family. Everyone here thinks we have money, but until you see the money up in the Northeast where Margaret is from, you haven't seen money."

Suddenly, the truck slows, and he wrenches the steering wheel to the right. We're now on a dirt road. Orange dust from the clay clouds around us, and I grab the door handle to hold on. Bouncing in the dirt ruts, headed to the creek. As I throw my second empty can in the back, I sneak a look at Caleb, and it looks like he might be crying. This stops my heart and makes my mouth actually drop open. I never imagined if you had money and looks and a good family, you ever cried. If I had money and looks and a good family, I sure wouldn't ever cry.

We stop when the dirt road stops at the creek's edge. Later in the summer, when the creek dries up, these roads connect on the other side and go to hunting blinds and old cabins, and you don't have to go all the way down to the bridge to cross. But now with the spring rains, the creek is full, and the roads end with just enough room to turn around. We sit for a minute, letting the dust die down.

Caleb turns off the engine. "This okay with you?" He doesn't look at me as he explains. "Neither of us want to go home. I want to keep drinking, and I shouldn't be driving."

My hand is on the door handle, and before I can think of anything to say, I pull up on it and the door opens. Dust settles around my feet as I drop from the high seat. Caleb opens his door, and I close mine. Sunlight bounces around the red clay and the fresh green grass. In only a few weeks the grass will be long, stringy, and dull green as the creek dries, but right now everything is fresh and soft. At the water's edge, I find a place to sit and kick off my shoes. My shorts are tight, and I try to pull my shirt to hide that the top snap won't stay snapped.

He sits the beer case on the ground beside me and then drops down with the grace and ease of an athlete. He unties his shoes, and I notice he's not wearing socks. Funny, but that, not the brand new truck, or the way he talks, reminds me how different we are. My daddy and my cousins would rather die than wear a pair of shoes without socks. I try to picture my daddy with his white legs in a pair of shorts and those dock shoes, and I start laughing. Crazy laughing. Laughing where you're out of breath, laying-down-to-breathe laughing. And I can't even figure out a way to tell Caleb, 'cause he won't understand. Won't understand how wearing shorts is out of the question for my Daddy and the farm boys around Piney. How having a farmer's tan from wearing short sleeves out on the tractor is a thing of pride, not a joke. How even the pink stripe in his shirt is too much pink, and wearing a collared shirt on a Saturday means you must be going to the doctor. The big doctor, the one at the hospital. He looks like an ad you'd see on TV, sitting there with his tanned legs, long-sleeved, button shirt and those flat little shoes.

When I think of how I look, my laughing stops as suddenly as it started.

Screw it. Who cares what I look like? This is just a weird thing that's happened and will never happen again. I pull the rubber band off my hair and shake out the curls that should have been washed before I went to work today, and then I pop the top on another beer.

6

"There's no reason at all to change our schedule. Her being here doesn't mean anything unless we let it. We do water aerobics at four every day." Pearl however ends her statement by yoo-hooing across the gate before she unlatches it. "Rebecca? Are you there?"

The ladies are inside the fence, before they notice their hostess laid out in the chaise lounge with white earbuds in and her eyes hidden behind sunglasses.

Huddled together between the pool and the gate, they wonder what to do. Pearl's repeated calls are going unheeded.

"No wonder," Ruth says. "I can hear the music all the way over here. Pearl, go shake her."

"Me? Why me? You go wake her up." Pearl sinks her hands into the pockets of her terrycloth cover-up.

Esmeralda huffs. "What is she thinking lying out in this sun? Don't they know about skin cancer in that backwater town she came from?"

A sigh from behind them breaks their concentration and they look behind them. The orangey-red hair, frizzed in a halo, circles around, wrinkled face that lights up in the afternoon sun. "Remember being that carefree?" A deeper sigh joins with, "Remember being that young? Coating yourself in baby oil and butter?"

"Oh, Marie, hush. She's not *that* young," Pearl admonishes, then growls, "Who's going to wake her up? Or are we just going to leave her there?"

A masculine voice pushes through the group. "I'll wake her up, although I'm not exactly against leaving her just lying there." He yells as he moves past the group, "Hey, honey, you got an audience of old biddies wishing they still looked like you." Magnus Llord walks through the gate and across the pavers. He stands over Becca Sue, reaches down, and pats her thigh.

"Magnus!" Ruth hisses. To the ladies, she adds under her breath, "He's such an imbecile."

"You want her woke up, right?" He pats her thigh again, but this time leaves his hand there. "Time to get up, sweetheart."

Becca Sue's eyes pop open, and she stretches her arms above her head, giving everyone a show of her thin body, only minimally covered in a bright pink, polyester bikini. "Hey, y'all. Mister, you need to get your hand back where it belongs," she says as she pulls both legs off the lounge on the side away from Magnus.

"Honey, just waking you up like the ladies asked." Magnus throws his towel off his shoulders and dives into the deep end of the pool.

Pearl sniffs. "We should've made the neighborhood requirements fifty-five and above *and married.*"

Becca Sue straightens up and adjusts her bathing suit bottoms. "He's not married?" Pursed lips and suspicious eyes meet her look. "What? I'm just asking. So, I guess y'all want to go swimming?"

"No, we're here to do your landscaping," Esmeralda grouses. "It's time for our water aerobics. We pay a lady from the Y, and she'll be here in a bit. We just wanted to come let you know."

"*He's* here for water aerobics?" Becca Sue asks, pointing at Magnus swimming laps along the far side of the pool.

"No," Ruth answers. "He's just here to be a bother to our instructor Jane, and he stays in the deep end once we start. By this time in the afternoon, the shallow end is in the shade. We hope its okay with you that we are here."

Pearl shoves Ruth and whispers, "Don't ask for permission."

Becca Sue shrugs. "Fine with me since y'all take care of the pool, right? I don't know about any of that. Hey, and thanks again for the groceries and supplies. I went down to the Walmart and got other stuff. Like this bathing suit." She turns to show off her purchase. "I've never bought a bikini before. Isn't it awesome?"

"Well..." Ruth drags out. "You did also buy some sunscreen, right?"

"Of course. The good kind that smells like coconut. See?" As she walks toward them, brown spray bottle in hand, the ladies meet each other's rolling eyes.

Pearl explains, "Sunscreen, not tanning lotion. Look, you're probably already burning."

"Hey, y'all!"

At their water aerobics instructor's greeting, the ladies heave a sigh of relief and turn away from Becca Sue.

"Jane, come meet Becca Sue. She's, um, she's the, well, owner of this house," Esmeralda stammers as she takes a couple steps toward the gate where the instructor is coming in.

"Here, let me set my stuff down." Jane places her bag and two floats down next to the table, and extending her hand, walks toward Becca Sue. "Becca Sue, right? Hi, I'm Jane Simmons. Are you going to join our aerobics group?"

Jane's white cover-up floats behind her, and her one piece black swimsuit moves with her athletic body. Her hair, in the same type of bun as Becca Sue's, looks sleek and polished, and her tan makes the bright pink toenail polish at the end of her wedge sandals glow.

Two women the same age and same size could never look more different, and the women are not the only ones who noticed.

"Hick meets Chick," Magnus observes from the side of the pool where he hangs with arms folded on the side. He holds one hand up to shield his eyes for a better look, shakes his head, and pushes off into a lap of backstrokes.

Marie laughs at his statement until Pearl shoves her with her shoulder. "Stop it. That's not nice." Pearl adds under her breath, "True, but not nice."

Becca Sue no longer looks as tall as Jane, her shoulders caved forward and her back bent, as if bowed from thousands of such comparisons. Ignoring Jane's outstretched hand, Becca shuffles away. "Naw, not today. I've got to... got to go in." As she turns to the house, she shakes her head back and forth and picks up speed. "Bye, y'all."

"Poor girl," Ruth says as she takes off her terrycloth cover-up. "Poor girl."

Pearl begins the struggle of putting on a swimming cap, then abruptly declares, "I'm going to get that girl to join us." She pulls the flaps down over her ears and then folds them back up so she can hear. "Go ahead and start, if I'm not back out here when you're ready." She marches to the door of the house and without a pause flings open the French door. She hollers, "Becca Sue?"

Inside the house she's met with cool darkness. "Becca Sue? It's Pearl. Where are you? Seeing as there's no furniture out here, I'm assuming you're in the bedroom. I'm coming in." With a quick knock and a small pause, Pearl announces her entrance. "There you are. Scoot."

Becca Sue lies with her head flopped to one side—or so Pearl thinks, since her body is fully covered by a new duvet. "What do you want? I'm trying to take a nap."

"No you're not." Pearl perches on the edge of the bed. "Come out and do water aerobics with us. It's real easy and fun. Besides, you've already got on all your suntan lotion, right? And Jane's really nice."

Becca Sue's mass of dirt-colored hair pokes out first, and then her screwed-up face. "What's she doing here? Isn't everybody supposed to be old? Y'all said everyone was, like, over fifty-five or something."

Pearl shakes her head. "She doesn't live here. Why does it matter how old she is?"

Becca Sue flops over, away from Pearl. "It doesn't. I'm not

coming. I'm taking a nap."

Pearl stands up. "Okay, suit yourself. But you won't get any more fit or tanned or nicer, lying in this dark house in bed. You said I remind you of your fifth grade teacher? Well, good, just like you should've learned in fifth grade—stand up straight, look people in the eye, and smile."

Pearl grabs onto the door knob as she steps out the bedroom door. "And don't think just because you're younger than the rest of us that live here that you look that much better. I'm here to tell you, you don't!" Jerking on the door knob, she slams the heavy door and then marches across the living room grumbling to herself. Throwing open the French doors, she announces, "The princess is taking a nap!"

With the slamming of that door being even louder than the last one, it's debatable if anyone was actually sleeping.

7

White wings lift a big bird gently over the pond, skimming the weeds near the side, and then, with powerful strokes, it lifts up into the sky. Against the pink sky, the bird disappears. The moss hangs from the trees and dips into the water at the edge of the lake. There's no breeze and the humidity is heavy, so I pull my hair up and off my neck. As I straighten my legs and lean back in the pool chair I'd dragged to the back of the patio near the pond, the words leave my head and finally come out of my mouth.

"Why did I act like such a jerk?"

I drop my hair and reach for my red Solo cup of wine. The Walmart had a liquor store attached to it. Florida is really different, different in a good way when it comes to Walmart selling wine, but not so much in other ways. "Maybe I was just tired. Shoot, I slept all afternoon."

After a big gulp of wine, I pop a couple Ritz crackers piled up with spray cheese in my mouth. I take another drink, wipe my fingers on the towel I brought out with me, and lean my head back in the chair. Tears push up in my eyes. Why did I even begin to think I looked good? I know better. Sure, I'm not fat now, but I'll never be pretty. Too much like my daddy's side of the family. Momma always talked about how she knew the first minute she seen me I was going to be all like the Cousins family and none like her side. Everyone in Piney talked about how odd it was with us that the mother was prettier than the daughter.

My words ride on a sad sigh, "Except Caleb."

Caleb and I just had fun. Laughed and drank and rode around on the old backroads all summer long after we met. It was like living in a country song. Even the romantic parts—after we got to be good friends, we turned into lovers, and Caleb really, truly loved the real me. I don't care what people said.

And still say.

"Caleb Mason, what is this piece of white trash doing on my front porch?" Gloria Mason stood on the front porch of her huge house, staring down at me and her son. We'd had a picnic on the front porch, because it had rained all day, and then I guess we fell asleep. Caleb's folks weren't supposed to be home from their European cruise for another week. It probably didn't help we were all wrapped up in the white comforter from her bed. And nothing else.

And just like that, he saw me through his mother's eyes. And I saw me, too. For some reason I'd forgotten just what I looked like all summer. In Caleb's truck or swimming in the river or in his bed, I became Caleb Mason's girl, and we all know what Caleb Mason's girl looks like.

So first, I watched his surprise, as he saw me like his mother saw me, then the wave of horror as he remembered. I wasn't just his girl.

I was his wife.

"Hey there."

I bury my face in my towel to wipe away my tears, so I can turn around. The deep voice and the clinking of glasses tells me it's that old guy who always has a glass nearby, the one swimming here this afternoon. He fancies himself a playboy, I think.

"What do you want?" I ask, but change my mind about turning around, so I stare out at the lake.

"Just want to say, 'Hi.'" He stands in front of me and looks down at me over his sunglasses. "I brought some wine." His shirt is tan with small, green palm trees stitched all over it. His shorts are dark, and he's wearing those flat boat shoes Caleb was so fond of.

I pull my feet closer to my body, so I can hide the old neon green nail polish I've been picking off my toenails. "I already have some wine." I take a drink to show that I'm not just making it up. "Of course it's not in any fancy wine glass, but it works."

Another drink to emphasize how well my red Solo cup works is interrupted when he reaches down, lifts it to his mouth, and takes a swallow. "Well, by god, it does work doesn't it? Who would've ever imagined?"

Looking up, a laugh slips out before I can stop it. And with my laugh, his grin grows. "Here, hold this," he says as he sets the bottle beside my chair and hands me both the wine glasses and my cup. He moves over to the closest chair, lifts and carries it over to sit beside mine. "There." He sits, and then looks at me through the dark sunglasses, made even darker without the sun in the sky. "May I join you?"

"A little late to ask permission, isn't it? Besides, you sure you want to hang out with a 'hick'?"

He grimaces. "Oh, you heard that."

"Yeah, but screw it. I am a hick. Got the red Solo cup and the neon green nail polish to prove it." I toss back what's left in my cup and then toss it toward the lake. "So, you planning on opening up that bottle, or is it just a prop you carry around the neighborhood to pick up stray hicks?" I hold up both glasses, and he reaches down for the bottle.

With a smile, he unscrews the cork and pours hefty amounts in both glasses. With the top back in place, he sets the bottle on the patio and takes one of the glasses. He lifts his sunglasses to sit back on his head and leans toward my chair. As he clinks our glasses, he salutes the darkening sky. "To neighbors," he says.

After a sip, I relax, unfurling my legs and placing my feet on the patio. "Where do you live?"

"There, that kind of yellow house." He points across the lake to the left. "I was sitting on my screened porch when I saw you out here."

"Screened porch would be nice. The bugs are starting to come out."

"That is one thing that's good about it. Also, no one can see inside it, so you don't have to wear clothes."

I sit up. "You're making that up. You don't sit over there naked." I look at him. "Do you?"

That grin again. "Sometimes. You just never know."

"So your name, Magnum? Like that old Hawaiian show or the gun?"

"No, Magnus. Close though. Magnus Llord."

"And you're not married?"

This time he grins and cocks an eyebrow when he turns to me. "No, ma'am. Single. Divorced a couple times, but no current attachments."

We each take a couple drinks and I try to keep from asking more questions, but I can't help it. "So, why do you live here with all these people that are married? You don't fit in."

"Thank you, my dear," he says with a bow of his head. "You are so right. Two years ago, I had a scare with my heart and panicked. I retired from my law firm, sold my home, and bought this mausoleum for a ton of money, thinking I needed a quiet place to fish and read and die."

"Then you didn't die."

"Exactly. I didn't die, and now I, like everyone else here, am stuck. We all paid top dollar before the market crashed, and so we can't sell without losing our shirts, pants, and jock straps."

"But why did you choose here? Seems pretty dead to me."

He nods and bends down to pick up the bottle of wine. "At the time, I thought just being alive was more excitement than I could stand. Some of the folks here were friends up home and they talked like this place was paradise, so I bought it sight unseen. Here, hold this." He hands me his glass while he opens the bottle.

"Sight unseen. Kind of like me getting here."

He pours us both full glasses and nods. "Yeah, guess so. What *is* your story?"

"No," I say while shaking my head. "Not goin' to talk about poor, poor pitiful Becca Sue anymore. I left everything up in Piney. Everything. And that's that. Done."

"Fair enough." Magnus lies back in his chair, and when I look over I realize it's harder and harder to see him. I'd covered up with the towel, but I'm still keep swatting bugs away from the only skin I'd left exposed. "Why aren't the bugs biting you?"

"Lawyer blood."

We laugh, and he sits up straight in his chair. "Honestly, I sprayed myself down with poison before I walked over here. Bugs love me." He stands up. "I'm sweeter than you think."

I can't see it, but I know he winks. Law, I love a man that winks. He reaches down, picks up the bottle, and then takes a few steps back toward my house. "You coming?"

So I uncurl my legs from under my blanket, pick up my still-full glass, and walk towards him. "Where we going?"

"A swim. I always come over here and take a swim before bed. Me buying a house without a pool is a sure sign I thought I was dying."

The underwater light has the pool area glowing turquoise. A slight breeze causes the water to ripple and then echo ripples of color on the walls of the house. It's enchanting, and at the edge, I stand mesmerized by the light, the color, the movement—then it all goes dark. "Hey, what happened?" I call into the darkness.

A splash is my only answer for a bit, until suddenly, a voice speaks close to my feet. "Figured it being dark would make you more comfortable, since I'm not wearing a bathing suit."

Small pricks of light in the sky show me the stars, but there's no moon. The sound of Magnus' breast stroke tells me where he is as he goes back and forth in the night. When I slap at another mosquito, Magnus opines from the other side of the pool. "I don't believe mosquitoes swim. You should come in."

And so I did.

8

"And then she started gutting and cleaning the fish." Magnus shakes his head. "Disgusting, but all the fishermen started giving us free beer. Like we were a couple of good ol' boys." He leans forward and points his cigar at the men around the glass-topped table. "Best fish I've ever eaten. Anywhere."

"What I wouldn't give for a picture of that—Magnus Llord in a backwoods fish camp. Probably get you disbarred back in New York if you hadn't already retired," Dr. King opines.

From his wheelchair, Pearl's husband, George, says, "Interesting. I'd like to hear more about this fish camp. Sounds like a great seating for a book based in Florida."

Magnus laughs and nods. "Who knew there was more to the state of Florida than the beach? And here I thought I was the one with so much to teach her."

Dr. King taps his long fingers on the table. "Seems you and Becca Sue are spending a lot of time together. Seems you've gotten pretty tight in only a week."

"Aw, lighten up, Eason, Just a couple kids having fun," Magnus says with a big smile. He sticks his cigar between his lips.

Eason's look of grandfatherly disapproval fails to move Magnus, who draws deep on his cigar, tilts his head back, and blows out a stream of smoke.

"Don't you think it's a little early for cigars?" Pearl comes through the back gate waving another floppy hat, this one white, in front of her face. "George, Eason, did you men finish cleaning the pool filters? They looked filthy yesterday at water aerobics."

George Manningham nods, then scoots his wheelchair away from the table. "Later, men. Got some folks to kill."

Pearl stops waving her hat and plants her hand on her hip. "George, I've told you to quit saying things like that."

Her husband shrugs as he rolls out the gate and away from the group. His top-of-the-line chair moves smoothly and speedily toward the road. Pearl huffs at his back and comes to the table. "You understand, of course, he's talking about characters. Characters in his book."

In his soothing, doctor-voice, Eason answers her. "Yes, we understand. We all understand. He just says things like that to upset you, Pearl."

"I know, I know," she declares as her hat goes back to waving. "Eason, you simply must tell me sometime why I let him get to me." She pulls over a chair into the spot vacated by her husband's wheelchair and leans on the table. "What do you think?"

Magnus stands up. "Well, this is my cue to move on." When he stands up, Pearl takes note of his short robe. Royal blue silk, obviously expensive, but hardly outdoor wear.

With a tsk, a shake of her head, and an attempt to not watch him walk away from the table, Pearl admonishes him. "You wore that all the way over here?"

Magnus stops at the French door leading into Becca Sue's house and turns back to the table. "Don't you mean all the way 'out' here?" Arched eyebrows emphasize his grin as he opens the door and goes inside.

Pearl draws her hand to her throat. "Oh my. Did you men know he, uh, he came from inside Becca Sue's house?"

Looks around the table confirm their surprise matches Pearl's.

"Ruth was right," Eason says with a widening of his eyes.

"Ruth?" Pearl asks.

"Yeah, she said she was worried about Magnus taking advantage of Becca Sue, but I just couldn't see Magnus wasting time on a girl like that."

Pearl stands and sputters, "She's not exactly a girl, and who is he to treat Sybil this way? I'm going home to call her and tell her she better get herself back down here, if she doesn't want some tramp from the boonies taking her place."

"Ruth says Sybil left because she didn't see a future with Magnus. Maybe she doesn't want 'her place.'" As Eason finishes talking, a loud laugh comes to them from the darkened window nearest their table. With only three housing layouts in the neighborhood, the realization they were sitting outside Becca Sue's bedroom hits all at once.

Quickly everyone stands and gets busy pushing chairs in and talking about their day. Out the gate and down the path, the chatter dies away. Only goodbyes are heard, as one by one they peel off at their lonely-looking houses set apart by scrubby, bare lots and gaps in the sidewalk.

Eason opens his front door and welcomes the rush of cool air and darkness. "Ruth? Where are you?" A search through the house leaves him checking the screened porch last. "Here you are. Well, you were right."

Ruth folds shut the book in her lap and blinks her eyes to bring them back around to her husband. "Right? About what?"

He sighs, and then sits in the chair across from hers. "Magnus and Becca Sue. They are, well... they *are*. When George and I got over there first thing to clean the pool, Magnus was already sitting there. You know he sometimes gets there early to swim, so we didn't think anything of it. But then Pearl got there, and you know how she can be. She noticed his robe, and we hadn't even noticed it wasn't a swim cover-up, but a real robe. Even as we worked around the pool with the filters and such. Anyway, he went right into the house, and let us know that was where he had come from, too."

"I told you! I don't know why you are so surprised. She's needy, and he's a man always on the prowl." She picked her book back up. "So, did you see Becca Sue? What did she say?"

"We didn't see her, but we heard her laughing. There we

were, sitting outside her bedroom window. We all left. Pearl's going to call Sybil."

Ruth pulls her finger across the page and murmurs, "Sybil will be the least surprised of all."

"George! George!" Pearl rushes into her house, neither appreciating nor noticing the quiet, the cool. She rushes through, straight past the guest bathroom, and throws open the door to George's office. "You're never going to believe—"

"Magnus is sleeping with the hick. Now, since I guessed can I go back to work?" George never looks up from his computer; matter of fact, he never even stops typing.

"How did you know?"

He finally looks up. "How did you *not* know?"

She stammers for a moment, and he goes back to typing, but not without a parting shot: "Give Sybil my love."

9

So now they all know.

"Good. Good. Good," I say to the big mirror lit up all the way around, well, except for where the bulbs have burnt out. That was my mistake with Caleb, not letting anyone know we were together. Of course, back home I was worried about what people would say or think; here I don't care.

"Don't care a bit," I declare to no one, as I turn off the mirror lights and walk through the darkened bedroom into the blinding sunlight of the living room. Magnus left saying he wasn't eating in my filthy kitchen, and that suits me fine, too.

"I don't care if the kitchen is filthy." But then I realize I don't have any more paper plates. Well, if you don't count the ones spilling out of the trash bag. "Someone should clean this up," I say to the empty house, but turn my back on it when I realize there is still a packet of Pop-Tarts in the last box on the shelf. There's nowhere to sit in the house except on the bed, and well, I've spent too much time there already today. "When someone gets done cleaning the kitchen, someone should wash my sheets," I announce. Hmmm, good help *is* hard to find.

Taking a seat on the fireplace hearth, I scoot back to lean against the stone surrounding the grate. Its light gray blocks are smooth and cool. The hearth is a polished light gray stone, and so tall my feet lift off the floor as I slide back.

Opening the foil packet, I look up and see from this vantage point how incredibly thick the dust is on the floor. As I munch on my chocolate Pop-Tart, I look at the tracks forming paths in the dust left from the month the house sat empty and closed. From the doors leading to the pool, to my bedroom, to the kitchen.

Reminds me of my folks' trailer. Momma never did like cleaning, except for her clothes. Those she kept perfect: all on hangers, in plastic bags, with boxes for her shoes and boots. Daddy didn't clean, of course; that was for women to do. At least that's what Irene, his step-momma would say whenever she came by. "Rick Cousins, what do you stay married to that woman for if she can't do her job of keeping things cleaned up? That's a woman's job."

Luckily, no one ever thought I was woman enough to do it. And then when Caleb and I moved in with his folks, they had a maid and a cleaning crew every week. Shoot, the weekly cleaning crew saw more of that house than I did.

A suite, you say it like "sweet," is what we had there, and as pretty as it was, it might as well been a prison. Caleb left each day to go to work, and I was to either be in our suite or not on the property. And that wasn't just a feeling. Those were my instructions, written on a piece of creamy stationery with Mrs. Mason's name at the top. Always felt lucky his mother and father let me use the main stairwell.

The maid brought me my meals, and I waited every night for Caleb to come eat dinner, but he was always out working late. I'd eat, watch TV, or read, then go to sleep. At first Caleb would come home late at night, and we'd talk or make love, but then he got his own suite.

Until the kids came to live in Georgia.

Law, those kids were sweet, just four and five, and so well-behaved. Mrs. Mason was not having them living in her house, no way, and just like that, I was needed.

When I hear the unlatching of the pool gate, I realize it's time for water aerobics. I jump up from my seat at the fireplace and stand to the side of the big windows. There they all are—sneaking looks at the house, probably afraid Magnus will

come strolling out in his birthday suit. Not that that would be
so bad, he looks amazingly good for someone that old. Wonder how long it will take before one of the nosiest ones, Pearl
or Esmeralda, comes looking for me.

Maybe I should go see Mrs. Bell. She sent me a chicken
casserole I've been eating on since I got here, and I should go
thank her. I edge around the room to stay out of their sight,
and then slip out the front door.

Ouch! The front walk is hot, and I didn't put on shoes. Oh
well, I just try to get across the blazing concrete fast and stick
to the grass or the mulch, although the hard corners of the
mulch hurt almost as much. By time I make it to Mrs. Bell's
front door, I'm out of breath.

She finally opens the door. "Rebecca, what a delight!"

"Well, I wanted to come thank you for the casserole."

"Come in, come in. Let me get you a glass of tea."

Her kitchen is a pretty yellow, with white dishes rimmed
in sky blue in a big cabinet beside a table with a bouquet of
bright sunflowers. She points me to sit down at the little table, and I settle on a cushion. I'm afraid to touch anything; it
all looks so pretty, and I feel like I don't belong here. My hair
is not attractive when it's clean, and it's not clean. It's pulled
back into a ponytail, and the dirt has managed to keep the ponytail from frizzing out like a cheerleader's big pompom. My
shorts and shirt may not look dirty, but they don't smell clean.
Not something it would be possible to notice in my house, but
here they smell awful.

"I made some scones; something must've told me I would
be having company," Mrs. Bell says. "Please have one."

"Thank you," I manage to say, but reaching for one, my
dirty fingernails glare at me. So, I quickly get one onto my
plate and try to keep her talking so she might not notice my
hands. "Scones? I've never had a scone. Like a flat kind of biscuit?"

Mrs. Bell laughs her sweet laugh. She breaks open her
scone and spoons strawberry jam onto each piece. I do the
same, and have to admit, after sampling, that they are pretty

good.

"This kind of reminds me of my grandma's strawberry freezer jam and homemade biscuits. Of course, those we ate hot."

"Freezer jam?" she asks.

"Yeah, real sweet, and easy, too. Keep it in the freezer, and so you always have homemade jam on hand." The scone is good, especially compared to my earlier, foil-wrapped breakfast, but now that I'm thinking of Grandma's biscuits and jam my mouth is kind of dry. A sip of tea doesn't help much as it's unsweetened. What's the point? Plain ol' tap water is just as good as unsweetened tea. Better even.

Fresh coffee, hot biscuits, cold, sweet jam. I'm tearing up remembering my grandma, Momma's momma. She lived closer to town, and so I'd go to her house after school every day. Her front porch was my favorite place in the whole world. Her dying when I was twelve meant no one in the world thought I was the best, well, until Caleb. With Grandma and Caleb both gone, there's no reason to miss Piney.

As the memories flood my brain, they come out my mouth, and Mrs. Bell and I sit there and eat that whole basket of scones while I talk.

"There go the ladies from the swimming class thing." I point out the window beside the table, and I don't even try to hide my fingernails. By now, I'm sure she's seen them since I tend to wave my hands around when I talk. "Guess it's time for me to go home."

My eyes wander around the kitchen and how beautiful it is, how clean and bright and welcoming. How good it feels to sit here. "I love your house."

"Well, dear, the only problem I have with it is there's too much stuff, but I can't figure out what to do with it all. I'd take it down to the thrift store, but I can't haul bags like that."

Looking around, I can't see a thing I'd get rid of. It's all perfect. Then I look at Mrs. Bell's face. She's smiling real big.

She reaches over and lays her smooth, white hand on top of my dirty one. "Will you help me? Your house is practically empty, and I do have some nice things I'd like to give away."

"Oh, *your* things in *my* house? I don't think so. It's, ah, it's pretty dirty."

She pats my hand, and her smile fades. Her voice is strong and really reminds me of Grandma. "Dirt is not a real problem, is it? It's more like a choice."

She stands up. "Dear, I need to lay down a bit. Let me walk you to the door, so I can lock it behind you and take my nap." At the door, she smiles and waves at me. "You decide what you want to do and let me know. It's your choice." She closes the door, and I make sure I hear the deadbolt lock. I guess everyone worrying about her safety has gotten to me, too.

The concrete is still warm, but with this side of the house now in the shade, it's tolerable. The bugs in the trees are going ninety, just like they did in the summer at home.

Home. Guess this is really my home now. The smooth white walls, gardens full of rocks and tropical looking plants, big windows—none of that says "home" to me. Pink flowers, spread open like dinner plates, cover a bush at the end of the driveway. I stick my nose up to one, but it doesn't have a smell. There's another bush like it beside the gate to the back, and walking up to it, I find it doesn't smell either. The back gate is open, so I go through it and close it behind me.

"There you are." When I turn, I see Magnus swimming in the pool. "Your car was here, but no sign of you. I brought dinner."

My stomach holds onto the scones, and the warmth of Mrs. Bell's house wraps around me. Dirt is a choice, she said. A look through the glass doors, doors covered with smears and dust, tells me cleaning fairies didn't choose to show up. Magnus climbs out of the pool and walks over to the table. "I have boiled shrimp, a loaf of bread and a bucket of beer on ice. You're lucky you got here, I was about to start eating without you." He takes the bags from the table and sits them on the edge of the pool next to the bucket of iced beers, and then walks back into the pool. With a couple gyrations in the pool he flings his bathing suit onto the pavers at my feet. "Figured this way we can eat in the nude. What do you think?" He lays out the paper bags on the edge of the pool and sets the food on them, opens a bottle of beer, and after sticking a slice of lime into it, holds it up to me. He grins.

"I think tomorrow sounds like a good choice," I say. I walk into the pool with my shorts and t-shirt on. They don't stay on long, though, and when I fling my underwear onto the edge next to his bathing suit, I laugh. "Well, I'm planning on doing laundry tomorrow anyway."

Tomorrow is an awesome word.

And choice.

10

"For God's sake, Becca Sue, it's after noon. Get out of bed! Look at this pigsty."

Becca Sue pulls back as the man jerks on the bedclothes. She manages to hold onto the sheet to cover herself. "Magnus?"

"No, Magnus Llord hightailed it out of here right after he answered the door naked. Get up, and I mean now."

As the man pulls open her curtains and floods the bedroom with magnifying sunlight, Becca Sue catches her breath. "Caleb? Caleb, you're..."

The man turns away from the window and sighs. "No, Becca Sue. No, it's me, Jameson. Come on." Caleb's younger brother walks out the bedroom door and closes it behind him.

Becca Sue looks around for a minute, then remembers getting into the pool in her clothes yesterday. With a hunt around the room, she manages to get dressed in a pair of cut-offs and an old Mountain Dew T-shirt.

She wipes her face on a wash cloth that smells like mildew and goes to the bathroom. One look in the mirror suggests that her hair is beyond hope after going to bed with it wet last night.

She tosses her head at the mirror. "Who cares? Who cares what Jameson Mason thinks? He's the one that got me into this," she says as she stomps out of the bathroom, past her bed, and pulls open the bedroom door.

"So, Jameson, what's going..." And there, sitting on a pile of luggage are Caleb's children. Tears wells up in Becca Sue's eyes. "Cab. Maggie."

But her walk across the floor stops with a shake of Cab's head. "This place is disgusting. No way are we staying here. Mother would die. Grandmother would burn it down."

Maggie bites her lip. Her eyes had softened a bit at Becca Sue's approach, but with the word "Mother," the softness fades into blankness.

Jameson comes out of the kitchen, striding between Becca Sue and the kids, and turns his back to his niece and nephew. "The kids are here for the summer. Margaret is in South Korea for two months, Audrey is due to have the baby in a couple weeks and can't take care of them, all their grandparents are indisposed, and I don't have room in my townhouse. You have the perfect place, and it will be like a vacation for them to stay here in Florida."

Becca Sue protests. "But I don't have furniture or anything."

Jameson runs his hand through his dark blonde hair and then rests it on his hips. Tall, he never bent his back or hunched his shoulders, he always used his height to shore up his position or take control. Now he used it to assure he was in charge.

"I figured you wouldn't have outfitted rooms for the kids, so I have a shipment of furniture being put together by Mother's decorator this afternoon. It will be here tomorrow."

He reaches his hand down to Becca Sue's arm, but hesitates before he actually touches her. When he does, he grabs her arm and pulls her into the kitchen. There he lowers his voice and uses his height to bend over her. "What in God's name have you been doing here? All these years Mother was apparently right about you. Now I'm worried about what kind of influence you are for Cab and Maggie, but I don't have any choice."

He releases her and turns around looking at the spilled garbage, dirty dishes, unclean counters. "Do I need to hire a cleaning crew, too?" He throws up his hands, and his voice drops back to a whisper. "And what about that cretin of a playboy answering your door naked?" His arm sweeps to the counter. "And the beer bottles, liquor bottles, filthy bedroom?" He shakes his head. "Mother always said you were a slut, but Caleb almost had me convinced you were a saint. Guess I know which one was right, don't I?"

Becca Sue flinches as if he'd slapped her, but ends the flinch with a nod. Then she drops her head and mumbles, "I know, Jameson, I know."

He pauses a moment, but then plows into the living room. "Cab? Maggie? It's all going to be fine. Your furniture will be here tomorrow, so that gives Becca Sue a day to clean things up."

Cab stands up with a fierce intensity. "Uncle J, take us back with you. We won't make any problems for the wedding. We'll share a room at your place if we have to. Please."

Jameson shakes his head, his short, styled hair never moving out of place for long. "That's just not possible, Cam. I'm sorry I didn't make sure things were set up before we got here, but you know things can't always be what we want them to be."

He walks over and hugs his nephew and niece, and then picks up the briefcase sitting beside their pile of luggage. "Becca Sue, you'll find more than enough money to take care of the kids this summer added to your account. You know there was already money there for furniture, right? And hopefully this time when you shop at Walmart, you'll buy some cleaning supplies, instead of just wine and bikinis. Now, I need to get out of here before these crybaby neighbors come crawling over here to complain some more. Goodbye, kids. Call if you need me."

Jameson walks across the empty room, opens, then closes the heavy door behind him. Becca goes to sit on the fireplace hearth. Cab and Maggie rest back on their suitcases. The silence grows until Becca Sue asks, "Y'all mentioned a wedding. Who's getting married?"

Maggie sighs. "Uncle J. He's marrying Cecelia Mattle."

For the first time all morning, Becca Sue's head raises completely up. "Jameson is marrying the governor's daughter?"

11

"Well, I thought it was one of the old biddies bothering you! Figured a shot of me in the buff would keep them from ever ringing the doorbell again." Magnus lifts the bag of garbage he's just filled and carries it out to the garage. Back inside, he leans on the kitchen counter. "What I really can't believe is that I let him get away like that. I'm truly off my game that I ran on home like I had something to be ashamed of in front of that scumbag." He groans. "I used to eat boys like that alive in the courtroom. Guess the kids standing there distracted me."

My stomach falls. "Cab and Maggie saw you, too?" I throw an empty garbage bag at him. "Here, start another bag."

"Done with the vacuuming!" Esmeralda announces from the front hall.

"How can she be this chipper about cleaning?" I ask. Didn't mean for her to hear it, but there she is in the doorway.

She tugs on her long black braid and answers, not a bit of chipperness lost. "This is how we made all our money. Esmie's Cleaning. My mother and aunts always cleaned houses, and I just took it to a whole new level. Sold the company for four million dollars and got out before the market fell."

"You and Patrick?" I ask. I think of them as the odd couple: she's so dark and Italian, and he's so Irish. Right down to the red hair and the name.

"Pshaw," she exclaims with a wave of her hand. "He doesn't

know how to clean. I'll take my vacuum out to my car and be back with my mop." She hikes up the vacuum, which is practically as tall as she is, and marches out the front door.

"Huh," I say to Magnus, who is already tying up another bag. "So, what does Patrick do?"

Magnus looks a bit more like his old self as his grin grows. "He's a kept man. She won't marry him because she doesn't want him to have any claim on her money. They've been together for years before they came here. And she's not stretching the truth about selling her company. It's one of the rare, true rags to riches story."

Behind me Pearl clears her throat and makes me jump. "Some people will just settle for whatever they can get, right, Magnus? And then others want a commitment, you know, Magnus?"

Pearl is giving him the stone-cold teacher stare, and when Magnus looks off center, I turn to her. "What's going on?" Then I turn back to Magnus. "What's she talking about?"

I catch him snarling at her, but then his grin slides back into place. "Jealousy. Pure jealousy."

"Never!" Pearl huffs and leaves the kitchen. "Master bath is done."

When I turn back around, Magnus has moved up to me. He wraps his arms around me. "Baby, just ignore these old crones."

I push him away. "'Baby?' Uh, no. And these 'old crones' are cleaning my filthy house. Maybe not for me, maybe just for the kids, but still. Don't call them names." I pick up a roll of paper towels and a bottle of glass cleaner. "And don't call me 'baby'".

Esmeralda vacuumed all the cobwebs from the high ceilings with some magic attachment wand, so my living room looks a little less like a haunted house. However, the windows and glass doors are still barely see-through. Spraying the blue liquid on the first window, I look through it for the kids. I'd told them to get their swimsuits on and hang out by the pool while I cleaned. Magnus showed up about the time they were changing clothes, all ready to have it out with Jameson. He would've left if Pearl hadn't shown up about that time to see what was going on with the strange car in the driveway. She told him he'd be helping clean, since he'd helped make such a mess. Then she called Esmeralda, saying it was about time she had something to clean besides her already immaculate house.

Cab, stretched out on one of the chaise lounges, looks like his uncles. Tall, muscular, blonde hair tending to brown. He'd always been cute, and now at fifteen he was the boy all the girls in Piney dreamed about. The way they'd always dreamed about his father. The way I'd always dreamed about his father.

Maggie sitting on the edge of the pool, with her head slumped, staring into the water looks sad. Cab always pushes bad things away. He's Mr. Sunshine. His sister, on the other hand, holds onto all the sadness and grief. And being a teen-ager sure doesn't help.

Her hair doesn't have the blond highlights of her broth-er's and father's, and it doesn't have the tilt toward red of her mother's. It's just brown. She does have her maternal grand-father's famous green eyes, but they are too large and too re-markable for her young face. She refused to put on her swim-suit. Poor thing doesn't realize there's not one thing wrong with her body, but she's had a lifetime of people telling her how to make it better, so how could she know it's perfectly fine?

And now they are here for the summer, I think as I clean the windows. What am I going to do with them? For the last few years they've grown away from me. They looked at me like their grandmother and their father, a necessary evil. As they got more into sports and their friends, they were rarely home. And when they were, I was so out of fashion for them. Occa-sionally, I could entice Maggie to watch a Lifetime movie with me, but that hadn't happened in forever. Then when Caleb asked me to move out, so they could redecorate for Audrey and the new baby, I didn't see them at all. Well, besides the funeral.

Pane after pane of glass, I clean and remember. Remember how sweet they were. How they wanted me over their mother, their grandmothers. Only their daddy came before me. I took them to school. I talked with them over cookies when things went wrong. I helped with their homework until they got way too smart for me.

And here they are.

What in the world am I going to do with them?

Cab pulls one of the white plugs out of his ears and waves his arm at me.

I open the door. "Hey, Cam. What ya need?"

"Food. We're hungry."

Maggie joins in. "Can we go to the beach to eat? Uncle J said the seafood is great down here."

"Sure. Um, I guess get changed, and yeah, we'll go get something to eat." I close the door and walk off to find Pearl. "The kids are getting hungry, so I'm going to take them out to eat. We'll stop by the store later to get some food for here."

Pearl finishes rinsing out the tub in the guest bathroom, then turns off the water and stands up. "So, these are your ex-husband's children, and his family just decided to dump them on you?"

Chewing the inside of my lip, I avoid her eyes and nod.

She collects her cleaning supplies and puts them in a bucket. I move to the side so she can pass me. "Well, isn't it ironic that the very man who sold us our homes in a 55-plus community now requires us to care for his children?"

I catch her eye. "Not 'us.' Me. I can take care of them."

Pearl doesn't hide her eye roll this time. "Please! You can't take care of yourself, much less two spoiled teenagers. Look at the mess this house is in. Look at who you spend your time with. Jameson Mason has done a lot to earn my disdain, but he topped it all today dropping off his own niece and nephew into the hands of someone fully incapable of caring for them. Of course, we have to help you. And, of course, he knew we would."

She huffs down the hallway, and as I follow her, while sighing, the door to Maggie's room silently closes. Knowing Maggie heard Pearl does nothing to help my frustration.

In the living room, Magnus has keys in his hand. "I borrowed Patrick's truck and have the garbage loaded in it since we don't have such creature comforts as trash collection in our forgotten little corner of the world. I'll take it out to the recycle place he told me about." He waits for Pearl to go out the front door, and he leans a little closer to me. "So, get the kiddies in bed tonight, and we can have our midnight swim?"

I push him away. "No. No midnight swim. The kids are here. Thanks for your help, but you just go on home. I'm taking Cab and Maggie for some dinner."

"Fine. Fine by me."

He steps away, and I reach out for his arm. "Magnus, I'm sorry. Really, but well..." My arms fall to my sides.

He smiles, and then winks at me. "Okay, I'll give you a little space, and we'll figure something out. Don't want you to get lonely."

Cab comes around the corner and stands with his hands in the pockets of his khaki shorts. His curly hair is so much like his daddy's was, and he's wearing those cute little boat shoes that still tell you who's a farm boy and who's a money boy.

Before I can tell him about how much he looks like his dad, he frowns at me. "I thought you said we were getting changed. Aren't you going to change? We're starving." His scowl isn't cute. Neither is his tone.

A swallow makes my words squeaky. "Oh, yeah, guess I don't have time for a shower."

Magnus lifts his eyebrows at me, and then with a little shake of his head, he turns toward Cab. "Nice to meet you and your sister. Have a good dinner."

Cab only grants him a nod and then turns toward Maggie's closed door. "Margaret Bernice, come on."

Magnus leaves, and I rush to my room. Cab called her Margaret Bernice just like her grandfather does. Bernice was some old relative, and Maggie hates to be called by her middle name. Her grandfather does it just to aggravate her, and I'm thinking Cab does too. Poor girl.

My hair didn't magically clean itself, so it's still dirty and wired from sleeping on it wet. I pull it back into a ponytail with a yellow rubber band and then look for something to wear. Never did get around to doing laundry either. In a corner of the room, I find some blue jean shorts that aren't cut-offs. They are faded and wrinkled, but my one shirt still hanging in the closet is long so it'll cover them. The green shirt is just a plain t-shirt without any writing on it. It's hanging up because I spilled salsa on it last week, and I washed it out in my bathroom sink. The front is clean, but wrinkled from where I wrung it out. Once it's on, I try to smooth out the wrinkles while I slide my feet into a pair of flip flops. I avoid the mirror and hurry out to the kids.

"Okay, let's go. There's lots of fast food. You sure you want seafood?"

Cab scoffs. "We don't eat fast food. Do you have any idea what that does to a person?"

"Uh, no," I say. "But okay. I just don't know many places."

Cab goes toward the front door. "Doesn't matter, I looked online and found a place. I'll drive."

I laugh as I grab my purse. "Sure you will. Maggie you want to drive, too?"

Maggie shrugs and answers. "Cab drives all the time, Becca Sue. He's had his permit since Christmas."

He stands with the front door open, one hand extended for my keys. Well, he has to learn somehow. I lay my keys in his opened palm and wait for him and his sister to leave the house. When I pull the door closed, I feel strange, and then I recognize the feeling. Relief. I feel relieved, but I'm not sure why.

12

"Um, I don't think you can just pull up here like this," Becca Sue says.

Cab put the car in park and got out in answer. Maggie leans up from the back seat and quietly says, "Its valet parking." She then lets herself out of the back door, just as a young man in black pants, a stiff white shirt, and a bowtie opens Becca Sue's door. Halfway out of the car, she notices the young man's hand she should've taken, instead of pushing herself out of the low seat by grabbing onto the door frame. She gives him her other hand and then is twisted around so that she comes out like she was crawling backwards. Then, she leans back into the car to pick up her purse. By time she is standing beside the car, purse in hand, both Cab and Maggie are watching the show with frowns.

Cab sighs and walks toward the brass and glass doors. He doesn't blink when two men on either side open the doors for him to enter. Maggie nods a thanks to the young men, and her blush at the good-looking men brings a smile to Becca Sue's face. She reaches up and nudges the girl's shoulder. "They've got some hot guys here."

Maggie's shy smile disappears, and she moves away from Becca Sue. Hurrying a bit, she catches up to her brother's stride, and Becca Sue scurries along, bringing up the rear. Polished wood, shiny brass, and seductive glass fill the wide room, with everything leading to an open expanse of windows that overlooks the ocean. Becca Sue comes up to the kids who are talking with a lady (also wearing a bowtie) at the little stand beside the next set of doors.

"Cab Worth Jameson. We have a reservation for three."

The young lady nods and answers, "Yes, Mr. Worth Jameson. We have a table beside the window, just as you requested. Lea will show you to your table."

"Hey, Lea?" Becca Sue whispers, as she reaches up and touches the woman's arm. Lea pauses. Cab and Maggie stop abruptly and look back at Becca Sue. "Where's y'all's bathroom?"

Lea directs Becca Sue to the side hall off the main lobby. As she starts that direction, Becca Sue looks over her shoulder. "Mags, you wanna go to?"

Maggie quickly shakes her head and turns to follow her brother. At the table, Cab chooses a seat on the side, then directs his sister to the center seat. His shoulders relax for the first time since they arrived in Florida. "You sit between us."

"How did you know about this place?" Maggie asks.

"It's the Ritz. Thank God I did my homework, or Becca Sue would've dragged us to some crab boil place with filthy restrooms and Styrofoam plates." He pauses while the waitress pours water in their glasses. "And that's another thing. Becca Sue, what a hick name. I'm going to give her a choice, Rebecca or Susan. She can pick. Or, hell, she can come up with a whole new name for all I care, but I refuse to continue calling her that hillbilly name."

"Wow, this place is amazing," Becca Sue says as she slides into her seat. "Look at this view." She reaches across the small, white-clothed table and reached for Cab's hand. "Honey, you did real good, calling ahead like that. We like got the best table here."

Cab pulls his hand away to wave at the waitress. The small blond who'd poured their water flows to his side. "Yes, sir? Are you ready to order?"

"Could you please tell us your specials?" His smile at the girl causes her blue eyes to widen...

"Oh, certainly." She licks her lips as she straightens her shoulders and takes a deep breath. She smoothly tells the table, mostly Cab, the specials. Becca Sue ignores the waitress and mainly just stares at Maggie and Cab. Her brow creases further and further, until she is practically wiggling by time the young woman walks off.

"Who are you two? You are so... so polished. So grown up." Becca Sue's creased brow relaxes into a wide grin. "Cab, you talk just like your grandfather, asking for the specials, making reservations. And Maggie, you're so put-together. Look at that dress, so simple, and yet you make it look like you're the president's wife or something. And that silver barrette in your hair matches your sandals and bracelet. My, my, you are both something."

Maggie blushes and reaches out with both her hand and a genuine smile. "Thank you. It's good to see you too."

Cab nods, but swallows any pleasant look that tries to cross his face. "Yes, thank you. Thank you for noticing we are growing up. We are aware of our place in life and appreciate our families and what..."

Becca Sue smacks the table. "I know. Calling yourself," she squares her shoulders and lowers her tone, "Cab Worth Jameson. But it did get us a good table."

"Becca Sue!" The fifteen-year-old Cab makes a quick appearance, but Cab quickly hides again, clearing his throat and looking down at his lap. "Please don't hit the table like that. And about your name. Don't you find Becca Sue a bit, uh, a bit backwoods? A bit country? Which would you prefer? Rebecca or Susan?"

Maggie stares at her lap, and when the blonde walks up to the table to take their orders, Cab is the only one ready.

Maggie quickly asks for whatever the first special had been, and Becca Sue points at the first shrimp entree. Cab places his order, complicated and full of flirting. The waitress flirting back says she has no idea how young he is. He watches her walk away. Her walk says she knows he's watching.

"Rebecca. You can call me Rebecca."

Cab picks up his water glass. "Wonderful. Rebecca it is." He pushes his glass through the air toward the center of the table, and it's met by Becca Sue's and Maggie's glasses. "To Rebecca."

"And to Caleb and Margaret, since we're no longer using nicknames." Suddenly, there was only one glass lifted. Cab's face twists in fury, and Maggie's face flames.

"You *know* we don't like being named after our parents," Maggie whines.

Becca Sue shrugs and drinks her water. "I could call you both Junior, but it might get confusing."

"My name is Cab. Not Caleb and definitely not Junior." Cab slams back in his seat and crosses his arms across his chest.

"Ooh, bread. Thanks honey," Becca Sue says to the young man who sits a cloth-lined silver basket on the table. She waits for him to walk away, then reaches to unwrap the basket.

Maggie sighs. "We forgot to say 'no bread.'"

"Why would we say we don't want the bread? It's free, isn't it?" Becca Sue asks as she places a warm yeast roll on her plate.

"As someone who recently lost so much weight, you'd think you would understand what bread does to your body. Mother really doesn't want Maggie eating bread."

Becca Sue places her butter knife, just loaded with creamy butter from the china bowl, onto the side of her plate. She looks up, then back and forth between the siblings. "Oh, yeah, guess that I should watch it. But y'all are young and you'll burn it off. Cab, you're skinnier than either your daddy or your uncle were at your age. And, Maggie, why darling, you're just beautiful." She looks deep into both young people's faces, but only Maggie's allows any entrance.

Cab crosses his arms on the table, leans on them a bit, and then turns to stare out at the ocean.

Maggie watches him look away, then slides a shy smile at Becca Sue. She reaches over to the warm yeast roll on Becca Sue's plate and breaks off half. She smells it, closing her eyes as she lifts it to her face, and then she takes a quiet bite.

Her green eyes grow round, and they shine. She encourages Becca Sue to eat the other half.

   With the gray-blue waves rushing to cover the endless sand behind the wall of glass and the cool rush of jazz music float-ing on the air conditioning, two young women from Piney, Georgia silently eat warm rolls.

13

Probably only a handful of people can say that a meal at the Ritz with an ocean view was one of the worst meals of their lives, but I am one of those people. I'm so mad at Cab I could chew nails. He's turned into everything there is to hate about rich people—rich, *beautiful* people. He didn't care one bit to embarrass me in that place.

People kept looking at us, and that made me so nervous I jabbered on like some crazy blue jay. Shaking my head at how stupid I must've sounded, I lift my wine glass for a shot of forgetfulness. Through my wine glass, the glow of the pool makes everything a turquoisey kind of blue. You won't see me out there at the Ritz again.

Once when I was with Caleb, and he still liked me, we went to a fancy thing with his folks. It was just like tonight. Me embarrassing everybody. Guess I was so excited to see the kids I forgot I don't belong in places like that.

We didn't even stop at the grocery store on the way home because I was in such a hurry to get away from Cab. I just couldn't think! Now, by myself, with my glass half-empty, I see how I let things get out of hand.

It sure didn't help when I told our little blonde waitress that he was only fifteen. Yeesh. If Cab could've come across that table and strangled me, he would have. She still passed him her phone number when we were leaving. And yet...

Gotta admit as upset as I was, well... it's a relief someone is here to tell me what to do. A fifteen-year-old tyrant is better than trying to figure things out myself.

My phone buzzes, and I look down at the text from Magnus that pops up. I sit down my glass and pick up my phone. "Hey. I saw your text and figured it was just easier to call you. Yeah, we're home."

"So how was the Ritz?"

I had picked up my glass, but didn't get a drink before he surprises me with that. "What? How did you know where we went?"

"Oh, I hear things. Things like Roger Worth's grandkid acting like a big shot. Who does that kid think he is?"

"He doesn't think, he knows. So folks here know his up-north grandfather? He really must be a big deal."

"Bigger than big."

"Well, guess my summer is planned now. Take care of the kids. Keep them out of trouble, and maybe have a little fun with them. It'll kind of be like back in Georgia when they were little."

The silence on the phone stretches long enough for me to unfold my legs and hang them into the water. Finally I ask, "Magnus?"

"But we were having fun, weren't we? The kids won't take up all your time, will they?"

Now the silence stretches on my side. "Magnus, who's Sybil?"

He answers immediately. "A woman. She's in my past. Gone. Not a very *fun* woman. Where are the kids?"

"Inside watching stuff on their laptops. They're sacked out in sleeping bags in their rooms."

"Come over."

"To your house?" Very interesting. He's never invited me over there.

"Yes," and I can hear him grinning over the phone. "Can Becca Sue come over and play?"

I down the rest of my wine and stand up. "Okay." I end the call and, leaving my glass on the patio table, slip out the side gate.

Having to walk around the lake means it takes about ten minutes to get to Magnus' home. Which means ten minutes I argue with myself about what I'm doing. Finally, at the foot of his driveway I almost convince myself to go home, but I heard the Manningham's door opening and Pearl telling George she was going out to walk their dogs, Freddie and Scooby, and would be back soon. The thought of more eye-rolling sends me dashing up to the dark alcove of Magnus' front door. I knock and then try the door handle. When it opens, I slip inside, hoping Pearl had missed the quiet opening and closing of the door.

"Magnus," I whisper. "I'm here."

"Why, yes, you are. Come on in, won't you?"

"Sorry, I was trying to keep Pearl from seeing me. I'm only going to stay for a minute... gotta get back to the kids, you know." I catch my breath to take a look around. "Wow, this is beautiful."

Low lights and lit candles fill the room with a beautiful golden glow. There are books everywhere and pictures, large pictures that I don't like. That modern art stuff that makes no sense. The furniture is big and heavy, not really Florida furniture at all. A warm scent, like the expensive powder Mamma got one Christmas from a customer, fills the house, and the wide, thick couches look made for laying on more than sitting. "Oh, can we sit in here? I'd thought we'd sit on the screened porch, but I want to sit on that green couch."

Magnus motions for me to sit. "I'll get you a drink."

Carpets lie on top of carpets, and after my bare floors, it feels like walking on clouds. There are two couches facing each other, one green, one dark red. The chairs are a deep gold. All of the furniture has wide, plumpy cushions, and when I sit on the green couch and slide back, my feet leave the floor. Half lying, half sitting, I melt into the velvet fabric. "Oh, Magnus, this is amazing."

"It is, isn't it? Here, I made you a martini. Have you ever had a martini? Watch it, it sloshes out of the glass."

"How can I drink this? I can't even sit up." But he hands it to me anyway, and I take a quick sip to help with the sloshing problem. "Ooh, that's, um, that's different tasting. Good, I think."

Magnus sits and glides back beside me without spilling a drop of his. "Well, I knew you liked olives, so figured this couldn't go too wrong."

We recline and sip, and slowly my mind comes around to what all happened today. Jameson, the kids, the Ritz, Magnus' home. *Jameson.* "Did I tell you Jameson is marrying Cecelia Mattle, the Georgia governor's daughter?"

Magnus tilts his head at me. "Is he really?"

"Yep. This summer, I guess, because the kids were talking about it like it would be happening soon." I manage to pour some more martini into my mouth and swallow. "Yep, everybody is somebody. Jameson marrying the Governor's daughter, Cab and Maggie are Worths and belong at the Ritz, and then there's me. I'm nobody. I'm just the babysitter. And Pearl says I can't even do that." A tear rolls down my face, and Magnus lifts my glass from my hand.

He sets our glasses on the low, square coffee table, and then moves back next to me. "Of course you are somebody." He slides his hand up under my shirt. "Somebody I'd like to know better."

I giggle and stretch out so that I'm lying in the corner of the huge sofa. "Okay, sounds good to me. This is the nicest couch I've ever sat on. Or laid on."

Then the giggles really get going, but I manage to get the words out, "Or *been* laid on."

Magnus starts laughing, too, and we dissolve into laughing and kissing and touching. Sinking into the green plush fabric, I give into the luxurious feelings. Jameson thinks he's somebody, but he's not. No, he's not.

Really he's not.

14

"We are going shopping this morning. There's really nothing to eat." Maggie greets Becca Sue as she emerges from her dark master bedroom into the sun-filled living room. "Cab's gone for a run, but he left his list, so we don't have to wait for him."

Becca Sue sways in the sunlight, blinking her eyes. "Sure. When's the furniture going to be delivered?"

Maggie unfolds herself from her seat on the floor next to her plugged-in laptop. "Uncle J texted this morning and said afternoon." Becca Sue looks around the room and sees her phone lying on the mantle. She picks it up and looks at it. "He didn't text me."

The girl shrugs, and then screws her mouth up like she doesn't want to say what she's getting ready to say. "Uh, do you have a key for the back door?"

Becca Sue points to the glass doors on her right. "These doors?"

Maggie nods and Becca Sue answers, "I don't know. There's a set of keys in the kitchen, but I haven't really figured out what they are to. Why? Do you need a key?"

"No, but you might. I mean, Cab wanted to lock you out last night. We didn't know where you were. I guess you went for a walk, and so Cab said we couldn't just leave the door unlocked. I told him I'd wait up for you, but well, it got so late." Maggie turns to walk in the kitchen. "So I just left it unlocked and went to bed. Cab wasn't happy when he found it unlocked this morning."

"Ooh, I should've locked it when I came in, I guess." Becca Sue follows the girl into the kitchen, and out of habit opens the refrigerator.

Maggie whirls around. "No, what I'm telling you is it *won't* be unlocked for you to come in whenever you feel like it anymore! You'll be *locked out*! You would've been locked out last night if I hadn't stayed up waiting on you." Her face heats up, and her eyes fill with tears.

Becca Sue closes the refrigerator door, and reaches an empty, limp hand towards the upset girl. "I never even thought of you waiting up on me. No one has ever really cared when I came and went, honey. It just never crossed my mind." She turns her hand over like an offering.

"Don't. I'm fine," Maggie says as she turns away. "I'm going to the bathroom, and then I'm ready to go."

Becca Sue sighs and then looks down at her shorts and t-shirt. The same ones she put on to go to dinner. Same ones she put on after picking them up off Magnus's floor around 2 a.m. Same ones she put on after picking them up off her bedroom floor this morning. "Guess I should change clothes. Wonder if Cab did any laundry when he was obsessing over locking the doors last night?"

Pulling a hank of hair towards her nose she sniffs as she walks back into her dark room. "Well, at least my hair is clean. Magnus' shampoo smells awesome, and that conditioner made my hair so soft." Holding up a pair of gym shorts, she looks for stains. "Hair stuff probably belonged to that Sybil."

"Who's Sybil?" Maggie comes out of the bathroom and leans on the door frame.

"Ah, just some lady that used to live here. I don't really know." She spreads her hands out a bit and looks around when Maggie flips on the overhead light. "I have to do laundry this afternoon. Need to make sure there's detergent."

The teenager looks around, too, and then turns away saying, "I'll go check the laundry room."

"Okay, hey, have you had breakfast? Want to stop at Chick-fil-a? I love their biscuits." Becca Sue collects her sandals from beside the glass doors, her phone from the mantle, and her purse from the kitchen counter. "Should we just leave the back door unlocked for Cab?"

Maggie rolls her eyes. "No. We figured out the garage door code from the house paperwork Uncle J told us about on top of the refrigerator. Cab can come in that way. You do have a front door key, right?"

Becca Sue opens two kitchen drawers before she opens the one holding the key ring. "Here it is. One of these works, or did when I got here." She dumps the keys in her purse. "We'll figure it out when we get back if Cab's not here to open the door for us."

"So you usually just leave the doors unlocked when you go out?"

Becca Sue grins. "Don't be so uptight. We never locked the doors in Piney."

Maggie shakes her head and opens the front door. "That's because we had housekeepers at both houses. They locked and unlocked the doors." She stops on the sidewalk and turned. "Lock the door. It has to be locked."

Becca Sue digs the key ring out, studies it for a moment, and then tries several keys before she finds one that turns. "There, locked up tight. All to make you happy."

"And to keep us safe. We don't even have a security system; anyone could just walk in."

"Walk in and do what? I don't have anything worth stealing."

Maggie slams her car door. "But aren't you scared someone could come in and hurt you?"

Becca Sue maneuvers the car out of the concrete driveway. "Hurt me? Why would someone want to hurt me? No one's going to bother me in this neighborhood."

"Never mind." Maggie opens her window a bit to let out some of the hot air. "For some reason you're not scared of anything, but me and Cab are, so the doors need to be locked from now on."

"Okay, no problem."

At the entrance to the subdivision, they turn right and immediately dip into a huge pothole. The rest of the road is just as bumpy and in bad repair.

"Uncle J says this is a shame," Maggie says. "The county promised to fix this road when Daddy bought all this land and wanted to develop it." After half a mile, the road ends at a stop sign and a smooth, newly black-topped highway. The median spreads out, making the highway look extra wide, mown grass with purple and pink crepe myrtles forming a tall, flowery divide. Palm trees line the sides of the highway along with strips of white concrete sidewalk. Shops with colorful canopies and bright glass windows sit separated from the highway by large parking lots filled with shiny cars.

On the left, past a few parking lots and two intersections, Becca Sue turns into a Chick-Fil-A and parks. Inside they order, and while Maggie gathers napkins, straws, and a table, Becca Sue gets their food at the counter.

Seated at their table, Becca Sue puts hot sauce on her chicken biscuit, and after a few bites they both slow down to talk about the people around them, playing a game Becca Sue started when the kids were little. Each trying to top the other with stories of what the lives of the customers around them are really like. The more outrageous and original, the better.

After a few tries Maggie warms up to her task. "I haven't done this in so long," she says with a laugh, hoping the young couple near the window didn't hear her.

Becca Sue takes a cautious sip of her coffee. "I still do it, but I have to do it in my head since there's no one to talk to. I've missed you and Cab."

Maggie's happy face slides away, and she bites on her straw. "I miss my friends in Piney." Her brows tighten. "What about your friends in Piney, Becca Sue? I bet you miss them."

"Friends? Well, not really. I had, I mean, *have* my cousin Jen, but she's married with a baby. Naw, when I married your Daddy, he was all I cared about, and I kind of never really had friends anyway. And, you know, I didn't really fit in with all *his* friends. They kind of did things on their own. And I had y'all. Cab and you were a handful, but a lot of fun."

Maggie's eyes focus on Becca Sue. "Your hair looks soft this morning. I like it."

Becca Sue reaches up and smushes a handful. "It is soft. I have to find out what kind of conditioner that was."

"Why don't you know what kind of conditioner it was? Didn't you buy it?" Their eyes lock, but Maggie's look away as realization crosses her face. "Oh, it wasn't at our house."

They each take another bite, and then Becca Sue swallows her mouthful with a drink of coffee and grins. "Our house. You called it 'our house.' That's really nice."

Maggie grins, too. "I guess I did. Okay, tell me about the people in *our* neighborhood. What's the old lady like next door?"

Becca Sue leans forward. "They're *all* old."

Laughing and talking furiously about their new neighbors and then moving on to talk about the new folks in the restaurant makes the time melt away.

"Okay, on to shopping. You said you have a list?" Becca Sue cleans up the table and collects all the trash on her tray, while Maggie gets the list out of her purse. They study it, Becca Sue looking over the girl's shoulder, as they walk outside.

"Wow, it sure is hot here. I thought back home was hot."

"Careful the seat don't burn your legs." Becca Sue cranks the car and twists the air conditioner knob to high. She puts on a pair of big sunglasses with white frames. "Like my new sunglasses? I love them!" Becca Sue says looking into the rearview mirror.

Maggie laughs. "You're fun. I missed you. No one's been fun back at home."

Becca Sue pulls through the parking lot. "Well, I can't imagine it's been easy losing your dad like that."

"Yeah," Maggie draws out the word while she peeks at Becca Sue. Maggie's eyes fill with tears, and she leans back against the seat and closes her eyes. "Miss Audrey's been real upset and Grandmother Mason yells a lot at everybody, especially Uncle J. He kept trying to find ways to keep out of Grandmother's way, but you know how she sneaks up on you. Me and Cab took to just staying at friends' houses, well, *I* stayed at friends' houses."

Maggie's emphasis on the word "I", causes Becca Sue's eyebrows to pop up. "Where did Cab stay?"

The girl leans up and then toward the driver's seat. "The club. You know, the Country Club. He was hanging out at there with the college kids and some other people."

"Uh oh. That bunch was always hopped up on something."

"Yeah, uh oh. Hey, where are we going? We've passed like four grocery stores."

"Umm, I like one out here better."

"Really? This doesn't look at all as nice."

Manicured medians, canopied stores, and parking lots full of shiny new cars were miles behind them. Weeds, fresh and green and swaying in the breeze—but still weeds, line the road. No lawn or sidewalk on either side. Cracked pavement meets the waist-high weeds, which slope down into a ditch of dark, almost black, water. Old houses with old cars in their yards mix with old businesses with old trucks in theirs. The first fairly large intersection has a gas station, a check cashing place with bars on the window, and a sad-looking daycare center anchoring an old strip mall. On the other side of the intersection, Becca Sue slows down and turns right, into another dilapidated strip mall with a Reddi-Mart grocery store, a barber shop, and a Dollar General.

A handful of cars in the parking lot surround a rusty grocery cart corral. Becca Sue pulls in next to the cars and lifts her purse up from the floorboard. "You ready? Got the list?"

"I'm not shopping here." Maggie looks around them. "This doesn't look safe. Or clean. There's probably more drugs sold in this place than groceries."

"Well, haven't you turned into a little snob? Here I thought it was just your brother." Becca Sue opens her car door. "I'm the one who drives, and this is where I want to shop." She gets out and slams the door. At the front of the car, she stops to see what Maggie is going to do, and then acting disinterested in Maggie, she smiles and looks around. Three men sit on a bench at the other end of the store, and when she smiles at them and waves, they don't smile or wave back. They just continue to stare. She turns and bends down to look through the windshield. "What are you doing in there?"

The girl points to her side of the car, motioning for Becca Sue to come to her window.

"Great, now what?" At the passenger window she's met with a hand sticking out the four-inch opening, and in the hand is Maggie's phone.

Becca Sue puts her purse onto her shoulder and reaches for the phone. "Hello?"

"Becca Sue, what is going on?"

"Jameson?"

"Yeah, I just left court because Maggie called me, and I thought it was an emergency, but she tells me she doesn't like the store you want to shop at?"

Becca Sue sticks her tongue out at the girl behind the window. "I'm driving, and this is the store I want to go to."

"She says it's not safe. You wouldn't take the kids anywhere unsafe, right? And she was ranting about unlocked doors? Have you taken leave of your senses?"

"No, I have not 'taken leave of my senses.'" Flipping around to present her back to Maggie, she sees the men from the bench are halfway across the parking lot and coming towards the car. "Hey, I gotta go. I get it. Go back to court. We're leaving. Bye." She hits the end button as she swerves around the hood of the car and races to her door. She jerks it open, slides into the seat as she tosses Maggie's phone back to her. "Lock your door."

"Why are they coming over here?"

"I don't know. Where are my stupid keys?" Becca Sue takes a quick look up to see the men now only a few spaces away from the car and so she dumps her purse onto the floor board. "There they are." Maggie scoops up the keys and hands them to Becca Sue, who quickly starts the car and pulls away. Waiting to turn left onto the highway she takes a deep breath and tries to laugh. "Guess I overreacted a bit, huh? Those guys were probably just going to their car?"

"I don't think so. They're going back to that bench they were on." Maggie whirls back to face her and demands, "What is wrong with you? Why did you bring us here?"

Becca Sue shouts back. "Because this is where I belong. Not in that big house, not at the Ritz, not in those fancy shops. I'm not like the rest of you. Those stores up there scare me to death." She drops her head onto the steering wheel, no longer looking for a break in the traffic.

"How can a store scare you, but leaving the doors unlocked is fine?" Maggie asks quietly.

Becca Sue lifts her head, puts on her blinker, and pulls out onto the highway. Sunglasses in place, she drives back the way they came. Weeds disappear, sidewalks unroll, sparkly windows wink in the mid-morning sun, and she doesn't say a word.

Pulling into a bright shopping center with well-lined spaces, shiny metal cart corrals, and well-dressed ladies leading full carts pushed by teens in green aprons, she parks. "Here. This is where I should've brought you to begin with."

Maggie licks her lips and fingers her list. "Does this place really scare you?"

Becca Sue stares at the girl through her sunglasses for a moment. "No, that's silly. Let's go."

At the entrance they are greeted by several people, and they take a cart from the clean, open area leading into the flower shop section. There a woman says "Good Morning" and hands them coupons for gluten-free something, which she proceeds to tell them about. Maggie pays attention to her, but Becca Sue's eyes dart along the front of the store. She reaches out and pats Maggie's arm. "I'll be right back."

Past the floral shop, at the corner of the front wall, Becca Sue darts into an alcove with the sign "Restrooms" above it. In a stall, she barely gets the door shut and locked before she drops toward the toilet and throws up her biscuit she'd enjoyed so much earlier. She wipes her forehead and then face with a wad of tissue and then throws it in the toilet, stands up and flushes everything away.

Washing her hands she finally looks into the mirror. "Scared of a store? No, that's silly. Right?" She lays her hand on her stomach and closes her eyes against the tears swelling there. "I hate these people, and I hate this whole place. I do not belong here." Her stomach lurches, and she runs back into the stall. "God, I hope there aren't cameras in here, but Lord knows these people like to watch everything like hawks." She only gags, but then she laughs. "Bet they didn't know they'd have anything as gross to watch as Becca Sue Cousins."

15

"Law this is probably the most exciting thing that's happened in this neighborhood since that bull jumped on that cow right when Miss Bell's preacher visited." I let the front curtain fall back into place. The moving truck has only been here about half an hour, but already the house looks totally different—full of furniture, boxes, and people. Apparently after Jameson's visit last week, he added to the first shipment, so now we have living room furniture, a dining room set, a kitchen table and chairs. All that in addition to the kids' rooms being outfitted just like they wanted.

"Nobody asked what I wanted," I mumble, "but it's still all pretty. Looks just like Caleb's mother's house." Which means I can't help but gag a bit.

"Oh, Becca Sue, this is just lovely! Someone has very expensive taste." Pearl helps the mover take the brown paper off the living room couch.

"Yeah, it's pretty. Just not what I'd get, but this way I didn't even have to go shopping." *Even though I was kinda looking forward to shopping. I'd have gotten some fun furniture.*

Pearl smooths her hand across the couch. "This is fine fabric and very classy. You should be very grateful to these people; they are treating you extremely well."

Ruth King makes her way around the boxes in the front hallway. "She's taking care of their most precious possessions, of course they should treat her extremely well."

"Oh no, Miss King. They have just as nice furniture up in Piney." I spread my arm across the room. "This is all nice, but it's not their most precious possession."

Ruth grabs my arm. "No, dear, not the furniture. The children."

I shrug. "Oh, well, that's nothing. That's just, well, what I do."

Miss King shakes her head and presses her lips tight. She seems angry, but not with me. She doesn't know much about the Masons, if she thinks they think I'm doing them any big favor. They just needed a babysitter, and shoot, Cab and Maggie are doing a better job taking care of things than I am. The truck driver tried to give me the lists of what all they'd brought to make sure it was all there, but Cab took it instead. Besides, when I saw that it was just like the furniture in his grandmother's house, I immediately lost interest.

"Make way, folks!" a man yells, and we move away from the hallway. "Got the entertainment system here. Where do you want it, ma'am? Where's your cable outlet?"

"That's huge. Cable outlet? Um, well, it would be..."

"Right here. Move, Becca Sue." Cab brushes by and points to the wall beside the fireplace. "This corner here."

"Master bedroom? These are for the master bedroom, which way?" another man asks.

"Here, in here." I step over the paper in the floor and to the man with the wrapped-up furniture on a dolly. "Are you sure, though? All the bedroom stuff is for the kids' rooms."

"Not this. We have things for three bedrooms, a girl's room, a boy's room, and a master. So, where do you want this in there?"

I lead him into the room and start by picking up clothes from the path of the dolly. "Um, what is it?"

"Looks like a dresser? There's a couple more pieces marked for here, as well as some boxes."

I throw the pile of clothes into my bathroom and then motion for him to put the dresser down between the two windows. He leaves without unwrapping it, and that's just as well.

"Don't even get to pick my own bedroom furniture." Tears well up. I wipe them away with the backs of my hands, while I finish collecting all the dirty clothes in the room. Blinking and swallowing down the pity, I preach myself a little sermon. "Be grateful. You're getting new furniture. And if you'd paid attention you'd known Jameson put money in the account for you to shop. Anyone would be grateful to have people taking such good care of you. Like Miss Pearl said, the Masons are treating me real nice." A hiccup, and I'm picturing the big, old furniture Caleb's mother always filled our house with. Dark, heavy, antique-looking stuff, unless it was white with gold trim. Whatever it is, it will be old-looking.

"I'll just put these on the bed. Looks like bedclothes," another man says as he puts two boxes down.

Bedclothes? That old witch, she doesn't want me to have anything I like. Just like my wedding. She paid, so she got to pick everything out. My dress, my shoes, the food, even the wedding ring Caleb finally bought me. I told her I wanted a gold band, so she told me gold was tacky and made him buy me a silver one. And everyone just kept saying how thankful I must be. How good the Masons were being to me.

Just like now.

After another two more pieces of furniture and some more boxes are placed in my room, I step out to see the living room practically set up. The ladies have unwrapped all the furniture and emptied most of the boxes.

"There you are, Becca Sue," Esmeralda calls out. "We have Maggie's room done, and it's beautiful. She's so happy. Cab needed the technical men to put his room together, lots of wires and TV stuff, but they'll be done soon. Have you finished with your room? I'll come help you since everything here is almost done."

I wave her off. "I'm good. I'm not going to unwrap it all right now."

"Oh, yes, you are. No stopping until this house looks like a home. And let's see what the grandmamma has picked out for you. She has a very good style, very much like a New Yorker.

Very much."

"An *old* New Yorker," I breathe out with a sigh.

Miss Esmeralda squeezes my waist. "True, sweetheart, but old is better than nothing. In just one day you have gone from living like a street girl to a woman of class. *Expensive* class."

"Yes, I know. I'm very grateful."

"Pshaw!" Esmeralda spits and then waves her arms at me. "Be grateful for the job, never the pay. You earn the pay. I've raised teenagers, there isn't enough expensive furniture in the world to make me do it again. This," she sweeps her arms around living room, "this is all how they say they are grateful *to you.*"

Finally, something makes me laugh. "Oh, no, ma'am, you don't know the Masons. They are never grateful to other people, especially to someone like me. That's truly right off *Hee Haw*, them being grateful to Becca Sue Cousins."

She stops and studies me, then slaps my arm before turning into my bedroom. "We need to work on that."

And at the door to my bedroom, I am floored. Plum floored. My mouth hanging open and everything. The moving man is pulling off the last piece of brown wrapping from the most beautiful, creamy-white chest of drawers I've ever seen. Then I gasp when I see the dresser matches it, except its drawers have been put in place and the top row of little drawers are baskets that slide into the slots. The mirror to go above it sits in front of the window, and it's a huge rectangle. The handles for the drawers are not the old brass like Mrs. Mason likes. They are that pretty soft silver, and the wood has little marks in it like it's been sitting all these years in some grandma's house just waiting for me.

"Oh, look at the headboard!" Esmeralda has unwrapped the big flat thing beside the bed, and now I hurry over to see it. Individual boards make it look simple, and yet the shine of the paint, and how big it is, tells me it's not as simple as it looks.

"The nightstand!" And I kneel to look at the little table with two drawers, one of them matching the baskets on the dresser. "It's beautiful, all beautiful."

Esmeralda pulls out a box cutter from her back pocket. "Now let's see about these boxes." The first box is light, and once it's opened she sets it in front of me. "See what's in there."

Through layers of paper I pull out two small quilted pillows. They are perfect. Off white and soft-yellow quilted squares with little blue embroidered flowers scattered across them. "Oh, do you think this is what the bedspread looks like?"

With a single nod, Esmeralda pulls out a clear plastic bag with the quilt to match inside. "So, this you like?"

"I don't think I ever dreamed anything this beautiful existed."

"See? I told you. They are grateful."

I lay the pillow down on the bed and smile at her enthusiasm. "No, it's just an accident. You don't know how much I disgust Caleb's family. If they couldn't stand me when we were first married and he still loved me, then they surely don't give a hoot about me now that he's gone. It's just a mistake, but I don't care." I caress the pillow in my lap. "I'm so happy. It's more than I ever dreamed of."

16

"**B**reaks my heart," Ruth says to Eason. "That young woman has no self-value whatsoever. You should've seen her with that bedroom set. You'd have thought it was made of pure gold."

Eason reaches over and pats his wife's hand before he picks up his tea and takes a sip. Their view from the terrace at the Ritz's Ocean Club is all sea and sand. "Glad you ladies could help her out. We poor men missed all the action with our golf game." He takes another drink and then watches the condensation run down the glass for a moment. "And, honey, don't feel too sorry for Becca Sue. According to George she slipped out of Magnus' house about four this morning."

Ruth pauses in unfolding her napkin, then lays it gently in her lap. "What was George doing up at 4 am? And he doesn't golf, so when did you talk to him?"

"He met us for drinks at the clubhouse afterwards." He smiles at his wife and shakes his head. "Honey, you know George often writes throughout the night. You can't get too sentimental about this girl. She's, well...she's not the type of person you're used to dealing with. I'm afraid she might be more, well, more capable than we might think. Ah, here's our food."

Ruth purses her mouth and nods as the waitress sets the plates down. She stares at her dinner until Eason finishes talking to the waitress. She gives the young woman a minute to walk away. Then, she barely opens her mouth as she challenges her husband. "You think I'm being played? How dare you, Eason King. I'm not some stupid housewife who never interacted with people unlike myself."

Eason nods as he unwraps his utensils and places the white cloth napkin on his lap. "Of course. I'm sorry you took it that way. Let's not talk about Becca Sue when we have what looks like scallops seared perfectly, a view to die for, and the best company around. Okay?"

His wife takes a deep breath and looks out to the ocean rolling in and out below them in the late afternoon sun. "Okay, but I do worry about her."

"Agreed, but let's put your willingness to help others behind us for the evening. Plenty of time to talk about Becca Sue later. I'm blessed to have such a caring woman for a wife."

Ruth smiles at her husband, but the hand on her napkin tightens its grip.

"Magnus is over there, again. George, did you hear me?" Pearl yells from her kitchen window. "He's out at her pool."

The whir of his mechanical chair alerts Pearl to her husband's presence, and she turns around still drying her hands on a kitchen towel. "You'd think she'd tell him to stay away now that those children are living there. You are not going to *believe* what her family up in Georgia sent her. Thousands, tens of thousands of dollars, worth of furnishings. Safe to say that tramp has the best furniture in the entire neighborhood. Just to take care of a couple very well-mannered teenagers. You won't believe it." She turns back to the window. "You saw Magnus today? Did you mention his late night visitor?"

"Have you never met me? Have you *ever* known me to nose into other people's business? Would I dream of stepping into your venue?" George moves to the patio door. "I'm starting the grill. Kabob's should be ready to put on in ten, right?" Once outside he pushes the door closed and Pearl looks after him smiling.

She chuckles out loud. "My venue." Her left eyebrow raises to an arch. "Right."

"What are you doing here?" Becca Sue stands looking over the edge of the pool.

"Swimming. What are you doing?" Magnus lays on his back and pushes away from the edge.

"Nothing." She sits on the side and lowers her legs into the water. "You missed all the excitement today."

"Golf games wait for no man or woman. I hear you got a load of furniture."

"Yeah. I may never see Maggie and Cab again. Their rooms are totally outfitted. Cab even has a small refrigerator, not that I got to see it. He wouldn't even let me in the door, but I saw the movers carrying it in. Maggie has her own TV and computer desk."

Magnus swims up and grabs her feet. "You feeling lonely? Want to come swim?"

He tugs on her feet, and she laughs. "Not now. Want a sandwich? I bought bananas and peanut butter today. Want me to make you a banana sandwich?" She pulls her feet up and brushes the water off them.

"Yuck! Why would I eat a banana sandwich? Didn't they have any deli meat or cheese?"

"Of course. We bought some ham and turkey, too, but nothing's as good as a banana sandwich. So, want one?"

"Maybe some turkey, but no way would I eat some redneck sandwich with fruit on it."

Becca Sue stands up. "Mr. World-Traveler, eating food from every dirty street market, even when you can't pronounce it and it hasn't been washed, but who's afraid to even taste a banana sandwich. You are so limited, so sheltered." She tsks and shakes her head as she walks to the house.

"Hell, that's true. Okay then, bring me a banana sandwich. Or maybe just half of one." He laughs and pushes a splash of water in her direction, then swims toward the deep end. "Can't believe the hick is getting me to try a banana sandwich. Yuck."

After several laps, he gets out and dries off, then wraps the towel around his waist and stretches out in the chaise lounge. When he sees Becca Sue approaching the doors he gets up and jogs over to open it for her. "Looks like you've got it all there."

"I think so," she says as she places it on the table. Sandwiches, chips, and a couple beers. "None of that fancy beer," she explains. "Bud Light is the official beer of banana sandwiches."

Magnus spreads his hands. "Whatever you say. You're the chef tonight. Kids eating banana sandwiches, too?"

"Oh lord, no. They're more stuck in their ways than you. I made them ham and grilled cheeses. That's what took me so long."

Magus twists off the cap from his beer. "Do they want to join us? There's plenty of seats."

"Naw, I took plates to their rooms. That's how they usually ate at home, too. The Masons are not real big on family dinners except on Sundays and holidays." She takes a bite into the bread and closes her eyes. "Mmm, that's so good."

"So, what exactly is on this?" He holds up half of his sandwich and stares at it.

"Crunchy peanut butter, sliced bananas, and the secret ingredient which I'm not telling you until you eat two bites. I've learned the hard way. It's a deal breaker sometimes." She takes another bite and struggles to keep from laughing out loud at his look of horror.

"I didn't bargain for 'secret ingredients.'"

"Just one! Don't be a big scaredy cat. Take a bite."

After a deep breath, Magnus takes a bite and chews carefully. As he chews, and through his swallow, he nods. "Okay, not bad." He takes another, more confident bite. "There is something, something tangy. Two bites, what is it?"

"Miracle Whip. You know, the salad dressing. Some people swear by mayonnaise, but I love the tang from Miracle Whip."

Magnus grimaces and looks at his sandwich again. He takes a swig of beer and after a little pause takes a big bite of his sandwich. "Just call me a redneck, I'm going native!"

Becca Sue laughs and throws a potato chip at him. "And when you reach the gourmet level you can stick a potato chip or two on the sandwich. Gives it a satisfying crunch." Becca Sue pushes a chip onto her sandwich and laughs during her crunchy bite. "See?"

Magnus leans with his elbows on the metal patio table, then picks up his bottle of beer by the neck. He tips it back for a long drink. Setting the bottle back down, he crosses his arms on the table. "Want to go out somewhere? The kids don't need you here. You said they are barricaded in their rooms."

Becca Sue licks her forefinger, and then uses it to collect the potato chip crumbs from her paper plate. "I don't know. Where you wanna go?"

"Let's go to the beach. Take a cooler and a couple towels, just like teenagers."

"Naw. Here, hand me your plate," Becca Sue says with her hand out. "I don't like the beach. All the sand and stuff."

"You don't like the beach? How can you not like the beach? You *moved* to the beach." Magnus crumbles up his paper napkin and stands up.

"Yeah, I guess I figured a house in Florida was somewhere near the beach, but I never thought about it." She shoves all their trash into the empty potato chip bag and stands, too. Just as she gets to the door Magnus stops her.

"Wait. Now that I'm thinking about it, we've never gone toward the beach when we've gone out. We always end up in some podunk, redneck town in the middle of a bunch of pine trees and pickup trucks."

Becca Sue yanks open the door, and halfway through it

turns to look at him. "Oh, now you're complaining? Fine. I knew you were just playing around with the hick. Remember, you called it. I'm just a hick. Nice to meet you, Mr. La-Ti-Da." And dismisses him by pulling the door behind her with a quick tug and slam.

Magnus shrugs and drains the rest of his beer. After setting the bottle back on the table, he turns and walks down the side of the pool. Underneath the pergola, he ambles out towards the lake, and then makes his way home along the edge of the lake.

The sun hangs just below the highest branches of the tall pine trees along the western end of the long, narrow lake. Pink and yellow brushstrokes don't blend with the still-blue sky. Florida: summer skies that don't color until the sun hits the low, far horizon, but then explode into reds, oranges, purples. That wasn't something the pines allowed a view of from the little lake.

Turtles dive in at his arrival in their area. A couple wild ducks check him out for bags of old bread, but quickly head off when they see he is empty-handed. When he reaches his own backyard, he stands beside the water and watches as dark steals the light from the very air around him.

"Dammit all to hell. I don't need her to go to the beach." Magnus stomps through his thick, manicured grass and flings open the door to his screened porch. "Wouldn't be any fun with a hick like her, anyway."

The lengthening shadows darken the neighboring screened porch but do nothing to keep a pair of ears from hearing Magnus' eruption. Once the slam of the ex-lawyer's door reverberates through the nearby yard, the listening neighbor pushes a button which lights up a cell phone. "Hello, Sybil? You might want to plan a trip back to Florida sooner rather than later." A few moments pass before the call ends with a quick "Goodbye," and George tucks his phone back into his pocket.

"Sooner would be much better than later," he mumbles as he lights his cigar.

17

"There really isn't going to be a discussion. I'm going out, and that's that." Cab grabs a bottle of water from the fridge and leaves the kitchen.

"Come back here! You have to tell me where you're going? Who you'll be with?" I dump my trash and Magnus' into the garbage can, and then hurry into the foyer where Cab already has the front door open.

"You have my phone number if you need me. Oh, and if you call Uncle J, I'll tell him you left us here alone last night with the doors unlocked and didn't come home from your booty call until 3 a.m." Without even closing the door, he walks across the front patio and down the sidewalk. He passes my car and jogs as he gets closer to the small red car waiting in the street. I get a quick glimpse of the blonde from the restaurant last night in the driver's seat. Cab jumps in, and the car roars off.

I close the door and lean on it. "Well, at least he didn't just take my car."

"He's taken cars before." The little voice makes me jump.

"Maggie, I didn't see you there. What do you mean? He's taken a car even without a license?"

"Yep. That's a big reason we got sent down here. Grand-mother thought he would be away from 'the bad kids' who were ruining him." Maggie pulls her hair behind her head and flips a rubber band off her wrist onto the impromptu ponytail as she walks into the kitchen. "Guess that didn't work."

I sigh and join her at the bar in the kitchen. "From my experience, if a person wants to get into trouble, they don't have any trouble finding it."

"Are you going over to Mr. Magnus' house tonight? I saw he was outside earlier."

"No, he's doing something else. What do you want to do?"

Maggie's smile curls, and she bats her eyelashes. "Well, Uncle J says there is the most amazing ice cream place down town. Let's go get ice cream."

I shake my head. "But we bought ice cream today. We have three different kinds. And cones and sprinkles. To go out and get ice cream would be silly." But in my head all I can hear is me saying, "No. No to shopping in the nice shopping center. No to going to the beach. No to getting ice cream."

The girl I've practically raised stares up at me for a minute, then rearranges her smile back onto her face. "Sure. That's true. We don't need to go out." She jumps up from her stool and at the refrigerator opens the freezer door. "What do you want?"

I take a deep breath. "Salted Caramel."

The dark head comes back into view as she pulls back. "But we didn't buy that one, remember? Just chocolate, moose tracks, and chocolate mint."

I wink. "Then I guess we'll have to go to the ice cream shop."

This time the smile doesn't have to be arranged. It just appears. "Really?"

I nod, and she darts off. "All I need are my shoes," she yells.

My stomach starts churning, and I wonder if I'll be able to keep any ice cream down. "I'll just focus on her and I'll be fine." Maybe I'll just stay in the car.

Open car windows and classic rock turned up loud help me to not think about where we're going—onto the nearby island where well-to-do folks take vacations. Plus, Maggie is chattering about Jameson and Cecelia's wedding in August.

"She's so beautiful, isn't she? She should've won Miss Georgia, but Grandmother said since a blonde won it last year, Cecelia lost because she's a blonde, too. And don't tell Grandmother," she says—like I'll be talking to Mrs. Mason any time soon—"but they're not going to live in Piney. Not at all. Uncle J says he saw what that did to my dad and his marriage, so they're going to live up in Atlanta. Grandmother is going to have a fit, but Uncle J says he doesn't care. Although he says Cecelia is a lot stronger than you, so she'll be able to handle Piney and Grandmother better."

Well now, hearing that they talk about me and how weak I am sure isn't helping my stomach. We turn left onto the most horrible street in the world. On our way to the Ritz the other night we drove down it. I swore I'd never find myself here and yet... Isn't that how scary movies begin?

Thousands of white lights fill the trees on both sides of the streets. Lit shop windows display crafts and clothes and purses, and people sit at street side tables eating dinner. A nightmare, right?

Monsters dressed in cute skirts and sundresses, or collared sport shirts and ironed shorts, wander the sidewalks and gather in groups around little black wrought iron tables with food and drinks. Then, on the next corner, the shop of torment and torture with cheery music and colored lights. Barrels of wrapped candies anchor the door, and through the window, the smell of fudge and caramel and vanilla is stomach-churning. It's full. It's always full of those people, the monsters. Of course, they don't look like monsters to most people. They look like the people you want to be around, or be like. But, I can't even imagine that. I don't belong here, with them. Ask anyone in Piney, and they'll tell you.

Maggie's eyes shine as bright as the shop windows and twinkle like the lights in the trees. "Isn't it wonderful?"

"Yes," I dismiss her. "So here's a twenty. Bring me a scoop of salted caramel, or if they don't have that, then just anything caramel or chocolate."

"But you're not coming in?" There's not even an attempt to reapply her smile this time. "I thought we could get our ice cream and then walk around. Look at stuff."

"There's traffic behind me. Jump out, and I'll drive around

the block. I'll look for a parking spot, and we'll see. Now go." I push the money towards her, and she gets out. Looking in my rearview mirror at the cars behind me, I push the thought of her sadness away. "She's just a kid. She'll get over it." Down the rest of the street, and then around a couple blocks, I keep my focus straight ahead and never let my eyes drift to the sides where there might wait an empty parking place.

Back on the corner where I dropped her, off she's waiting. I shrug and push open her door. "Couldn't find anything. Those look amazing."

She concentrates on eating her ice cream, something bright pink and orange, and seems to enjoy just looking out the windows as I hurry to the side street that will take us home. We pass a couple empty parking spots, but I pretend to not see them.

And she does, too.

Pulling into the driveway, Maggie opens my glove box and pulls out a little remote control, points it at the garage door and it slowly rises.

"How did you do that? Where did you get that clicker?"

"Cab found it on top of the refrigerator with all the other house stuff. Uncle J told us it was all there." We creep into the empty space, and she asks, "Didn't he tell you when you moved here?"

My shoulders slump. "I didn't even know about this house until the morning of the funeral. Jameson told me stuff, but I don't remember. All I could think was that it was a way out of Piney. Out of watching Audrey grow more pregnant. Out of living with my folks in that nasty trailer." I shove open the door and get out. In the garage, I laugh. "Honestly, he could've told me he'd buried gold in the backyard and exactly how to find it, and I wouldn't have heard. So how do we close this?"

"Buttons are over here by the door." Maggie pushes one, and the door begins closing. "Didn't you ever use the garage door opener at Dad's house? I mean, yours and Dad's house?"

"Well, of course, but Caleb told me 'Here's the clicker, push this button.' He showed me the buttons on the wall. And then we always had a housekeeper and lawn people. I never had to figure anything out. Things just happened."

In the kitchen, we both grab bottles of water out of the refrigerator. "Want to watch a movie?" I ask.

"Don't think so. I'm going to Skype some friends back home."

"On your computer?"

"Yeah, we can talk and see each other." She walks into the living room. "Wait, do you even have a computer or an iPad or anything?"

"No, I don't need anything like that, and wouldn't know what to do with it if I did." I sit down on the couch and pick up the TV remote. "I'm good with books, I guess. Although it sure is nice to have TV again."

"Well, before I go home, I'm going to get you on the internet. Get you on Facebook so we can talk when I'm back in Piney. Good night. Oh, and thanks for the ice cream. It was delicious."

"You're welcome. Good night, sleep tight." My thumb flicks the buttons and the channels roll by. The only muscle I'm allowing to move is my thumb, but my heart is about to jump out of my chest. I don't want to be on the internet. I don't want to talk to anyone in Piney. Why? I don't know. Why does it make my heart thump like this? I don't know.

Sure, I have furniture and TV and a new bedroom set, but it's not worth it. I want to go back to eating Pop-Tarts on the fireplace hearth, drinking all day and screwing my brains out all night. I want my heart to stop freaking out. Now.

Channels continue flashing by until I suddenly stop the parade by mashing the off button. Chilly darkness, accented only by the light from the pool, makes me shiver. Why did I think this place was an escape? That people would leave me alone and let me just live my life?

Of course, Maggie won't drop the internet idea. She'll push to go *into* the ice cream store, Cab will push every one of my buttons, make me set rules for him, and then enforce them. Esmeralda and Pearl will show up to do white glove tests on my floors. They act like they're just helping, but they really just want to get in my house and tell me what to do. Magnus will want to go the beach, where we'll run into his fancy friends. And eventually he'll see. They'll all see me like I really am.

Maybe I should just go back to Piney. Momma and Daddy already know. They know the real me.

The hole that opens up in my chest is bottomless, like the sink holes up by the bog at home. One minute it's all solid, and the next, it's just wide open blackness. The blackness makes me move, and at the refrigerator I don't even stop to look, just grab the open bottle of wine on the door. I dump the melted ice from my plastic iced tea glass from this afternoon, and take them both outside as quickly as possible.

The magical heat wraps around me. Like a damp towel that's only been in the dryer a little while, the air is warm and wet and heavy. I suck it in, and its heaviness fills my chest, fills the darkness, destroys the cold. Every hair on my head, my body, lifts at the moisture and welcomes it. I pour a glass of wine and take a long drink. It adds a wave of heat from the inside, and my muscles relax. I pull off my tee shirt and let the wet air touch me further, and after another long drink I pull my phone from the pocket of my shorts.

"Hey. Did you go to the beach?"

Magnus pauses before answering. "Yeah."

The black hole, the pounding heart, are almost gone. "Want to come swimming?"

This pause is even longer, but he finally ends it the same way. "Yeah."

"I'll be waiting." With the phone laid on the table, and the rest of the wine in my glass, I take off my bra, shorts and panties, and walk into the warm water.

"There. Everything will be better now."

18

"Becca Sue! Get up!" Maggie accents her yelling by banging on the bedroom door. Magnus pushes the groggy woman towards the edge of the bed. The room is in full darkness.

"What? Maggie? What time is it?"

Maggie opens the door just a couple inches. "It's Cab. He's in jail. Get up." She pulls back from the door, but her manners make her mumble, "Hello, Mr. Magnus."

The man in the bed growls a bit and rolls over to face away from the door. "Get the details, and I'll come help out in a minute. A drunken Yankee lawyer is better than no lawyer at all, I suppose."

Becca Sue shuts the bedroom door and goes into the bathroom, pulling on a long T-shirt and panties as she does. Splashing water on her face, she reaches for her washcloth. Magnus will share her bed, but not her washcloth. The counter shows he's also sharing her bathroom. The month of June rolled out its final two weeks, replaying that night of the ice cream drive-by. Cab partying every night. Magnus, with some help from the wine, keeping Becca Sue's emptiness filled. Maggie worrying and staying out of the way. It all happened over and over and over again.

Now July 4th is only 2 days away.

Becca Sue leaves the bathroom and sees Magnus is sitting on the edge of the bed. "Thanks for helping. I'll see what I can find out." She softly closes the bedroom door behind her. Maggie is waiting two feet away.

"He's in jail. Here." she holds out Becca Sue's phone. "It was outside, so we didn't hear it ring. He didn't call me until a few minutes ago, but by the time I got it, he'd just left a message. No one answers when I call it back; it just makes a weird sound. He left you messages, too, but I didn't listen to them." When Becca Sue just stands there, Maggie frets with her hands. "Hurry!"

Taking the phone, Becca Sue stumbles into the kitchen and leans on the counter. "its 4 a.m. Wonder when he first called?"

"His first call to you was around one. Guess y'all were already in bed."

Becca Sue concentrates on her phone, but starts chewing the inside of her mouth, as red begins creeping up her chest and neck. "Can you get me a glass of water? My head is pounding." She squints in the low light from the light under the sink. "Uh oh."

"What? What happened?" Maggie clutches an empty glass to her chest.

"My last four calls have been from your Uncle Jameson. Looks like Cab finally called him." Her voice is rough. "This is *not* good."

Maggie runs tap water into the glass and turns to give it to the young woman. "Not good? He's our uncle. Someone has to help Cab."

"I've tried and tried, he won't listen to me," she says while at the same time listening to the messages. "Nothing more on the messages. Just that he's in jail. Of course, by the last couple he sounds really mad."

"What did Uncle J say?"

Becca Sue sighs and drinks the full glass of water. She finishes and puts the glass in the sink. "Not much. Just a lot of yelling on those, too."

"Underage drinking." Magnus walks into the kitchen. "I called the station and explained the situation. Apparently, he and his friends were making quite a scene out at the Ocean

Club. One of the girls slapped one of the club security officers, and another girl claimed one of the club security guys of groping her. Left the club management with very little room to maneuver so they called the local cops."

Magnus leans on the counter beside Becca Sue and rubs her back. "Seems like all these nights he's not been coming home until morning, this little group has been raising Cain all over the island. It's half rich kids with names, and half locals." He takes down a glass and fills it with water. "I need to go home and get something better than my swim trunks or shorts to wear, then I'll come pick you up. If we get down there quick, we may be able to avoid a big mess."

He drinks all of his water, shakes his head, and heads to the living room. "You said Jameson called? Call him, and tell him I'll let him know what I find out. I'll be back in ten." He slips out the sliding door and jogs toward the lake.

Becca Sue stands motionless for a moment, and then turns toward her bedroom. "Mags, can you call your uncle and tell him what Magnus said? Thanks."

Maggie rolls her eyes and silently screams at the closed door Becca Sue is hiding behind. The girl retreats to her room, but takes out some of her frustration with a good, old-fashioned door slam.

"There's no way my grandfather is coming down here. I doubt if Grandmother Mason has even told him. He's not allowed to deal with serious things." Cab stands up. "I need to get some sleep. I don't know what everyone is so upset about. Things just got a little out of hand."

Glaring, early morning sun pours into the living room, outlining every wrinkle and sag on Magnus' and Becca Sue's faces. Maggie's young face is twisted in concern, and her eyes squint tight against the harsh light. Cab looks like the young god he believes himself to be. The sun highlights the blond hairs on his tanned arms and the streaks of blond in his hair. The rumple of his clothes could've been professionally done to keep him from looking *too* perfect.

He tips his head to Magnus. "I do appreciate your trouble, having to leave a warm bed and all," his eyes cut to Becca Sue, "but I'm sure once they got all the names straight, the right ones of us would've been released. The ride home was nice, at least. I've no idea how long it would've taken to get a taxi. Good night, all." He turns and heads toward the hall.

"Worth." Magnus drops the word into the bright room. "Not Mason, your Grandfather Worth."

Cab stops and turns only a quarter of the way around. "Is coming here?"

"Yes. You see, he and I go way back. Of course, I couldn't get his grandson, his only grandson, out of jail without letting him know."

Cab turns fully around now. "You had no right to do that."

Magnus shrugs. "Roger seemed quite appreciative. Said he'd had a couple reports from friends running into you and your little tribe down here the last few weeks. Said he'd been planning a trip down anyway. They should be here tomorrow."

The young god looks like he is going to be sick. He turns around, slinks down the hall, and closes his door with a small click.

Becca Sue leans up and pats Maggie's back. "Well, your grandparents will be happy to see you."

Maggie stands, and when she turns to look down at Becca Sue and Magnus, her tears have had time to run down her face and drip onto her shirt. "Happy? They won't be happy. How could you do this?" She tears across the living room, and her door closes with quite a bit more than a click.

Becca Sue and Magnus sit in silence as the dust motes swirl in the flood of sunlight. Becca Sue stands up. "Want a mimosa? Sounds like someone should toast the end of the world."

19

"Why did you put on heels?" I ask, as I try to balance a wobbly Maggie as we walk around the lake. "We would've walked on the road, if you'd have said something. Oops!" I blurt as I almost jerk her arm off when her heel gets stuck in the ground. "Just take them off and go barefoot until we get closer."

Up ahead, Cab turns around to walk backward and face us. "Not likely. Mags knows darling Grandmother Worth is most likely watching right now from their dear friend Magnus' windows and comparing her to her *other* granddaughters. I as the only grandson, though *any* comparison is welcome at *any* time, can never be found lacking. I could be heading over there right now buck naked and dear, dear Grandmother and Grandfather Worth would believe all young men should follow suit. Right, Mags?"

"Shut up!" she yells just a bit too loud, if they really are watching.

"Ignore him," I say. "You are beautiful, and of course, if they are watching, it's because they can't wait to see you." I smile and try to make her wobbly progress look more graceful. Just in case. "Your dress is perfect with your hair, and remember, you have your grandfather's eyes. Everyone says he has the most amazing green eyes, and so he has to love seeing them in his granddaughter's face."

"But you've never seen them. The other girls," she whispers

as our heads are bent together.

"And I probably never will. Your grandparents are here to see you and Cab, and the others are far away. They belong to your mother's sister, right?"

"Yes, Aunt Helen. Wow, would you hate Aunt Helen." Maggie giggles. "She's an ice queen, and she really hates Cab, since she only had girls."

"Well, maybe she can get a sex change operation for one of them." We laugh, and as she relaxes, our walking becomes easier.

Cab can't hear us talking, but he keeps looking back when we laugh. He finally drops closer to us and advises, "Get all your laughing out now. You won't be laughing soon."

I watch Maggie's face fall, and I hiss at him, "*You* should be the one worried. You're the one that was in jail last night." I reach out and lay my hand on his arm. "Cab, remember what I'd always say when you were little. Admit when you're wrong and then apologize."

He jerks his arm away and stares at me with cold eyes. "Apologizing is for losers, and Cab Worth Mason is not a loser."

We arrive at the back of Magnus' home, and Cab runs onto the screened porch and then into the living room.

Magnus holds the screen door for us. "Maggie, don't you look pretty. Your shoes may not be great for walking around the lake, but they are perfect for you."

She smiles at him and takes a deep breath. I reach for his hand, but he moves to open the big French doors for Maggie. I follow her, and we walk into the lovely living room with the jewel-tone furniture. The room is full of people.

Magnus goes across the room and speaks in a low voice with a tall man in a cream-colored jacket. The man's hair is blonde with an esteemed touch of gray, and when he lifts his head in the direction Magnus motions, his green eyes blaze across the room. They are truly remarkable, and I'm mesmerized.

I put my hand on the small of Maggie's back. "There's your

grandfather."

She takes a step in his direction when he lifts a hand. "Margaret. Good to see you," he says and then turns completely around to a woman standing behind him.

Maggie stops cold. "It's Aunt Helen. Why is she here?" The girl's eyes fly around the room, then stop at a little group near the front entrance. Cab appears to be holding court with three teenage girls and, as I take a step closer to Maggie, I see tears forming. "No, they can't be here."

An elegant woman, with gold jewelry lying in the plunging neckline of her white dress, steps to us and takes one of Maggie's hands in her own. "Dear Margaret, how are you?"

"Fine, Grandmother Worth."

My head explodes. *Grandmother?* This woman looks like she's as young as me. Her hair is a perfect red, not clay-colored like mine, and not that artificial purple-red so many young people choose. Her boobs are nestled in the deep V of her dress like balloons. She's gorgeous and, wait, she's not said one word to me.

"Hi, I'm Becca Sue Cousins Mason," I say as I stick my hand out.

She tilts her head in my direction. "Yes, I hear marrying cousins is quite popular in the South. Leave it to Caleb to go running from his marriage to my daughter to a relative."

"But he, he didn't. He..." I stammer.

"Dear, does it really matter?" She gives me a cold shoulder. For the first time I really get that saying. "Margaret, we will get together again, I'm sure, while we are on the island. We understand you have accommodations with Miss Cousins, so we won't make you move everything. Wonderful to see you again, my dear." She leans to tap Maggie's cheek with her deep red lips and then moves through the room to Cab's side. Once there, she puts one arm around the blonde girl next to him and links her other arm into Cab's.

Maggie watches and barely contains her tears. "Can we go?"

"Go? We just got here, honey."

She turns to face the screened porch and talks to me with her head tilted down. "But you can see it's not me they want to see. Believe me, no one cares if we leave."

I pull open the door we'd only moments before come through. "Go sit on the porch for a minute. I'll bring you something to drink, okay?" She nods and steps out into the heat of a July afternoon. "I'll be right back."

On the edge of the crowd, I wonder who all these people are. In the kitchen, as I put ice in a glass and then pour lemonade over the ice, I study the crowd in the adjoining room.

Helen stands post at her father's side. She looks like Cab and Maggie's mother, except she only has her father's cool blondness set amidst a sea of tanned skin, none of her mother's red hair and creamy skin. Cab and his cousins look like they are shooting an ad for Gap Teen or something. The girls all have strikingly blonde hair hanging down their backs, and while I can't see their faces, I can see their shorts are tiny. Like Barbie doll clothes, so small you can't imagine a real body could fit in them. Of course they don't look vulgar; they are much too expensive to be vulgar. The other people, I count five, are a range of ages, and while none have approached Cab they all seem to be sneaking peaks at him as they mingle around the room. Magnus has disappeared, so I move on out to Maggie.

"Here you go," I say, handing her the lemonade. "Are you okay?"

"Better. Ready to leave when you are."

"Okay, let me go look real quick for Magnus. I'll be right back."

Back in the room, I stay to the edges and don't make eye contact. Magnus still isn't around, and so I dart down the hallway. In the past couple weeks, I've become familiar with his home so I know where the master suite is. Just want to let him know Maggie and I are leaving.

At the master bedroom door, I push it open just a bit, then it's pulled open wider from the other side and I step back.

"Yes?" The woman holding the door is older than me, with dark hair cut short. She has on black slacks and a sleeveless black turtleneck with a beige sweater pulled over her shoulders.

"I'm sorry. I was looking for Magnus."

She looks down at my sleeveless white shirt and short khaki skirt. When she gets to my green flip flops, she pulls her eyes back to my face. "Let me guess. You're that Betty Joe."

"Becca Sue."

The woman sighs and shakes her head. "No idea where Magnus is. I'll tell him you were looking for him." And she shuts the door in my face.

I move down the hall and through the room, again along the walls. I return to the porch and to Maggie. "Come on, let's go."

She follows me off the porch, and at the edge of the yard, she jogs to catch up with me. I look down at her feet and her shoes in her hand, and say, "Now that Cab is there, no one's looking outside anymore, right?"

She smiles at me, and it causes me to slow down and smile a bit, too.

"Did you find Magnus?" she asks.

I say, "No," but even as I do I replay what I saw reflected in the standing mirror in the corner of his bedroom, Magnus behind the door, behind the woman who lied to my face.

20

"Must be water aerobics time," Maggie points at our pool when we get closer.

"Shoot. Just what we *don't* need. All of them wanting to know what's going on. But I guess we can't help it."

"Maggie, that dress is adorable on you," Esmeralda's nasal voice calls from the shallow end. "And I love your hair pulled away from your face like that."

Becca Sue pushes Maggie to walk faster, but the girl stops at the edge of the pool. "Thank you, Miss Esmeralda."

Ruth chimes in as she continues moving her Styrofoam-covered weights back and forth. "I do like being able to see your face. Your eyes are just remarkable."

Maggie smiles and shakes her head to let her hair fall around her shoulders. "Mother bought my dress in New York."

Esmeralda nods. "I can tell it's very expensive, and cut so very well."

Becca Sue wanders toward the doors. Her green flip flops make little noise.

"Why did you leave Cab over at Magnus' house? Who are all those people over there?" Pearl shouts from where she hangs onto the deep end ladder.

Maggie folds her arms around her waist, being careful to hold her shoes away from her dress. "I'm going to go change." She walks past Becca Sue, but her head stays bent.

As soon as the door closes behind the girl, Becca Sue turns

and nods at Ruth and Esmeralda. "Thanks for saying Maggie looks good." Becca Sue shoots a mean look at Pearl and heads back toward the door.

"What? I asked about her brother! She'd already been told she looked good. What was I supposed to say?" Pearl asks as she climbs out of the pool.

"Pearl, we're not done," Jane the instructor admonishes from her seat on the side of the pool.

"Well, I'm done. I can't concentrate with all this activity, and us not even knowing what's going on in our own neighborhood." Pearl picks up a towel from the lounge chair and dries herself. "Did Cab get arrested last night? We deserve to know what type of hoodlums live here."

"Ignore her, honey," Ruth says from just below Becca Sue, as she places her weights on the side of the pool. "Pearl's just forgotten what it's like to be around teenagers. They do stupid stuff and get into trouble."

"Not all teenagers!" Pearl admonishes.

Esmeralda shakes her head as she does some stretching exercises in the shallow end. "Ruth is right. They all do stupid stuff, sometimes bad, sometimes not so bad. It's the nature of the beast."

Becca Sue steps toward the pool. "Oh no, Cab might be a little wild, but he ain't no beast. He didn't even have to spend the night in jail."

"He *did* go to jail. Told you." Pearl nods at the other ladies. It's fascinating how quickly the busybody changes topics. "And is that his Grandfather Worth over at Magnus' house? Vivian Worth, his grandmother, is absolutely stunning. She is always in the society column. We should have a party for them. Magnus will know what we should do."

She picks up her bag, and before she can get her shoes slid on completely, she stops. "Oh, maybe the Worths will buy the development! They have that kind of money, and it will help out their grandchildren." She hurries to get her shoes settled. "We must talk to Magnus. This could all turn out so well. Thank you, Jane. Bye, everyone."

Esmeralda joined Jane sitting on the side of the pool. "We cleaned for Vivian Worth's daughter's family. That woman was cold, very cold."

"Helen?" Becca Sue says. "I saw her over there today. Her daughters are here, too."

"She was just one of our accounts. I never met her or her children, but our ladies did not like her at all. Never once gave them a Christmas bonus or tip."

Ruth speaks up. "So, if I may ask, where is Cab, if he's not still in jail?"

Becca Sue points across the lake. "Still over there. Maggie felt really out of place. Maybe I should go check on her."

"Becca Sue?" Jane causes the young woman to stop her turn towards the house. "That skirt looks really good on you."

"She's right," Ruth adds. "Very flattering."

Becca Sue looks down at it. "Thanks. Maggie and I ran into Walmart last week and bought some clothes. She made me wear it today." Her smile grows with each loud flip-flop towards the door where she waves and goes inside.

Jane stands up and stretches. "Do you think she was wearing a bra? How can a woman get to be her age and not know some things need to be put in place?"

"Jane!" Ruth exclaims.

"Okay, so I shouldn't have said that, but someone has to help that poor girl. She's a mess."

Esmeralda struggles up from the side of the pool. "You don't know the half of it," she laments as she shakes her head. "You ought to see the way she keeps a house."

"Eason says I'm not reading her right, and she does confuse me at times. Although, lately, my biggest question has been why would the Mason family trust her with those two children? They've been here two weeks and during that time Cab's been arrested, Magnus has slept over here most every night, and the drinking is never-ending. Poor Maggie even looks like she has gained several pounds."

Esmeralda sighs. "I can attest to the drinking *and* Magnus *and* that they eat fast food or frozen fast food all the time. I come over to clean and see all that, but what can I say?"

Jane slips on a black pull-over sundress. "It's just sad. Is there anyone we should notify? Their uncle maybe?"

Esmeralda spits to her side. "That's why Becca Sue doesn't look so bad to them. The whole family is evil. Jameson Mason is a rotten apple. What does he care about his brother's children as long as they are out of his way? Their mother is too busy. Too busy for her own children! Ugh, I have to go home. I have a headache now."

Jane and Esmeralda both leave as Ruth tells them she wants to swim a couple more laps. Silently she circles the pool, and just as she gets ready to leave the water she watches Becca Sue's bedroom window slide shut.

Ruth catches her breath. "Damn, she was listening."

21

"They're just jealous their boobs are old and saggy and need to be held up. Mine look just fine." *Of course, I am holding my shoulders high and arching my back.* I hold my breasts up and look in the mirror, turning for a side view. "Okay, maybe I'll look into a bra. Maybe a black one. Or a camo one."

Wearing a bra just always seemed like something *old* women did. Or women that wanted more in their shirt than they already had. Momma wore one of those push-up things, so she had cleavage for her customers at the restaurant. Said it paid for itself in one day's tips. I never needed help in the wanting more area, and Caleb always liked that he could reach out at any time and get a handful of real boob.

Magnus ain't getting no handful of real boob from that piece of skin and bones he was hiding behind in his bedroom. I walk out of the bedroom as I pull on a white button-up. I need to go see how Maggie is. Instead of checking on her earlier, I rushed into my bedroom to listen at my window and see if the ladies talked about that woman at Magnus'. I'm betting that's that Sybil. But they just talked trash about me. Old lady bitches.

"Jameson!" I pull the sides of the shirt together, but not quick enough to keep my ex-brother-in-law from getting a free show. "What are you doing here?"

"I told Maggie I would be here today. Why are you wandering around the house half-naked? Just getting out of bed? Scoot back in there and tell Magnus I need to talk to him."

My face feels like it's on fire, and it gets hotter as he stands there watching me button my shirt. My fingers fumble with the buttons, but he stays cold as ice, watching. Finally, I turn away from him in surrender. "He's not here. Cab's not here, either. He's with Magnus and the Worth family over at Magnus' house." I shove my elbow towards the back wall of windows. "Maggie is here, though."

He takes a deep breath, and then walks to Maggie's bedroom door, knocks gently, and tells her it's him. She says something I can't hear, but he enters, and closes it behind him.

The air conditioner cuts off, and the house is silent. I turn in a slow circle and all is clean, big, and silent. The only thing out of place is the suitcase beside the front door. So Jameson is staying. The ladies are right. I can't take care of Cab and Maggie, and now both of their families are here. I lost my one and only job. Probably lost my home, too.

In the kitchen, I open the cabinet beneath the sink. "Guess the party's over. 'Bout time to head back to Piney," I say out loud as I haul out the big bottle of gin. "Sounds like something to drink a toast to." Into a large red solo cup, I pour some of the liquor that smells like Christmas trees. I grab a handful of ice cubes and a small bottle of diet Sprite from the refrigerator. "I'll sure miss you, refrigerator." A shudder runs through me at the thought of Momma and Daddy's trailer and nasty refrigerator.

"You're talking to the refrigerator?" Jameson asks as he turns the corner into the kitchen. "Gin? Make me one, but have you got any tonic?"

I split the ice cubes between my cup and the one he picks up off the counter and holds out to me. "No, but there's real Sprite in there," I say.

"In the refrigerator you talk to? Why are you talking to the refrigerator anyway?" he asks with his head stuck in the conversational appliance.

I don't have to answer his stupid questions. "Just 'cause.

How's Maggie?"

He shakes his head and then motions to the front door. "Let's step outside."

On the front porch we lean against the wooden railing in the one shady spot and take sips of our drinks.

"So, you met the Worths, I hear."

"They even give Yankee a bad name, don't they?"

Jameson laughs. "Yes, they do. Guess they were pretty brutal to Maggie, as usual?"

"Don't know if it's *as usual*, but yeah, didn't give her the time of day. She tell you her cousins are here?"

He takes a drink and nods. "Yeah, aren't they something? Did you know they model? Every teen magazine Maggie picks up or clothing store she goes in to, at least one of them is staring back at her."

"Seems unfair they got all the best parts of the family genes." I fish a little bug out of my drink and flick it into the yard before taking another sip.

"But they didn't. They all wear contacts. None of them have Maggie's Worth eyes and only one is a real blonde. They are like dolls, all made to look alike." Jameson shakes his head a bit and then drains his cup. "Man, that was good. So, listen. I'm staying for the weekend. Cab is staying with the Worths, so I'll take his room."

"Why don't you just take the master? I can be out real quick-like and leave in the morning."

Jameson steps away from the railing. "Where are you going?"

"Home. I can't take care of the kids. You and the folks here have got business to do with these houses and this half-done neighborhood. I appreciate y'all letting me stay here to get over Caleb's dying and all, but it's time for things to get back to normal. I'll go pack."

"You can't leave."

"But the car's mine. Right? Caleb said it was mine when we got divorced." I push away from the railing.

"No, I mean yes." He reaches out and grabs my arm as I

brush past him to the front door. "The car is yours, but so is this house."

At the door, I turn to him and smile. "How can this house be mine? I know nothing about houses, and I know *absolutely* nothing about owning a house. I didn't even know about the garage door opener until the kids found it. People work hard to own houses, especially houses like this. I've done nothing, ever. I understand you wanted someone to watch the kids, but I'm no good for that anymore. They're much smarter than me and are part of a world I'll never figure out. I fitted in with Caleb because, well, because," I lift up my red cup, "because of the alcohol and the sex. But I don't have nothing to offer Cab and Maggie." I shrug off his arm and smile at him as I open the front door. "Everyone knows that. Everyone including me. It's been fun, and I'm real appreciative, but I should go home and let you folks get things straightened out."

Inside, I let the glass door close behind me, and the silence reaches deep into me. Silly girl, for a while I thought this would be my new home. Sunlight glinting off the pool reminds me of the hours spent swimming, how the water stays so blue and cool. Not like where I learned to swim at the lakefront. The fourth is tomorrow, and by time I get home, everyone will be down at the lakefront cooking out and waiting on the fireworks. And with the fifth being Saturday, everybody will party all night down there. It's been a long time since I was at the lake. Masons don't hang out where the water is dirty, smells like fish, and the people match it. Course, Masons weren't usually in Piney for the Fourth of July, anyway, but I wasn't never welcome on their getaways, either.

I fix another drink and head to my room to start packing. "Girl, it's time to get back to one world and stay there. High time."

I hesitate outside my bedroom door, and when my breath catches, I wait for the hole to open back up in my chest. As it starts opening, I release myself to the darkness inside, close my eyes, and push open my door.

"Hello, beautiful. You dreaming of me?"

"Magnus?" My eyes pop open. "What are you doing here?"

He's sitting on my bed, where he puts his hands behind him and leans back. "Waiting on you. Saw you out front talking to Jameson and figured it'd be best if I waited in here. Roger says Jameson is coming to stay for a few days, to represent the Mason side of the family."

I step in the room and softly close the door behind me. "Yeah, I guess so." I take a big drink, set my cup on the pretty, white bedside table, and step up to the bed. Magnus leans up and pulls on the hem of my shirt.

"Come here. All those fake people at my house made me miss you."

"Are they all still there?"

Warmth flows over me as he reminds me why I don't wear a bra, but just as the warmth pulls me onto the bed, there's a knock on my door. I stumble, fall to the bed, and his hand gets tangled under my shirt.

Which is the scene Jameson sees as he opens my door saying, "Becca Sue, you don't understand...Oh my God." He turns around and slams the door behind him.

My horrified expression is not mirrored on Magnus's face. He's grinning, and I push him away. "What is wrong with me? You're just marking your spot like some old mangy hound dog!" I jump off the bed. "Go home. Go home and tell Sybil I said she can have you. How could I let a man who would hide behind a woman in his own bedroom feel me up?"

"Oh, so you saw me?" He stands up. "Honestly, I just couldn't have a scene with Roger's family all there. Sybil is back, but not because I asked her. And as for 'marking my spot'? No. I don't believe in competition. You either want me or you don't. Besides, Jameson isn't any threat. He's too young and stupid to see you for who you can be." He takes my hand and holds it in both of his. "That was the truth when I said that all those fake people made me miss, and appreciate, you. I'll leave now, but tomorrow night you are going with me to see the fireworks at the beach."

He presses my hand when I shake my head and start to

talk. "No, we're not doing that. I'll pick you up at six. We're going shopping, then we are going to dinner, and then fireworks. That's it."

He pulls me to him, kisses my cheek and then drops my hand. "Good night. See you tomorrow."

In the living room, he shakes Jameson's hand and they talk about the neighborhood. I listen for a few minutes, then close my door. I pick up the novel I'm reading and go into the bathroom to run a bath.

Okay, so I can move out day *after* tomorrow, 'cause I have a date for tomorrow. A real date. I'm in the tub with my book and candles lit before I realize I left my drink back on my bedside table, and the next realization surprises me.

I don't really want it.

22

"We have to go, Maggie. Really, there's no way out," Jameson says as he carries the frying pan full of scrambled eggs to the table and sits it on the hot pad, then sits in the third chair. "It'll be fun. The Worths' boat is huge, and besides, seeing the fireworks from out on the water will be amazing."

I scoop out eggs for my plate and Maggie's. "And besides, your uncle has some business to discuss with your grandfather, right?"

Jameson shoves eggs onto his plate and ignores the question.

Maggie places her paper napkin in her lap. "Are you going, Becca Sue?"

"Yeah, right. Only way I'd get invited is if they need someone to clean up all the seasick barfing."

"Please, Becca Sue, we're trying to have breakfast," Jameson moans. "No one will be seasick. We need to be down at the marina by five. That gives us the whole day to relax here. We can swim or do whatever you want. Of course, you two sleeping until noon cut the day short. How many movies did you watch last night?"

"Three, a Julia Roberts marathon," Becca Sue answers. "Eggs are good. Thanks."

"It was fun." Maggie's sea green eyes shine at her uncle. "Just like we used to do. Dad and Cab would go off and play video games, but me and Becca Sue watched movie after movie."

Jameson nods. "Well, you can do it again tonight after we get back, but we are going on the boat." He takes a deep breath, and his niece's reluctant happiness is reflected in his face as he looks at Becca Sue. "I'm assuming you don't want to go with us, right?"

"You are assuming correctly. Besides, I have a date." She looks up in time to watch the happiness, reflected or otherwise, fall off her ex-brother-in-law's face.

"With Magnus?"

"Yes. A date. A real date."

Maggie beams and claps her hands. "Can I help you get ready?" she asks.

"A little late for a *date*, isn't it?" her uncle growls at the same time.

Becca Sue's face turns red, and she looks at the napkin clutched in her hand lying on the table. "So, the pool sounds like a great idea. I'll get this cleaned up and meet you outside. Okay, Maggie?"

Maggie jumps up from the table as Jameson takes one more bite of his toast and then pushes his plate away. "Well, at least we know you have several bikinis and plenty of wine for an afternoon at the pool."

"And how do you know that?" Cleaning up the dishes, Becca Sue doesn't realize Jameson isn't saying anything.

Maggie stops on her way into the entry hall. "Yeah, how do you know that?"

"Um, well, from the shopping lists."

Becca Sue turns to Jameson. "What shopping lists?"

Maggie tilts her head and presses her lips into a thin line. "Really, Uncle J? You're examining Becca Sue's bank account? You're acting just like Grandmother Mason. Even Dad didn't do that!"

Jameson stands up. "I've got some calls to make. And keeping a close eye on my, I mean, our, um, well, *the* money is just smart."

Maggie stomps her foot. "It's not smart, it's spying. Tell him, Becca Sue."

Becca Sue has deflated. "But it is smart," she concedes. "It's his money, their money. They should keep an eye on it. I guess you see everything when I use my card at the store?"

Jameson's eyes spread wide at the open look on Becca Sue's face. "Yeah, but well, you should have privacy. I'm sorry."

"Privacy? I grew up in a two-bedroom trailer without a cent to my name. What do I need privacy for?" she laughs. "Besides, Maggie's right. Your mother always knew everything I did. No big deal." She shrugs and laughs again as she carries an armload of dishes to the sink.

Behind her back, Jameson and Maggie shake their heads and walk away.

"Well, there's the funeral dress." Only Maggie's mouth moves in the hot afternoon sun, as it beats down on the pool area. She and Becca Sue occupy both lounges.

"Wear black?"

"Black is very fashionable. You know, like 'the little black dress.'"

Becca Sue lifts her head off the lounge cushion. "What little black dress? My funeral dress isn't exactly little. No, I don't want to wear it. It's my cousin's anyway, and black is for old people."

Maggie sits up and fans her face, her black one-piece bathing suit stretching tight across her stomach. "I wish mother would let me wear a bikini."

"My green one is hanging in my bathroom; go try it on. The pink one is in the dirty clothes, though."

"Mother says I don't have the shape for it. Bet the cousins are all going to be wearing bikinis on the boat today." As if the thought propels her, she stands and steps to the edge of the pool.

"Ugh. I'm not even going to be there and that made my stomach flip-flop. Hey!" Becca Sue shouts when the spray from Maggie's cannonball showers her. Maggie swims up to the side of the pool, and Becca Sue leans on her elbow to look down at the girl. "You really are pretty, honey. Those cousins of yours aren't normal. They're fake. You're not."

With her arms crossed on the hot pavers, Maggie lays her chin on them. "Why wouldn't you go in the ice cream store, but now you are going on a date at the club? I know that first night you went to the Ritz Ocean Club with me and Cab you were okay because you were kinda drunk. Are you planning on getting drunk to go tonight?"

"Whoa, maybe a little fakeness would be good for you! I wasn't exactly drunk." Becca Sue gets up and walks over to the wide step leading into the shallow end. She looks around for a bit and then sits on the middle steps, half submerged. "I don't know. Some of it is that Magnus is onto me. He knows I've been avoiding the beach and town like the plague. It kinda felt this way with your Dad. He made it okay that I didn't belong. Like he chose me anyway, so I could go anywhere with him and be okay."

"And with just me you don't have any cover?" Maggie asks.

"Yeah, cover." Becca Sue slides down to the next step so that only her head sticks out of the water. "Maybe that's it." She goes under and swims across the pool.

At the far end she comes up and hangs on the side like Maggie was doing on the other side. She says quietly, "So, what am I worried about? Magnus knows who I am and what I look like, and he asked me to go with him." Then adds louder, "Not like he's getting a pig in a poke."

"What?" Maggie laughs.

"A poke is what old folks call a sack, a paper sack, I think. So like a pig in a sack that you can't see through. Yeah, Magnus knows me." She dives under and swims toward the steps. When she comes out of the water, she has a plan. "So, let's do what we can with my hair. You can help me put on some makeup, and I'll surprise Magnus, okay?"

"Absolutely. He'll feel like he won the lottery!" Maggie exclaims.

23

"**G**ood morning."

"Shoot fire, you scared me!" *I'll just walk right past him and into the house like nothing's wrong.* "See you later."

"That door's locked." Jameson is seated at the patio table between the pool and the house.

I twist the door knob just to check, but when my hand gets no leeway, I turn to Jameson. "So how did you get out here?"

"Through the garage. There's a code, you know. Perfect for when you go running." He waves his hand at his shorts and shoes. "Or when you're out doing other types of exercise." Here he waves his hand at me. "Pretty fancy exercise clothes, by the way. I thought Maggie had you dolled up in your khaki skirt and a red shirt last night."

"Well, Magnus had other plans. Isn't it gorgeous?" In one fell swoop I became a believer in bras last night. Seeing what happens in the right dress with my boobs, and then what happens in men's eyes, made me a convert. I hold out my soft-beige high heels, looped over my fingers. "Shoes, too. So, do you like it?"

Jameson tries to look bored. "I guess its fine. Kind of bright, isn't it?"

"Is it?" I smooth my hands down the shiny green sparkles. "Reminds me of a mermaid's tail, but the women at the salon said it went great with my hair and skin. It is too bright, isn't it?"

Jameson opens his mouth like he's going to say "No" and so I wait for him to say he's mistaken, that it's perfect, that he approves. Then he shakes his head and looks back down at his newspaper. "Magnus must've liked it. Of course, he probably didn't see much of it once he got you back to his house."

"Shows what you know. We didn't go back to his house. We stayed at the Ritz." I jerk on the door knob. "What's that stupid code for the garage door?" I spit at him, marching past his chair on my way to the driveway side gate.

He sighs. "Okay, your dress is pretty, and your hair is, uh, very straight."

"And you're a jerk. What's the code?"

"One-zero-one-six."

"Really? I should be able to remember that, it's my birthday."

He shrugs. "Whatever. You might want to put your shoes on while you're on this side of the gate, since there's gravel before you get to the driveway."

"Yeah, right. I couldn't walk in these things on a solid floor. Gravel? No way. Plus, I think it would mess up the heels."

Through the gate, slamming it just for emphasis, I shift the ivory high heels to my left hand so I can punch in the code. "What is it about high heels and men? Magnus even wanted me to wear them when I got out of the car this morning." As the garage door lifts, I look at the shoes and smile. "Magnus may not have seen the green dress much once we got to our room, but these little puppies were front and center of the fun. Dress or no dress." I feel myself blush and wish I'd thought to say that to Jameson. *Show him I don't care a bit what he thinks.*

I tiptoe through the kitchen, but in the living room, it's obvious there's no reason to be quiet. "Up already?" I ask Maggie who's sprawled on the couch, her back to me.

"I slept here last night. I thought you were coming home to watch movies."

Shoot, that's right. "Well, we ended up staying out at the Ritz." She sits up and catches me before I can get to my room.

"Whoa, look at that dress! And your hair, I love it. Turn around."

"Okay," I say and slowly turn and pose. "Enough, I have to sit down. My feet are killing me. Just look at these shoes. Scoot."

"Where did you get this dress?"

"Told you Magnus wanted to go shopping? Well, we got to the Ritz, and he had a whole team of women waiting for me. We went into the salon; he didn't go, of course. They washed me and waxed me, did my hair, my nails, everything. It was like that scene in *The Wizard of Oz* where whole teams of people are working on making Dorothy as beautiful as possible."

Maggie squirms around in the blankets so her feet are lying in my lap. I massage them like I did when she was little. "They had three dresses for me to choose from, but this one was everyone's favorite because of my hair. Can you believe the color of my hair? It's always just been like mud, but now it's so glamorous."

Maggie squints. "I don't see much different in the color, but it is so shiny and so straight. How did they do that?"

I shrug. "Who knows? But you should've seen Magnus when I walked out. He almost fell over, and it was so weird. I always thought boys didn't like tall girls, but with these heels I was taller than most everybody, and they all said I was fantastic."

"Who's all?"

"His friends. We had drinks with a bunch of his friends, and I was fine." Gazing out the back windows I remember that I was more than "fine." Several of the men came onto me and tried to touch me, and even then Magnus was so proud of me, he didn't realize it. I'll have to tell him those men aren't really his friends. "But, hey," I switch tactics, "how was the boat?"

"Okay. Being okay to be tall must just be for older people because my sweet, cute, tiny cousins were the hit of the night. I hate them." She turns, pulls her feet out of my lap, and curls up facing the TV.

"Aw, come on, were the fireworks at least pretty?"

"I guess. Once it got dark, I could just hide in the corner and watch everyone, and, well, the fireworks."

"Did Cab have fun?" She doesn't answer, so I shake her leg. "Mags? How was Cab?"

She still won't answer, and then snakes one hand out of the blanket to get the remote and turn the volume up. I turn to focus on the TV. *I'll ask Jameson about Cab later.*

24

"Great tip on the Ritz salon! She hardly looked like the same girl." Magnus lines up his putt and swings. The ball rolls past the cup, and he growls, "Who thought a tee time this early was a good idea on the fifth of July?"

"It's only a problem if you're dating someone half your age who keeps you up late. Esmie wouldn't even go out to see the fireworks." Patrick's putt falls, and as he scoops his ball up, he starts walking away from Magnus. "Sink that, and let's go inside. This heat is suffocating. Reminds me of Esmie."

Thick Florida grass cushions Magnus' steps up to the clubhouse. Condensation on the windows points to the already great difference in the inside and outside temperatures, thanks to the heavy overnight humidity. He walks over to the table and drops into a chair. "Guess it's a good thing we did have an early slot, since it's already like playing in a bowl of hot soup out there."

Patrick wipes his forehead and nods. "I ordered us a couple Irish coffees. Told them to hold any whipped cream so everyone will just think its plain coffee."

"I don't need the calories from the cream, but what do I care if people know I'm drinking?" Magnus asks.

"Or screwing a backwoods chick. God, I need your life."

"Esmeralda might disagree."

"Of course Esmie would disagree. She disagrees with anything that might make me happy."

"Except paying your bills." Magnus sneers.

"Oh, speaking of screwing, isn't Sybil back in town?" Patrick leans on the table. His rich brown hair and beard, along with his youth, make him stand out in the room of mostly gray hair and clean-shaven faces.

Magnus stares the younger man down. "Yeah, Sybil is back in town. She's staying with Pearl and George."

But the stare doesn't faze Patrick as he lowers his voice. "You banging both of them? Like a smorgasbord, some of everything? Old, young, skinny, not so skinny, socialite, hillbilly."

Magnus stands up. "None of your business, you jealous SOB. None of your business at all."

He saunters out of the room and into the main hall. He talks to a half-dozen people around the room and then hands his ticket to the valet. Back out into the humidity and harsh light, he slips on his sunglasses and waits for his car. Into the thick air he wonders aloud, "Wonder if the jerk is guessing, or actually knows anything?"

"High heels? She was wearing high heels?" Ruth shakes her head. "Can't picture it. She looks awkward just wearing flip flops."

Pearl arches her already cosmetically-arched eyebrows. "No one was concerned with how awkward she looked. They were waiting for her breasts to fall out of the front of that dress, or maybe they were watching her walk and waiting for her to fall so that scrap of a Christmas decoration she was wearing would expose whether she had any panties on or not."

Ruth unfolds her legs from her reading chair and leans closer to her friend. "What did Sybil say?"

"Honestly? She didn't seem bothered at all, but she had to be crushed. Don't you think so?"

A door closing in the house causes Ruth to tilt her head that way. "Must be Eason. He didn't feel like going to the golf course this morning. Shoot, if he'd gone, he could've told us what Magnus has to say."

Pearl shudders. "That man is hurting two women in this neighborhood. It's about time someone stood up to him."

"Well, it won't be Eason. You know how he is about getting involved in other people's business. Look, let's talk at water aerobics tomorrow. Maybe come back here for some lunch?"

"Okay." Pearl stands up. "We have to do something. Oh, does Eason know if the Worths might be going to buy out the neighborhood, or at least get us moving forward again?"

"Eason says the economy is so weak, no one is going to take this on. Not with the road improvements needed and how far out we are." She sighs and shakes her head. "It seemed like such a good idea when everything else was being snatched up like cookies." As if on cue, the cows next door begin mooing and makes it impossible to ignore the smell of manure hanging in the saturated air. "How can we have managed our entire lives so well and then end up someplace this miserable?"

Pearl lifts her hands in the air and then drops them. "Who knows? We are definitely being punished. And on top of it, to have to deal with the hillbilly hussy..." Her hands lift and fall again. "Here comes Eason. I'll let myself out and walk around the house." She leaves out the screen door as she waves goodbye to Ruth's other half.

"What's Pearl upset about today?" Eason asks as he sits down and sees the woman in question is out of hearing distance.

"Magnus has taken his playing around with Becca Sue to a new level. He got her all dressed up, 'pimped out' as Pearl called it, and showed her off at the club last night. Apparently they stayed at the Ritz last night, too."

"It's just not any of our business, hon."

"Sybil was there, too. With Pearl and George. She saw it all."

"Pearl must be happy. She's the one that insisted Sybil

come back."

"She says she didn't. She says she never ended up calling Sybil. She doesn't know how Sybil knew."

Eason rubs his arm. "Hmm, Pearl's a lot of things, but she doesn't usually out and out lie." He looks away and then back to his wife. "So why did Sybil come back?"

Ruth shrugs, picks up her book, and looks for her place. "Guess we'll have to wait until someone asks her."

Eason laughs and stands up. "Let me know what she says."

He's still laughing as he closes the door on his wife's voice, calling, "Thought you said it wasn't any of our business."

His laugh and smile die when the door is shut and he's turned away from his wife's sight. "Damn you, George."

Jameson stretches out in his chair to dry his running shorts. Laps in the pool felt good after the heat of the morning sun and the heat of his talk with Becca Sue. The need to get in the water was so great he had kicked off his shoes and socks and thrown his shirt to the side just before he dove in.

Through the years his brother had talked about girls. He'd had them all, even during his marriages. His marriage to Margaret he said was to make their mother happy, and his marriage to Becca Sue was just a big ol' mistake. So saying "no" to the constant parade of girls through his wedded non-bliss was never part of his plan. Telling his little brother about them, however, and attaining a partner in laying South Georgia was a big part of his plan.

That part of the plan failed.

Jameson shook the water from his hair and grinned as he remembered spending many of his college years thinking he must be gay because he wasn't obsessed with girls like his brother. How that many times he'd get a girl alone, and then feel so guilty he'd end up just taking her home. This led to him gaining a reputation as a true gentleman, but didn't help his concern over being gay. Then it dawned on him being gay was more than not sleeping with girls, it meant liking guys, and that wasn't there.

By law school, he was dating occasionally, but being top of the class and, by that time, keeping his big brother out of legal trouble took all his time and energy. Caleb said his lack of women made him mean and mean was good for a lawyer. Besides, by that time he'd met Cecelia and knew she was the one.

He takes a deep breath, shakes his hands to rid them of dripping water, and lays them by his side. *That's it; think about Cecelia.*

She was in his class at law school, and brains in such a cool, blonde package made her hard not to pay attention to. Her family, especially her father, Tyler Mattle, made her *impossible* to ignore. Ty Mattle ran Georgia through his family's companies before he began running it from the Governor's mansion. He served two terms, then, as required by law, sat out four years before making history by winning again. The marriage of his daughter at the end of the summer would be the social event of the South, and then the Governor would begin the final year of his second eight-year reign. Plenty of time for his daughter's campaign.

The plan was for Jameson to be sleeping with the new governor by next November.

Shorts dry and the coolness of the pool fading, Jameson stands, picks up his shoes and shirt, and heads toward the side gate and the garage entrance. He rotates his shoulders and takes a deep breath. "Just handle this mess here, and I can get back home and back to my life and wife-to-be."

He drops his shoes in the garage and picks up his phone from the kitchen counter.

"Hate running alone" was the first text with a second right below it. "Hate showering alone." His smile, and need for a shower, grew as he read the many additional things Cecelia hated doing alone.

Jameson walks through the living room. Without looking up, he announces over the blaring TV, "I'm getting in the shower." No answer causes him to look away from his phone, and the texts leave his mind as surely as if he'd never read them.

Maggie is asleep on one end of the couch, curled up under a blanket. He groans, wishing the blanket had been at the other end of the couch where maybe then, a sleeping, sprawled-out Becca Sue in her fancy dress wouldn't be on view.

He groans again and turns. "Definitely, a shower."

25

"Thank God I'd covered up with the blanket," I say out loud to the mirror. "I was half-naked under there." Twisting, I pull the dress up where it belongs for one last look. "It is a hot dress. Can't believe how it makes me look. Guess it's time to take it off and quit playing Cinderella."

But it's not just the dress. My hair is straight and falls past my shoulders. The red is more brown, looks more like dirt than clay, and the little bangs they cut brush my eyes and make me look so young. Leaning closer, I examine the eye makeup. How just some stuff put on my eyes can make them look so different is amazing. They look kind of golden, not just dull old brown. "Magnus, I don't know how to thank you—Oh, wait. I do know how to thank him, don't I?"

I leave the bathroom and sit on the bed. Cleavage leaps up to say howdy, so I lay back on the bed. Yuck. This is how it always ends up. Me being grateful to a guy and sleeping with him to show him just how grateful I am. Yuck.

Why can't sex just be fun? Why do I always end up feeling like I'm paying them back for something? My hands run down my body. "But this is an amazing dress. He deserved last night."

And tonight. And tomorrow night.

"Yuck." I push myself up off the bed and push the dress down. The satiny black bra and matching panties cause another trip to the mirror. Hard to believe, but this is my body.

This really is me. Again, I'm a believer in bras now. I grab an old T-shirt off the back hooks on the bathroom door. Oh, yeah, that looks amazing. Makes me feel amazing too. After pulling on a pair of cut-off shorts, I go back out in the living room. Maggie is still cuddled up on the couch, but awake.

"I got you a blanket. Your dress was all twisted around, and you were asleep."

"Oh, thanks."

"Uncle J came in from his run. He's what woke me up."

"Okay." I sit down in a chair closer to the outside windows. "So, where's he now?"

"He's outside on the phone. Said he has to get things wrapped up here."

Guess that means I should start packing.

Florida light is so real, like something you could put in a bottle. From the soft shining tiles, to the bright blocks of sun against the top of the walls and ceiling, the big room feels full. Like if you were outside you could see the light in here coming out the windows.

I stand in the light-filled air and walk through it to the big glass doors. They're so shiny from Esmeralda's cleaning they don't look real, but like they are just harder slices of the light. Outside, the sun holds the high blue skies in place and pulls at the green. Trees, grass, flowers all seem to be reaching and growing while I stand here. The humidity here feels alive and like it's helping everything grow. At home the humidity just adds weight to every step, every breath.

I take a deep, deep breath. Think I could get used to Florida, but guess it's not meant to be. It's time to go home.

"Jameson?"

"Oh, hey. Um, you're up."

"Yeah, sorry about falling asleep on the couch, you know."

He shoves his phone in his pocket and walks over to the table and chairs in the shade. "No problem. Maggie missed you last night."

"I know, hate I forgot. Cab and Maggie are good kids, and they're going to be fine. I messed things up, but I am glad I

got to spend some time with them. I really appreciate it, like
I said yesterday, seriously. I really do appreciate all you and,
well, your mother, have done for me. Totally grateful." In the
shade, he looks so much like his brother it makes my throat
close up, so I turn away. "I'm going to go pack."

"Where are you and Magnus going now? You'll be back tomorrow, right?"

My hand turns the door knob, and I pull it open a bit as I
turn to face him. "I'm going home, and I'm most definitely not
taking Magnus to Piney." The thought of Magnus on the porch
of Momma and Daddy's trailer makes me laugh a bitter laugh.

"Running out on the kids? Scurrying back to Piney? Why
are you determined to not hear me?" He strides toward me.
"This is *your* house. This is home now. You can't go back to
Piney, because you live here now. Not in Georgia. Here. Do
you get it? This is your home."

He shuts the door, and my hand falls away from it. Maggie
makes eye contact with me through the shiny glass, which no
longer looks like light. It looks like solid ice. Even the midday
sun doesn't touch the ice also now in my stomach. "You can't
be serious."

"Completely. You own this. Matter of fact, you own the
whole development. You leave now, and I'll have you arrested
for abandonment. The taxes, the liens, the lawsuits, they are
all yours. You signed all the papers."

When I turn to face him, he no longer looks anything like
his brother. Caleb never let his mother show through his eyes.

Jameson can't hide it.

"But I don't know what to do with this house, much less the
whole neighborhood." I spread my hands out as I look across
the lake at the half-dozen houses scattered there. "I don't want
it."

"Too bad. You'll figure something out. I'd offer to help, but
you've got your own lawyer, don't you?"

"Magnus? You think Magnus is going to help me?" When
I spin to look at him, my hair flies out in a line and I really
like that. I pull my shoulders back and stand tall like my gym

teachers always begged me to. "I may be good in bed, but I'm not that good."

"Only good enough for a sparkly dress and a nice dinner?"

"Good enough for your brother to marry me." Guess standing straight lets stuff jump out of your mouth quicker, because even I'm shocked I finally said out loud what everyone in Piney has been saying for years. And just like that, the power of it hits me. It's always been a cause for shame to me, but in Jameson's eyes I see the truth. Caleb Mason didn't just sleep with me, he married me. "Yep, good enough to get the holy and perfect name of Mason added to mine."

Jameson shrugs it off. "Lapse of judgment on Caleb's part, and probably a little rebellion towards my mother."

This time I not only throw my shoulders back, I stick my boobs out. (The bra helps.) "Rebellion? Don't you ever wonder what that feels like? Cecelia Mattle? Bet your mother is happier than a hog in slop."

He smiles and shakes his head. "Smells a bit like slop here with all these impromptu cow pastures that you own, doesn't it? I'm leaving in the morning. Maggie is staying here with you for a few more weeks, and Cab will probably leave when the Worths do. Enjoy your time with them. This summer is your final attachment to the Mason family, and when they come back to Georgia you will never be a part of their lives or of any of our lives again." He jerks open the door and slams it on the other side.

He stops to talk to Maggie, and I turn to walk out to the lake. It has to be near a hundred degrees in the afternoon sunshine, but I'm chilled. The biggest thing I've ever owned is the car Caleb gave me, and I couldn't even figure out how to put it in the garage here. Now this all belongs to me? From the bits I've picked up, this place might be pretty, but it makes for some huge problems. Is it a gift or another Mason trick? Cold pulls at me from deep within and causes a shiver.

The black water of the lake reflects the stand of tall Southern pines in the stretch of empty lots across from me. Deep blue sky and a few lit-from-within clouds mirror themselves in the still water. Who's looking out from the scattered houses? Magnus? Pearl? George? One house is still and the windows shuttered. Abandoned, I've been told. The yard, once as manicured as Magnus' and the Manninghams' is covered in knee-high weeds. Florida doesn't need kudzu, everything here grows like a weed.

My eye catches on movement near the abandoned house. Sybil is looking at its back porch. She sees me and starts to wave, but stops and turns. She walks to the front of the houses, and I can't see where she goes next.

Sybil. She can't win. She can't have Magnus.

I can't deal with all this by myself, I have to keep Magnus now.

26

"But I thought I was leaving," Becca Sue practically shouts in the bright yellow kitchen. "I thought I was going home."

Mrs. Bell leans back in her wooden kitchen chair. "But don't you want this to be your home?"

"I don't know." With her head bowed, her hair falls and hides her face.

Mrs. Bell leans forward and pulls the shiny red curtain back. "I do like whatever it is they did to your hair. How they make curly hair straight and straight hair curly is fascinating. We always had to be happy with what the good Lord gave us because my father didn't believe in going to a beauty shop. Which was a good thing, because Mr. Bell loved my curly hair." She laughs and rises slowly from her seat. "But then he didn't have a choice, did he?"

"Do you know this Sybil lady?" Becca Sue asks while she picks up a hank of her hair and strokes it. "What's she like?"

"No, we're not going to talk about Sybil. That will come later. Right now we need to make some strawberry freezer jam. Scoot down to the store," she holds out a twenty dollar bill the young woman, "and buy what we need. Go on. Scoot."

Becca Sue stands up, tugging at her shorts at the waist.

"Looks like you need a belt, sweetie."

"Must've stretched out. They fit when I bought 'em. I'm going to see if Maggie wants to go to the store with me. Can I get you anything else while I'm there?"

"No, Ruth and I are going shopping tomorrow morning. Bring Maggie back over here with you. She can help with the jam."

Becca Sue crosses the yard to the street and then stays in the street past the empty lot full of weeds and critters. "Like our own little park for bugs and lizards and probably snakes." She walks around back keeping her head down, but looking sideways occasionally. "Wonder where Jameson is?"

She pulls open the big French door and slips in. She tiptoes to Maggie's room and softly knocks.

"Come in," a voice says inside.

"Hey, me and Missus Bell are going to make some strawberry freezer jam. It's real easy. You want to help? First, I gotta go to the store. You can go with me if you want."

Maggie lays back on her bed. "I don't know. Uncle J is taking me to dinner later." She sits up. "He's leaving tomorrow."

"Yep. Cab going to dinner with you, too?"

Maggie shrugs and stands to look in the mirror on her dresser. "Don't know." She pulls her hair back and cocks her chin. "I'll go to the store with you if you tell me what you and Uncle J were fighting about."

Becca Sue leans on the door and watches the girl preen in the mirror. "Okay. Deal. Are you ready to go?"

"Yeah. I can change before dinner."

They walk toward the front door, but as they near it, Becca Sue slows down. She turns and walks into the kitchen. "Show me the garage opener thing and where I can park the car when we get back."

"Okay," Maggie sighs. "'Bout time."

"Yep. About time."

"And it's even better when it's partly frozen," Becca Sue says as she pulls a spoon from her mouth. A spoon licked and sucked clean.

"Oh, with a hot biscuit to help it thaw. Honey, this is delicious." Miss Bell dips her spoon into the little glass bowl which a sample of the cooled strawberry jam lines with bright red, sugary goodness.

The young woman lays her spoon on her napkin. "So, what do you think will happen?"

"Honey, it's a mess. I tried real hard to reserve judgment on the Masons. I find it hard to believe people could be so uncaring about what happens to other people. But..." Ms. Bell's face fades into grayness so that the dab of strawberry jam on her chin remains the only bright spot.

"You're tired. I need to clean this up and let you go. I've worn you plum out." Becca Sue jumps up and finishes loading the used dishes into the dishwasher. "I'll get this started and you can lay down."

"I am tired, but come over here for a minute." She holds her hand out and Becca Sue rubs her own hands on her shorts. She walks over to the kitchen table beside the bright window.

Mrs. Bell takes her hands in her beautiful old ones. "From what I can see, you've been taken advantage of just one too many times by these people. You need to figure out a way to get out of this place and start a life of your own. Get a job, some schooling. They have used you, but you now can use them in a way. Use the time you have this summer to move on. At the end of the summer," the older woman shrugs and tries a weak smile, "at the end of the summer, let it all go bankrupt. Let the bankers deal with it. You don't really have any credit for a bankruptcy to hurt. Honestly, that's probably why they palmed it all off on you. Use this summer to get your feet under you, look for an apartment, and move on past these people." Her voice begins to fade, much as her color did earlier.

Becca Sue nods and tightens her grip on the old woman's hands. "Here, let me walk you to your bedroom." With one hand grasping Miss Bell's and the other around the woman's tiny waist, Becca Sue maneuvers through the kitchen and to the master bedroom. She drops her hand to pull back the covers and then seats her friend on the bed. Becca Sue slides off Miss Bell's shoes as the woman lays down and closes her eyes. Pulling the coverlet up, Becca Sue says, "You don't need to worry about me. And how could I just let it all go the bank when y'all have been so good to me?"

The air conditioner kicks on just as Becca Sue shuts the bedroom door. In the kitchen, she finishes loading the dishwasher and starts it. After wiping down the counters, she remembers the sampling bowl and spoon on the small, white-tiled table beside the front window.

She sits back down in her chair and scrapes almost a full tablespoon of jam from the bowl. The heat-filled light in the front yard makes the shade of the porch look even deeper and darker. Across the street is a long stretch of pasture where the cows now trod on development land.

Her land. How embarrassing when she'd told Miss Bell she'd never owned livestock, and now was an "official cowgirl." Miss Bell hadn't laughed out loud, but her eyes looked like they wanted to as she explained the land was rented out to cattle farmers. Miss Bell had also let her in on how there were taxes and contracts that came along with owning the subdivision. Things that bankers and developers deal with. Not stupid hick girls who've never even had a real job.

"Okay, okay," Becca Sue says out loud as she stands up. "She didn't actually say that about me." She takes the bowl and spoons to the dishwasher and wedges them in, then closes it and presses the start button. "But she was probably thinking it."

Becca Sue leaves the cool, quiet house and walks out the front. At the street, she notices the pavement has chunks crumbled off the edge where it meets the empty lot between her house and Miss Bell's. "Funny how different things look when you own them."

"Hey!"

She looks up at the shout from beside her house. "Hey,

Magnus."

"I need a swim."

Becca Sue nods and wanders around the side of the house. "Miss Bell really likes my hair this way." She walks past him as he opens the gate and motions her in. "Everybody does."

He doesn't say anything, just walks to the edge of the pool, drops his towel, then yanks his shirt over his head. As he tosses the dark green T-shirt behind him, he dives in and swims to the other end, where he turns and begins laps, beating the water with not only his hands, but his whole body.

Becca Sue watches from near the gate for a few minutes then goes to sit on the edge, legs dangling in the churning water. She leans back on her elbows and closes her eyes in the afternoon sun. The rhythm from the pool—stroke, stroke, stroke, the quiet as he touches the pool edge and then torpedoes underwater for a distance, bursting out mid-stroke—lulls her.

The sound goes on and on until one of the quiet moments lasts a little longer and shockingly cold hands grasp her thighs.

"What!" she exclaims as she catapults upright to find Magnus with his hands grasping the tops of her thighs, fingers reaching under the bottom of her shorts.

"Were you asleep?" His grin says he doesn't care, and one wet hand reaches up to pull her the low neckline of her shirt down. "That the bra I bought you last night?" She jerks on her shirt, but he doesn't let go. "Let me see it."

"No." A quick glance at the doors to the house doesn't tell her if Maggie or Jameson are watching due to the glare. "No," she hesitates. "Not here."

He caresses the outside of her shirt and pushes his fingers further under her shorts. "I want to get you pregnant."

"Pregnant? Are you crazy?" She pushes his hands away, but he manages to gather her hands into his.

"Let's have a baby. I never had a baby and you make me feel young. A kid would be fun. Don't you think it's time I had a kid?"

"Time? No, it's not time. You're insane. Besides, I don't

think I can get pregnant. Believe me, I sure wanted a baby with Caleb, but it never worked, and we were married ten years."

Magnus releases her hands and pushes away from the wall. "Great, just when I've decided to have a kid." He dives under the water and swims to the other end.

Like before, Becca Sue watches him go back and forth, but this time she sits tense and alert. After several minutes, she stands and goes to the shallow end where he'll turn. She slides into the pool, still dressed. When he reaches out to touch the wall, she grabs his hand and his forward motion causes him to ram into her.

He stands up, wiping the water out of his eyes. "What are you doing?"

She puts her hands on his waist and pulls him towards her. "You don't need a baby. You just need something to do. And I have a couple things you can do." She presses into him and looks up. "One is me, and the other is a surprise. A big surprise that I'll tell you all about after you take care of the first thing."

Magnus laughs and looks around. "Here?"

"No, silly, I have a room and a bed right through those doors."

"Isn't Jameson still here?"

She pulls him toward the stairs, and on the first one turns to him, her soaked shirt less than an inch from his face. "The Masons have cut me loose. Or, actually, have hung me out to dry, so why would he matter to me?"

Magnus shrugs and pushes her up the stairs. "Lead on, ma'am."

After picking up Magnus' towel and drying off a bit, they enter the house giggling and touching. The pool water stills, and the summer afternoon's only sound is the air conditioning pump cycling on. And the only one around to hear that solitary sound is Jameson Mason, from the garage side of the house where he's been leaning, and listening, for quite a while.

He pulls away from the house and walks into the dark, hot garage.

27

"If this house really belongs to me, then I can do whatever, or whoever, I want." *Yeah, that's what I'm going to say to him.* "He'll be sitting out there all smug and judgmental, and that'll put him in his place." My mouth in the mirror droops. "But what if Maggie is there?"

My bra is dry, and Magnus is gone. The bed wasn't kind to my hair, but I try to smooth it back down. Dressed, I leave the bathroom and lift the sheets back up to the top of the bed. As I grab the quilt, I sit down.

It wasn't even any fun.

For either of us.

We giggled and joked and squeezed and teased and... and managed to get through. Like neither one of us wanted sex, but we couldn't think of anything else to do. *This sucks.*

Might as well face the music. Before opening the door, I take a deep breath. *Why do I feel guiltier now than before?*

"Hey, y'all."

Maggie looks over her shoulder at me and rolls her eyes. "Uncle J isn't in here. You don't have to be all sunny and bright."

"Good. What ya watching?" I flop on the couch and curl my legs up beside me.

"*America's Next Top Model* marathon. I've already seen all of them, though."

Yet we keep watching and watching. Why we are sitting

here, watching these beautiful girls whine and backstab and wear amazing clothes and get their makeup and hair done for them, is beyond me. At the end of every hour, I make up my mind that this is the last one I'll watch. Yeah, every hour. All four of them.

Jameson finally comes in and saves us.

Well, somebody had to.

"Maggie, you ready?" He walks to the couch, picks up the remote, and turns off the TV.

"But wait, they were getting ready to announce who won!" Maggie and I both protest.

He turns to look at the black screen and then back at us. "You really care?"

Maggie answers by getting up and stretching. "Where are we going for dinner?"

"Wherever you want. Cab said he'd let you pick."

"Of course he did, so that way he can complain all night. Nope, your last night here. You pick." She looks down at me. "You want to come?"

"I don't think I'm invited, but no."

"I'll be dressed in a second," she promises as she heads to her bedroom.

Jameson sits down on the other end of the couch. His smile looks genuine, but he's nervous. "Listen, I think I better tell you something."

"Really? You have more to dump on me." I stand and put my hands on my hips, trying to remember all the good comebacks I'd been practicing. "It is *so* time for you to go home to Cecelia and your mama."

"Calm down, it's just that I heard you and Magnus..."

"If this is really my house then what I do whatever to, wait, whoever I want to... uh. Oh, just shut up." With a whirl I head to my room, but he catches me just as I get to the doorway.

"No, it's not just about Magnus. It's about any guy or, you know, about you getting pregnant. It's just that..."

"Oh my god, you can't be serious. You people have tried to run—no, you *have* run—every little bit of my life for so long.

Wait, you were listening?" With his hand around my upper arm, we are already close, but I lean closer to him. "You were listening to us talk? You are so sneaky. Just like Caleb always said."

He drops my arm and jumps back like I'd just spit out fire. "Caleb said *I* was sneaky? Me?"

"You were always sneaking around wanting to know what was going on. Even when Caleb wasn't there. You're just lucky I never told your brother how you snooped around always trying to catch me in a lie or doing something wrong. You are just like your mother."

Jameson shakes his head at me and takes another step back. As he does, he works his mouth like he wants to say something, then throws his hands up a bit and turns away.

I slide into my room, and just as I shut the door he says, "You probably can, you know."

"What?" With the door open only a couple inches, I stick my face out. "Probably can what?"

He turns, and the orange light from the low sun fills the room behind him. His face is dark. "You can probably get pregnant."

Maybe it's the descending darkness, but sadness makes me heavy, and I open the door a bit more. "Oh, yeah. No, we tried. We even saw doctors, but honestly, this is none—"

"*You* tried. Caleb had a vasectomy after Maggie was born."

Standing in the doorway, one hand on the door, the other on the door frame, my brain freezes. Stops completely. My body jerks when it overrides my brain and makes me take a breath. I close the door and sit on my bed.

The bed where I could've just made a baby. I jump up and like a faucet, tears flood down my face. I can get pregnant? I can get *pregnant*? Bubbles fill my stomach and make me want to laugh. I can get pregnant? But wait, then...

In the bathroom, I sit on the toilet. Then Caleb was lying all that time. But what about Audrey? He got Audrey pregnant. I fly through my room and the house, back to Cab's room where Jameson is staying. I fling open the door and whisper, "But what about Audrey? She's having Caleb's baby."

Jameson is just pulling on a shirt. "Yeah," he says when his head comes out the top.

"So it's not Caleb's baby?"

He sits on the bed and puts his face in his hands for a moment, then picks up a shoe from the floor. "It's only going to make you hate us more. I didn't tell you this for any other reason than I didn't want you being stupid and getting pregnant because Caleb was able to fool you all that time." He pulls on his shoe and then sets his foot up on the bed to tie it.

"So? Audrey's baby? It's not Caleb's, is it?" The laugh bubbles come back. Caleb didn't have to marry her. He didn't, they fooled him, and he played along. He really was all mine.

I turn away from the room and leave Jameson putting on his other shoe. Caleb just didn't want to lose me by telling me he couldn't have kids. That's probably what he was thinking. And I'm sure his mother didn't know her firstborn was done having children. Of course, he couldn't tell me. We had Maggie and Cab to raise. Of course. And Audrey? I never figured her for sleeping around. This time the laugh bubbles escape my stomach. And Caleb's momma will think that baby is her son's. Oh, how great that Mrs. Mason is fooled, too.

In my room behind a closed door, my thoughts come out loud, "And I've watched enough soap operas to know that it always comes out. Some rare disease, the true father showing up with proof. Oh, wow, Piney is in for some fun days ahead." I hug a pillow to my chest.

"Come in," I say to a knock on the door. I try to hide my grin, but I can't. Too many good scenarios going through my head featuring a shocked Mrs. Mason and an embarrassed Audrey.

Jameson sticks his head in the door. "We're getting ready to leave."

"Okay. Have fun." Go ahead, give him a full smile. So I do. "It's been good having you here, and thanks. I did need to know that. Knowing I could have a baby does change things." I nod and smile again. "Thanks."

He doesn't smile, just closes the door.

"Guess he doesn't think it's funny that as the Mason family lawyer he'll one day have to tell his mother she's been played for a fool by her darling firstborn son." This time the laugh bubbles plum knock me over, and I lay on the bed as they float from my lips.

Waking up, I realize my face is wet. Tears. Oh, I was crying in my dream. Sadness fills me up, and I remember the dream.

Caleb and I had a baby and then, oh, the baby died. A flash of anger stabs me, but I shake it off. It'll all be okay. Caleb needed me to want a baby so bad so his family didn't know the truth. He just didn't think it through, and he was a man. He had no idea how I felt. Rolling over, I force myself to forget all that and go back to sleep, but then a noise outside makes me lay still. Hearing it again makes me jump out of bed. I can't see anything out my window, so I creep out into the dark house. 1:30, my clock says.

The living room is quiet and dark. Maggie's door shows only darkness underneath it, so I walk to the French doors and look outside. Nothing is moving out there, then a man is standing inches from me through the glass. I yelp and so does Jameson on the other side of the glass.

He then adds, "Oh, hey. Thought I heard someone up. I'm sitting out here."

I open the door and smell the alcohol. "What did you do? Hide yourself out with a bottle of whiskey?"

He looks back at the table outside my bedroom window. "Whiskey or bourbon. Something like that. Come have a drink." He grabs my wrist and pulls me to the table. "Use my glass. We'll share."

A Mason boy asks you to drink with him in the middle of the night, well, of course I took a drink. Even with all my history, he's still one of the special ones. Good-looking, rich, smart, smooth, and he wants to have a drink with me. And after two good swallows, there's no part of my brain saying I should think twice. He picked me to drink with.

He refills the glass. "Reminds me of football games except it's hotter than hell out here, even in the middle of the night. You look real good, Becca Sue. Did I tell you that?"

"Thank you." My spaghetti strap top and girl boxers are kind of skimpy, but he's right, it's hotter than hell out here. "You know you've got a long drive tomorrow."

He lifts the glass and takes mouthful, holds it, then lets it rush down his throat. "Yep. Back to Georgia. Hey, why aren't you mad at Caleb after what I told you?"

I reach for the glass, and try his method of taking a mouthful, then swallowing it all at one time. Wow, that hits hard. "Guess I'm having too much fun thinking of how he fooled your momma and Audrey. Of course he fooled me, but I'm just a hick. But your momma? And won't Audrey be up the creek when her daddy finds out she was sleeping around, not just with rich college boys? 'Cause face it, there ain't but a couple rich college boys in Piney. Pretty much just you and Caleb." My giggling grows. "Too, too funny."

He chuckles for a minute, but it dies. He tilts his head at me. "You really think Momma doesn't know everything?"

"I thought she did before today." I lean on the table and watch his eyes travel down to my chest.

He slurs a bit. "You look real good. Did I tell you?"

I pour another drink and take just a sip this time. I stand up, and then hand the glass to him. The way he watches me fills me with more bubbles, maybe not all laugh bubbles this time. "Well, time for me to go inside. Thanks for the drink, and I'll make sure the door is unlocked." I know he's watching me, and I love knowing that. I'm so focused on thinking about him watching me, that I miss what he says. "What? I didn't hear you."

When I turn I see he's staring at the glass in his hand. Maybe he wasn't watching me. "What did you say?"

"The baby *is* Caleb's. Momma made him get the vasectomy reversed. She wanted Audrey's daddy's land real bad."

I walk back to the table, and this time he is most definitely watching me. I lift my shirt a bit, and he stares at my belly. Guess I could have a Mason baby, too. Looks like Jameson is ready to do it right out here, where it's hotter than hell. Bet the pavement is almost as hot as he is. Standing in front of him at his chair, I nudge one of his legs to the side with my leg and then move close to him, my bare leg between his tanned, muscled legs. He stares straight ahead, of course, that is where my hand is slowly raising my shirt inches from his face. My other hand clinches the bottle of Jack Daniels, and just as I have his full attention and I feel his hands on the sides of my legs, I step back.

"I'll take this," I say as my eyes cut to the bottle. "And don't wake me up in the morning when you leave. This is goodbye."

I leave the glass on the table.

Who needs a glass?

28

"Mr. Worth." Becca Sue steps back and opens the front door a little wider. The casually dressed man smiles, but doesn't enter.

Becca Sue smiles also, then clears her throat. "Um, you here for Maggie? I'll get her. Come in." She presses her hands down to flatten her hair. "I, uh, just got up, but I'm sure she's just in her room."

"Nooo, Maggie's not here." Now he runs his hand across the top of his hair and clears his throat. "Her Aunt Helen picked her up here a couple hours ago, well before noon." *Before noon* hangs on the air between them. "But I will come in, thank you." He steps through the open door and shrugs. "I've come to see you."

Becca shakes her head and tries to stretch her eyes fully open. "Oh, okay." She leads him into the living room. "I need to get changed and, uh, grab some water. Can I get you anything?"

Roger Worth stands for a moment, staring at the young woman. "No, nothing, thank you. I'll just have a seat." Seated, he leans his elbows on his knees, and concern deepens the wrinkles in his tanned face. He rocks forward onto the balls of his feet, and he stands up just as Becca Sue comes back in the room. "Look, this was a mistake. Maggie thought, well, never mind what she thought. I'll leave you now."

Becca Sue steps in front of him. "Mr. Worth, I'm so sorry I didn't know where your granddaughter was. Her uncle's been here." She looks around. "I guess he left, too." Under her breath she murmurs, "Thank God."

A loud laugh causes her to look up. Roger Worth has his head thrown back laughing. "God, I miss that."

Now all the concern is on Becca Sue's face, and she moves to the side so he can leave whenever he feels like it.

"Okay, unusual for me, but I've changed my mind again. May I have a seat?"

"When you smile, did you know your eyes look just like Maggie's? Yes, sit down. I just need to drink this and to sit... wait, can I get you something? Oh, you said no. Never mind."

"Wait, I will take a glass of ice water. Thank you." He sits back down, but this time leans back. He crosses one leg over the other and jiggles the foot hanging in air. His shorts are a stiff navy blue fabric and his shirt is a long-sleeved white dress shirt with the sleeves rolled up.

Becca Sue hands him his glass of water, and then doesn't wait to sit down before she drinks half hers down. "Not a good night for me last night."

Worth laughs again. "That's what Maggie said."

"No way. Maggie heard? Sh—sugar, I'm so stupid. Guess I should know by now when the word 'pregnant' is thrown around, a teenager is going to pay attention." She sits down in the chair next to his end of the couch. "But it was such a shock. I thought all these years I couldn't get pregnant, then James-on told me I could 'cause he heard me and Magnus talking about getting pregnant. Then I thought it was going to be a humongous scandal in Piney when Audrey and Mrs. Mason found out Caleb had a vasectomy. But, well, his Momma was behind it all."

"His vasectomy?"

Becca Sue looks up. Seeing Maggie's wide green eyes in the tanned face of such an important man talking about her ex-husband's vasectomy, she bursts out laughing. "No. Wait, it's not funny." Her laughter stops. "Not funny at all. I knew that family was running my life, I just had no idea how much."

She sits back and takes a drink, then lifts her glass. "Anyway, I spent the night drinking something much stronger than this."

"Okay, now let *me* explain. Maggie does not know, well, she didn't tell me anything about all this you were just saying. Maggie just told me how unlike everyone else you are. That you say what you are thinking and feeling."

"I know. I'm not a real good influence on her. And look at Cab. Guess I wasn't cut out to be a mother anyway."

"Hey, no, that's not it at all. You aren't at fault for how Cab turned out." He leans forward and puts his hand on her arm. "The rest of us are to blame for that. The Masons and the Worths. *You* are why Maggie is different. She practically idolizes you, mostly because you're the only person in her life that puts her first." He sighs, and pulls back from her. "I'm ashamed to say it, but it's the truth. Maggie says, and I'm beginning to agree with her, that you see, and know, more than you realize."

Becca Sue waits and thinks, then after several minutes, Maggie's grandfather stands up. "I want to make an offer to you, but I don't have many details. You're going to need to trust me and be willing to do some work." He walks into the kitchen while he's talking and sits his glass on the counter. "I need to walk around while I talk, so just listen for a bit, okay?"

She nods and sets her glass on the side table.

"I want to help you out with the development. Yes, I know you own it, and I have no idea what that's all about except Caleb wanting to just dump it." He strides across the living room.

"Not Caleb, Jameson." She claps her hands together and closes her eyes while she takes a deep breath. "Oh, everyone is going to be so happy you're are taking over. Oh, Mr. Worth, you have answered all my prayers. And everyone else's, too."

"No, now wait a minute. Nothing was said about 'taking over.' I want to help, and not in the way everyone may be hoping. Matter of fact, I doubt any of them are going to be happy in the least."

Becca Sue leaves her chair, and he turns from looking out

the back windows so that they face each other. "Just listen, okay? Anyway, whomever left all this in your lap obviously had no plan. The economy tanked, and they saw a way out of a problem." He tips his head at her. "Maybe several problems. But I've made my fortune seeing opportunities where others see problems. So—"

Becca Sue's stomach growls loudly. "Sorry."

"No, don't be sorry. Come to think of it, I'm hungry, too. Why don't we go to lunch?"

Her mouth falls open, and she scrunches her brow. "I really need a shower, I can find something here for us. Or I can wait to eat." She pauses and then asks, "Aren't you a bit worried about being here like this? With me?"

He smiles and pulls his keys from his pocket. "You take your shower, I'll go pick up lunch for us." He winks at her, then he walks toward the front entrance. "Becca Sue, if things happen how I want them to, you and I will spending a lot of time together. To hell with what other people think."

%%%%

"Who is that leaving Becca Sue's in that gray car?" Pearl asks the women walking up the street with her.

"It sure looked like Roger Worth. What would he be doing here?" a short, overweight, gold-haired woman asks.

"Oh, Marie, you've been gone on your big cruise; you left right after Becca Sue got here," Pearl laments loudly. "The Mason children are also Roger and Kathleen Worth's grandchildren." She pauses and with a twist of her head to look down at the shorter woman asks, "Wait, how do *you* know *Roger*?"

Ruth rolls her eyes at Esmeralda from their place behind the other two.

Marie lifts her shoulder on the side near Pearl. "You know we are in finance, right? I'm addicted to the money shows, like CNBC and Fox Business. When I met Harold I was a stock broker in his father's firm. Put myself through school, worked up the ladder, loved every bit, but Harold swept me off my feet and got me accustomed to a certain lifestyle." The short woman with a halo of blonde, frizzy hair places her hands on her squishy hips and sways like a beauty queen to the other ladies' laughter. "But that doesn't mean I didn't keep in the game. My portfolio is doing very nicely, if I must say. So, of course I know Roger Worth. He's on the business shows all the time. He's truly quite revolutionary in some of his thinking."

"Revolutionary in how much money he makes. Let's just hope he's here to buy out the subdivision," Ruth says in a low voice.

Esmeralda lifts her hands and face to the sky and in Italian lifts a prayer the others can't understand.

Pearl nods and adds an "Amen" anyway. They turn into the driveway just vacated by Roger Worth and his car, and Pearl's voice drops even lower. "Can you imagine the magnificent place the Worths would turn this dump into? No more water aerobics in a borrowed pool." She shimmies her shoulders. "Just imagine how amazing our clubhouse will be. And instead of looking down their noses at us, everyone closer to the beach will want to move out here. No more weed-filled lots no one will buy or empty houses falling apart. Wait until I tell George."

Ruth, Esmeralda, and Pearl greet Jane the aerobics instructor with big smiles and lots of whispered chatter. Marie slides her bag off her shoulder and takes it the table and chair by the house to sit it down. Facing the house, her frown causes her chin to double, maybe even triple. She takes a deep breath, pulls her frown up, and speaks quietly to the wall. "Hope I'm wrong, but this might not be good. Might not be good at all. I need to check some things out when I get home."

29

"It's from Mr. Magnus, isn't it?" Maggie guesses from her perch on the edge of my bed, watching me open the bag we just retrieved from the front porch. The tag just said "7 pm?", but seeing that the bag is from the shop where I tried on the dresses Friday night, it's a pretty good guess.

"Yes, it is." It's the black dress. Our second choice. Along with several pieces of soft tissue paper, I pull out a pair of black high heels. Maggie takes them from my hand.

"Can you even walk in these things?" she asks, skeptically.

With enough to drink, I think, but only say, "I walked in the other ones Saturday night."

"That's true. Here, try them on. Let me see them." I sit on the bed beside her, and she falls closer to me.

"So did you talk to my grandfather?" A glance to my right, and I see green eyes staring at me, just like the green eyes from this afternoon.

"Yes." Standing up, I hold onto her shoulder to get my balance. "There. What do you think?"

Maggie stands as I walk across the room toward the mirror, and she opines, "I don't get it. What's with the shoes so high you can hardly walk in them? Why do women wear them?"

In my shorts, I can see the way they make my legs look. My butt. Shoot they even make my boobs look bigger. With a smile, I turn around to her and lie. "I have no idea."

She flops back down on the bed. "So, my grandfather?"

I practice walking across the floor from the closet to the dresser. "Honestly, I didn't understand half of what he was saying, but it sounds like a good idea for him. Him and someone else." I drop down beside her. "Can't you talk him into just buying all this from me? He keeps talking about how no one will be happy with his plan. Why do you think I want to get messed up in something that's going to make the few people that still might like me unhappy?"

"Grandfather said you were 'perfect.' That without you his idea wouldn't work."

"Well, that's crazy. He's Roger Worth, for crying out loud. He has nothing to lose. Nothing." I twist around to look into her face. "Honey, in a month you and Cab will be back home in Piney with nothing changed. Your uncle made it very clear there is nothing back there for me. This is it. It's all I have, and it's up to me to keep it from turning into a trailer in the backwoods of Florida. A trailer no different from the one in the backwoods of Georgia I came from."

Maggie's eyes drop, and she looks at her hands in her lap. "He really did say you were 'perfect,' but I get it."

"Okay, well, go on and let me get ready. What time is Helen picking you up?"

"Soon. You know the only reason I went shopping with her and my cousins this afternoon was so Grandfather could talk to you?"

We both stand. "I know. That was sweet. Your grandfather is crazy about you. You know that, don't you?" I hug her and feel her let her breath out.

"I know. Just stinks that we have to not let Cab or my awful cousins know."

"But as he told me today, if they knew you were his favorite, they would be more awful to you. He also said that tonight he's going to sit you right next to him and quit doing such a good job of hiding how great he thinks you are, okay?"

"Okay. I'm going to wear the dress from my eighth grade dance. He'll love it." She darts out of the room, and I try to let her happiness about her dress infect me as I slump back onto the bed.

My dress, lying across the foot of the bed, is real stretchy. Real stretchy so it pulls at all the right, or should I say tight, places. The ladies in the salon all got real big eyes and stupid smiles when I came out in it. "And I wasn't even wearing these shoes." I pick the shoes up and then toss them behind me onto the bed. "Guess as you get older, being easy isn't enough." I head into the bathroom for my shower. "Now you gotta put easy into high heels and walk it around the block."

I used the shampoo and other stuff from the hair salon and, surprisingly, my hair is acting right. Not as straight as Saturday night, but tolerable and the color is still that nice brown. Maybe the curls are what made it look like red dirt. Staring in my mirror, rubbing smoothing cream (whatever that is) onto my hair, I remember that Mr. Worth said he knew all about red dirt. Said he grew up in Tennessee where they got red dirt, a little darker than ours in Piney. He don't sound like he's from Tennessee. Said he knew all about small towns, and not from the good side of the tracks.

"Come in," I say when Maggie knocks on my bedroom door. "Can you help me with my makeup?" Then I see her and gasp. "Look at you!"

She smiles and turns around for me to see all of her dress. The green fabric matches her eyes perfectly. "Cecelia helped me pick it out."

"Oh, well, we all know she has great taste. And is this how you wore your hair for the dance? Pulled back on the sides?"

She nods. "Cecelia said it makes my eyes stand out." She takes a deep breath. "I'm kinda scared. I've never wanted my eyes to stand out around my family." She moves to stand near me and look in the mirror.

Her bright hopefulness is something I've not seen in her reflection much. She has it rough at times with Cab being so gorgeous, but I can see her now as she grows up, maybe in a real smart college. Where her tallness and seriousness will be more than a match for all the cuteness. People will like her for who she is. My eyes shift to my reflection. Who I am has never mattered to anyone, so I've never much thought about it. She picks out my makeup and helps me apply it. When her phone buzzes, she looks at it. "They're here. And, oh yeah, Grandfather asked me to stay the night so we can watch the sunrise from the beach. My bag is ready." And she rushes out of my room. I follow her and peek around the door as she walks to her aunt's car with her head up and her hair swinging. Mr. Worth seems to think I've helped Maggie, but I think he's just trying to talk me into his little plan. Maggie's a good girl. She's going to be fine.

And I'll be fine real soon. I detour through the kitchen, pick up a glass, and grab a bottle of white wine from the refrigerator.

Maggie and her grandfather can talk all they want about ideas and being perfect and hard work. I know what it's going to take for me to get out of this mess, and there they are, right in the middle of my bed.

Black high heels.

Finishing my hair, I pull it back with one of Maggie's thick black ponytail bands. The lady at the salon talked about how I could wear my hair this way since my neck was long, and then she looked down at my boobs. Guess if you have big boobs in a low-cut dress, your hair doesn't really matter? Like a nice big deck on your trailer makes the rust just not matter. I get it.

I pull the dress down over my hair and the new lingerie Magnus also sent over, and it takes my breath away, not just 'cause the dress is tight.

"If Momma could see me now," I say to the mirror. She picked Susan for my middle name because she loved Madonna in that movie *Desperately Seeking Susan*. Believe me, I've never looked more like Madonna than right now.

"That's my dream for you, Becca Sue. Go out into the world and be somebody. Be pretty. Like Madonna." Then I turned out to not be pretty and ruined all of my momma's dreams.

Laughing is hard when your ribs are shoved into your lungs and every intake of breath means the dress is tighter, but I start laughing. Wonder if Mr. Worth, with all his talk about making dreams come true had any idea he would need to make me look like Madonna for the dreams to happen? No, I will not cry. With as deep a breath as possible, I suck in the tears and open my eyes to see again how good I look. Looking good for Magnus is what's important. Focus on that. Where are my shoes?

Shoes on, red lipstick on (also from the magic bag), smile on. There you go. Mama's dream come true. The big, shiny red smile droops into an 'O.'

Wait a minute.

He never said nothing about Mama's dream. Seemed to think I had dreams of my own. Huh.

The doorbell rings, and I down the rest of my wine. Magnus is here, and he's the answer to this mess. He's the only one on my side. He's the one who understands me and knows what I can and can't do. I just have to keep him on my side.

"Hey there. Look what someone left at my door today!" I release the door knob and twirl around as fast as I can in the heels on the tile floor.

"Girl, you look like a dream."

He gets one hand on my hip before I run back to my room, saying, "Just a minute" over my shoulder.

In my room, I close the door and stand with my back against it. Dream. I look like a dream? Why would he say that? What is it with everybody having dreams all of a sudden? Dreams are for the people in books. Dreams are for girls like Maggie. Dreams are for people who... who "aren't Becca Sue Cousins," I say out loud. I open the door. "Okay, I'm ready."

At the restaurant, we order wine, and I let Magnus order my food. For the first time it dawns on me I don't even know what I like best to eat. I never look at the menu. Caleb always ordered for me, even Cab has ordered for me. Huh. Interesting. While he orders, I have another swallow of wine and watch him hand the menus to the waitress. So, I had a menu, I just never opened it. My menu is carried away to be handed to someone else. I watch the waitress until she moves around the corner. Then I flip my head toward my date.

"Guess what? Caleb had a vasectomy, so maybe I *can* have a baby." Wow, good wine.

Magnus sits back in his chair. "What? Guess that was a shocker."

"Yep. So, my husband underwent surgery to keep from having a baby with me, and then his brother dumped their worst financial deal in my lap. I'm stuck here, and you are the only reason I fit in to our subdivision. They would've all dropped me if they weren't so all-fired interested in our sex life." I finish my wine and hold my glass out for him to refill it from the bottle at his elbow.

He fills my glass, returns the bottle to the wine bucket and then leans with both his elbows on the table. "Sugar, I've looked into the situation, and the best thing you can do is go bankrupt. Let the bank have it all. Come move in with me, and we'll go back to screwing and drinking and running around. I'm looking to rent a house at the beach. It's perfect for you and me, leave that bunch of saps behind us. You can dress like this for me every night, and we'll go back to playing. If you get pregnant, we'll have us a kid." He lifts up his half-full glass and moves it toward my full glass still in mid-air. I hadn't moved my glass or breathed since he started talking.

This is exactly what I wanted. Okay, dreamed. Right? Wasn't it? But that was with Caleb. How can I have no idea what I want now? But I don't. So I move my glass toward his, and the sweet clink brings a smile to his face. I take a deep breath. "A new life. A new dream."

"And maybe even a baby." He smiles even bigger and sets his glass down. "We need champagne."

30

"You might want to hold off on the champagne," Marie says through the screen door to the group seated on Ruth and Eason's screened porch.

"Harold. Marie." Eason rises from his chair and opens the door. "Glad you're back. Your cruise with the family went well? Grandkids all doing well?"

"We did have fun, but it's good to be back." Harold shakes Eason's hand. The two men are the tallest in the group, but where Eason's face is restful and encouraging, Harold's worries have, and still are, embedding themselves in his face. "Hope its okay we just came on around back. Sorry we're late, we were looking up some stuff."

Eason directs them to a wicker loveseat. "No problem at all. Pearl did bring over some champagne, but most of us are sticking with a cocktail."

"Of course, I brought over champagne," Pearl says. "Roger Worth spent three hours with that girl today. Unless he's throwing off Kathleen for that trash, he's buying her out. And saving us all."

Marie jumps up from the loveseat and walks behind it where a little room makes it possible to pace. "I'm afraid that, well, I'm just afraid."

"What? You were awfully quiet this afternoon. What have you heard?" Ruth stills the swing she'd been pushing back and forth with her feet, and leans forward. "Marie? Harold?"

Harold checks over his shoulder from his seat on the loveseat, and when his wife nods, he turns back to the group. "Roger Worth has some radical ideas. Not just in business or investing but in community development. Does everyone know what 'Enterprise Zones' are?"

Esmeralda answers, "I do. They helped us open up storefronts in some of the broken down areas of a couple cities. Tax breaks, leniency on some regulations, things that made it a profitable place to do business."

"Oh, that. Yes, yes." Pearl agrees and lifts her glass for a toast to her memory and looks at her husband. "Remember, George, when I was still teaching? Made a big difference in some of the communities where the schools were struggling. It created a tax base and brought in people who wanted to also help the schools. I never taught in one, but we heard all about it at those insufferable in-service days." She drinks her toast. "So that makes him an even better benefactor for our community. One who knows how to get things going again!"

Nods and murmurs around the room cause the concern on Marie and Harold's faces to deepen. Marie lays a hand on her husband's shoulder. "Well, Roger has spoken about taking it a step further in the face of recent economic troubles."

Harold adds, "Like into neighborhoods that have, well, failed."

Marie looks around as the nods stop, but before enlightenment arrives. "He suggests that the same tactics as Enterprise Zones be put into place in neighborhoods like ours."

Eason flips his hand in the air, as if needing permission to ask a question. "So new homeowners would be given tax incentives to build a home here? That could be good, but what would concern me is any leniency on covenants, even our homeowners' agreement."

"Ohhh," Ruth says. "Like the rule not allowing children. That could be overturned."

Pearl shakes her head at her friend. "No, it's not possible to just come in and change things already agreed to." Her smug expression fades when she looks across the room to see neither Marie nor Harold looking up in agreement. Both of their faces are hidden, and not only due to the darkening day.

Ruth stands up and takes a lighter from the table nearest her. As she moves around the room lighting candles, some watch her while others are deep in thought.

"There, I love the candles. With the sun down it feels much cooler out here. Anyone need their drink refreshed?"

Pearl rolls her eyes and asks, "What does it all mean? Why so dramatic about telling us this? I think we should go to dinner." She stands up. "We didn't eat earlier, so I'm starving."

Marie and Harold look up and smile, but none of their teeth show, and Eason groans. "You're not telling us what you really think. Now I know how my patients used to feel when I had trouble just coming right out and telling them what I was afraid of."

"I know what they don't want to say." George speaks up from his wheel chair. The candle on the coffee table in front of him reflects in the shiny metal of his seat and his glasses. "When you said neighborhood instead of subdivision it wasn't just a mistake, was it?" He looks from Marie to Harold. "No, didn't think so. You were too deliberate in your words."

Pearl explodes, "Words, schmords! You're such a writer. You do this all the time. Neighborhood. Subdivision. It's all the same..."

"Not really," George interrupts his wife. "Neighborhoods are more like a little town, maybe not a town, but, you know, not all the same." He lifts his head and hand to scan the view outside the room. "Look around you, everything's the same. Ten houses or a hundred, a subdivision says everything here is the same."

Esmeralda shakes her head. "Not exactly the same. I mean," but as she looks out at the other screen rooms facing the lake, she shrugs. "Okay, but that's for a reason. To ensure our, our neighbors are of a certain..."

"And it's important for property values," Ruth adds.

Marie clears her throat and speaks up. "Roger Worth *hates* subdivisions."

"So why would he want to buy one?" Ruth asks.

George unlocks his wheelchair. "To turn it into a neighborhood, a mixed use neighborhood, if I had my guess. Time to go home and do some research into Mr. Worth and his cockamamie ideas."

Pearl stops his movement with a strong hand on the wheel next to her. "But he wouldn't do that. You mean, apartments? Smaller houses? Surely not businesses, too. He wouldn't just change things for the sake of changing them. Once he knows how we, the residents feel...Right, Marie? Right, Harold?"

Marie comes back around and sits next to her husband. "Yes, he would."

"But what about Becca Sue?" Pearl asks. "He talked to her all afternoon. She's the key. We need to talk to her."

Ruth starts her swing swaying again. "Except Becca Sue doesn't really talk to any of us. Well, except Mrs. Bell."

"Okay," Esmeralda says with confidence. "We need to talk to Mrs. Bell. Ruth, you do that, and I'll see what I can find out from Becca Sue. I'm still cleaning the house. That Jameson paid for a weekly cleaning through the summer. I guess he figures she'll be bankrupt by then. Okay, time to eat. Anyone want to go with us to Casa Pablo? We can talk more over cheese dip."

After escorting the group out the front door and turning down the offers to join those going out, Eason returns to the porch where his wife sits surrounded by candlelight and summer night heat. The ceiling fan makes the candle light bounce around the room. He sits next to her in the swing. "A lot to think about."

"Just a couple hours ago, bankruptcy and the subdivision at the mercy of the bank sounded horrible. Now..."

"Now, it sounds doable. Even good." He pats his wife's hand. "And no one mentioned it, but Magnus can help us with Becca Sue. They were going out tonight. He delivered a bag full of goodies from the Ritz salon and shops today."

"Really? I thought he was going to talk with Sybil tonight?" Ruth pauses and presses her lips together.

"Sybil? Didn't she go back home?" Eason's voice is hard. "She was *supposed* to go back home."

"Pearl said Sybil just left for the one night but that she was going to talk to Magnus tonight at his house. Maybe she didn't tell Magnus and was just going to surprise him."

Eason pushes with his feet to make the swing go higher. "Well, from what I heard about what was in that bag, she better hope the surprise isn't on her. Maybe I should text George—"

"No, if Sybil gets hurt, that's her problem. Magnus couldn't have made it any plainer. He's moved on, whether any of us likes it or not."

"But Magnus doesn't, well... never mind." In the dark, the shadows move with the fan, the swing, and the breezes.

Moonrise was later than usual. By time it shone in the lake, the group from Casa Pablo was back home. Lights had flicked on in the houses, and then, in some, been put out again. The candles across the lake had been out for hours. Watching Ruth and Eason dance by their light before blowing them out made Sybil's eyes watery. Were they dancing to music? Or had they been together so long they no longer needed to have music to dance to?

She sighs and moves around in her patio chair on Magnus' screened porch. It was turning into a long night, and only after the neighbors' meeting across the lake was over did she realize Magnus wasn't even there.

The meeting. She'd watched the meeting, but couldn't hear the opinions or questions. Another deeper, sigh came as she realized that even without knowing the questions, she still had more answers than any of those gathered across the moon lit water.

One house had remained dark all night, until now. Sybil watches the lights inside come on and then sees two people walking into the softly lit living room. "Come home. Come home." She focuses her desire on the man walking outside to look at the pool. He stands at the pool, reflected in the blue light. She closes her eyes to make her words, and pull, stronger. When she opens them, he's no longer outside, and the only light in the house is in the end room. Staring at the dark house, she feels a vacuum take the place of her desire and will.

He's not coming home.

She picks up her phone and only needs to push a couple buttons.

"Hello, Roger? Count me in."

31

"It's a sign. Must be a sign." I kick my black heels into the corner, and in the little light from the bathroom, I find a pair of shorts beside the bed. I don't know what time sunrise is, but it's still dark out, so it must not have happened yet. When I drop the blind back in place, it crashes against the window sill, but no problem. No one to wake up. I pull on the shorts, my T-shirt from yesterday, and then slip on the flip flops I find in the bathroom.

My dress, bra, and panties make a trail that I follow, in reverse, to the living room. In the kitchen, I take my still-full wine glass from last night off the counter and pour the wine in the sink. The smell is awful this early. I do remember pouring it on my way to the pool last night. As I stripped off my clothes (no kids around), it had dawned on me that I wanted to get pregnant, that I wanted Magnus to be the father, and that I'd agreed to move in with him. So, I'd stopped in the kitchen for wine reinforcement and celebration. But I didn't get to the pool. Magnus came into the house holding his phone to his ear. His aunt had died, and he needed to get to New York. Now. While he sat in the dark dining room making calls, I went to bed. Well, more like passed out in my bed. He must've turned out the light, because when I woke at 5 a.m. everything was dark and still.

"Hon, you are out. Headed to the airport. Be back in couple days. I'll call. M" is scrawled on a napkin lying on the counter, directly beneath the counter lights, which I didn't even realize we had.

I pick up my keys and grab my purse. The garage light feels blinding when I press the button for the garage door. My stomach lurches at the idea of coffee. I'll get some later.

All I know is I want to see the sun rise over the ocean.

Dark heat wraps around me, and in the car, I roll down the window. There's a softness to the air, but no chill. Even the night critters are asleep, and the only sound is my tires on the asphalt, and then the sound of them hitting potholes, once I'm out of the subdivision. Mr. Worth says he can get this fixed, one of the things he'll work out with the county. Mr. Worth said a lot of things, and once I woke up at 5 a.m., those things wouldn't let me go back to sleep.

The red lights change, almost as I approach, but seem almost a waste with so few cars out on the road. Dim lights from the shops give the air a gray look.

Along the beach road, the houses are all dark. Even though these aren't the mansions near the club, these people don't get up to go to work either. Many of these are vacation rentals as the out-of-state license plates suggest when my headlights hit them.

At the first access road, I park and get out. At the top of the stairs over the dune, I see I'm not too late. The sky is not quite black, but there's no sign of the sun yet. Here and there, dark shadows of people walk, some with dogs. But most are alone. Guess, sunrise watching isn't a couples sport like sunset watching.

I kick off my flip flops at the bottom of the stairs I descend, and the sand is cool between my toes. Everyone else is walking near the water, but I'm not going that close. It looks big and dark. Honestly, until Maggie mentioned it last night, it never even occurred to me that the sun would come up over the water. I'm not a big fan of the ocean, so I just never thought about it, but then I dreamed about it last night. Dreamed a lot about it last night. Sunrise over water.

One time Momma and I slept in the car 'cause she and

Daddy were fighting. We ended up parking out by the lake, where I found out later everybody goes to make out. But that morning, I woke up and the sun was just coming up over the lake. Momma slept right through it, but I got out and leaned against the hood of the car. That was the most beautiful thing I'd ever seen.

I walk next to the dunes, far away from the waves, and the sky lightens bit by bit. I can't even tell yet where the sun actually is going to come up. With a little light, the water almost seems darker and bigger. I don't like the ocean, but I do like sunrises over water.

When the sky starts looking a little pink, I sit down against a dune. I cross my legs and lay my hand on my stomach. What if I had gotten pregnant last night? If Magnus's aunt hadn't died, we would have tried to have a baby. A real, live baby.

As the pink slivers intensify, they turn gold on the edges, and then I can see they are clouds.

Mr. Worth says I'm the reason Maggie is so good; he must think I'd be a good mother. Magnus thinks I'd be a good mother. Wait, did he ever say that, or was it more about him being a father?

Now the water looks silver, smooth silver with the waves only rolling most of the way in and not crashing. I don't like when they crash. The pink and yellow are filling up more of the sky, I have to look behind me to see any dark gray. I think I can see where the sun will come up. It's so bright there, like looking into a fire, not the outside flames, but down where the wood is see-through and hard to look at.

Mr. Worth wanted to know what my plans are. What my dreams are. Good thing he brought a big bag of chips to go with our sandwiches so I could keep eating and not have to answer him. He said he had dreams when he was in junior high. Knew he didn't want to be poor. Knew he didn't want the life his parents had. Knew he'd rather fail than not try.

Boy, I sure ate a lot of chips.

Then the sun shows just a bit, and what I thought couldn't get any brighter does. The light runs along the water, and the silver turns gold. It took forever to come up, but it seems to go so fast now. All of a sudden it's completely above the water, and it's shooting sparkles to ride on the waves. It's all I can do to not burst out laughing. Seagulls squawk and fly in circles as if they didn't see this yesterday, and the day before, and the day before that.

And, wait, where was I on those days? Those many, many mornings this was happening so close to me?

The laughter dies in my throat. Standing up I brush the sand off and start walking back. Shafts of sunlight strike the blowing grass on the dunes. Pink fades and the yellow turns into blue, and I walk back toward my car. On top of the stairs, I turn back toward the ocean. All this was completely dark when I got here. Now full daylight shows every wave, every person, every dune.

It shows everything.

32

"But wouldn't it be wonderful to have children around?" Mrs. Bell asks, but the way she takes a sip of her coffee and looks away from the women across from her, she doesn't seem to need an answer.

"You obviously didn't teach them for twenty-seven years," Pearl says. When she notices Ruth's stern look, she backpedals. "Of course, they are wonderful. I mean, I did teach them for twenty-seven years."

Ruth rolls her eyes, then carries on. "But what about our property values? Mr. Bell would want you to be secure, right?"

"Security is overrated." Mrs. Bell sets her cup down and pushes herself up from her chair. "You can be so secure that there is no longer anything left for you to do but die. A fly in a spider's web, when it's all wrapped up tight, is *very* secure." She walks to the kitchen and leaves Pearl and Ruth looking at each other.

After several minutes and the steady noise of dishes from the kitchen, Ruth calls out. "Can we help you with something?"

"Yes, come taste this." In the yellow kitchen, a blue plate sits on the counter. On it three biscuits are spread with a ruby red jam. Mrs. Bell takes one and then pushes the plate towards the other ladies.

"Uh, we're just going to eat these standing up?" Pearl asks.

Mrs. Bell laughs. "Oh, I guess I'm used to eating by myself. I eat standing up right here by the sink most of the time. No need for a napkin, you just wash your hands."

The hope of returning to the table, engendered by Mrs. Bell's laugh, dies when the other two women see she finds it funny, not a problem, as she takes a big bite of hers and lies it back on the shared plate.

Mmms and nods make up the conversation until all three biscuits are gone. No gentle eating or chatting while eating, due to their hostess' repeated encouragement to hurry. Then Mrs. Bell turns on the sink faucet, washes her hands and invites her guests to do the same by leaving the water running and backing away.

"Isn't this much more civilized than all those dishes and napkins and such? Mr. Bell never did think so, but then he never washed the dishes. Help yourselves to more coffee, if you'd like, and let's go back out to the living room. I have a question to ask you."

Whispers in the kitchen decide somebody needs to check in more often on the older woman, but eventually they seat themselves near her.

"So? What did you think?"

"Of?" Ruth asks.

"Of my biscone and jam?"

"Biscone?"

Mrs. Bell laughs and actually slaps her knee. "Yes, I've cooked both and they are similar, biscuits and scones, so the name is something I made up. I've always loved marketing. Why people name things what they do, and why people buy what they do."

"Well, they were delicious. And you're right, they were like a slightly dryer biscuit."

"The jam was particularly delicious. So sweet and so fresh."

Mrs. Bell smiles and leans forward. "Ladies, you have given me a new lease on life. All these years I stood behind Mr. Bell, and he was a wonderful provider and husband, but in my day when a girl got married, she didn't think about business anymore. My father and uncles owned a whole chain of stores, and I loved working in them. But once I got married, nope, off to be Mrs. Bell. Maybe if we'd had children I wouldn't feel this need, but I've been almost overwhelmed with a need to make my mark on the world, and as I've gotten older, it's gotten stronger."

Pearl and Ruth hold cold coffee, and blink.

Mrs. Bell stands up. "I had no idea where I could sell my biscones, but now I do. Right here in our new little town. Oh, ladies, this is going to be wonderful. Now, excuse me, but I have to talk to Becca Sue."

She pushes them out the door, and in the bright, hot light of the morning, the women begin walking down the sidewalk.

Ruth catches her breath. "Well, we did get her to talk to Becca Sue."

Pearl just shakes her head. "I suppose we should move on to Plan B." Her step falters, and she tilts her head toward her friend. "Except, do we have a Plan B?"

"Last time I did this, I ended up in a mess."

"You had reason to doubt Caleb, but you have no reason to doubt me, right?" Seated at the dining room table, Roger Worth gathers papers, and after a moment, he lays them in front of Becca Sue.

"Jameson, not Caleb, is who made me sign those papers."

"Yes, yes, but he's not the one who drew them up. Just sign here..."

"Caleb drew them up? But I thought... "

The man in the light brown suit taps his pen near Becca Sue's hand. "Ma'am? I need to get back to the office."

"Oh, sure. I just sign wherever the yellow marker is, right?"

"Yes," the man says and then looks across the table at Roger. "Still can't imagine how you got all this okayed and typed up so fast."

The casually dressed mover and shaker laughs and leans

back. "Paperwork can always be done quickly, if you have the right people. But mostly, with all the pension worries towns have now, they can't afford to look a gift horse in the mouth. Every couple decades, folks in Florida get greedy. If the beach towns are so popular and land so valuable, why not the land just a few miles inland? And if the economy stays strong, and there are no hurricanes, some people make big money. However, one bad hurricane season or the economy tanks, and everybody scuttles back to the beach. Just like the little crabs running from the tide. The town council couldn't get rid of all this fast enough when a way out was offered to them. A way out and a lot of money for the town coffers."

Becca Sue lays the pen down and sighs. "You were talking to them last week about all this, you said? Even before you and I talked."

Roger leans up and crosses his arms on the table. He stares at Becca Sue. "You were the last shoe to fall. I just needed to meet you and see if you could make it work. See if you *wanted* to make it work."

The large man in the suit stands up. "Looks like everyone got what they wanted." He walks around the table as Roger and Becca Sue stand up. At the door, he stretches his hand out. "Well, Ms. Mason, let me be the first to say it." He grasps her hand and smiles. "Welcome to Backwater."

"What?"

As Roger pumps the man's hand, he smiles at his new partner. "That's our name. The little town out at the main road decades ago was called 'Backwater,' so it made things much easier to take that name. Plus, it gives us a connection to the past. Thanks again, Jim, for coming out here and taking care of everything."

The door closes and Becca Sue walks back to the dining room table and sits down. "Now what?"

Mr. Worth collects his things. "I have a golf game to get to. One of the town councilmen wanted me to get him together with some of my friends. He's looking for investors for some business venture. After that, Kathleen and I are heading back to New Hampshire."

"What? You're just leaving?"

He sits down in the chair next to her. "Now we have to set things in motion. Me there, you here. I have a couple businesses already interested and a marketing firm is locating others. You'll see quite a bit more traffic in the area, but I should be back by the weekend, or at least by the next one. Cab will be coming back out here to live. He's going to cut his business teeth on this project, so you can talk with him about things. It's all going to be fantastic."

He stands, and she follows him to the front door. "But what do I tell people if they want to know what's going on?"

As he opens the door, he laughs. "Oh, don't worry. That will be the fun part. Maybe you should throw a party." He turns and leans against the doorway. "Seriously, Becca Sue, own this. You and I know something a lot of people don't, that most small towns stink. We have the chance to change that, to make something better. Better than Piney. Better than where I grew up in Tennessee. To make it work for everyone." He straightens up and takes a step back. "Be proud, okay? You're doing a good thing."

She waves and closes the door. She leans against the door and closes her eyes. "I live in Backwater, Florida."

Then she runs to the bathroom and throws up.

33

"I want to open a store. Here, take this," Mrs. Bell says as she pushes a plate into my hands. She uses her empty hand to grasp the door jamb and steady her step in my front door.

"A store? Here, let's go in the living room."

Mrs. Bell scuttles down the open hall wearing red capris, flat navy tennis shoes, and a flowing white shirt.

"Still dressed for the fourth, I see. So, do you want me to take you to a store?" I ask as I sit the plate on the coffee table and settle into a chair. Mrs. Bell sits only on the edge of the couch and grabs the plate to sit it on her knees.

"I'm not dressed for the fourth, this is for my store. My colors are going to be red, white, and blue. Our family stores used those colors. Mostly because my one uncle married into a family who owned an American flag factory. They got decorations for wholesale prices. Here, eat this." She lifts up the plastic wrap and hands me a biscuit.

"Um, okay." I take a bite, trying to catch the crumbs in my other hand. "It's good. Isn't it the biscuit, or you called it a scone, we had the other day?"

"Shoot, no, it should taste different. This one has parmesan on it. I need a variety if I'm going to stock a store."

"I'm not sure what you mean by stocking a store. You want to sell these?"

Her face falls. "Don't you think they're good enough? I have a darling marketing campaign worked out. So, how do I get in on your plans with that Mr. Worth?"

A flash of recognition. "Oh, you mean, Backwater?"

"That's our name? Hmm. Well, it fits. So where do we stand?"

"How do you even know about this?" I had thrown up, taken a nap, and planned to spend the afternoon by the pool, but I barely got my bathing suit on when someone was ringing the dickens out of the doorbell. When I saw Mrs. Bell through the little window, I thought she must be having a heart attack. Listening to her, it sounds more like she had a stroke.

She waves her hand at me. "Oh, Ruth and Pearl were over earlier bellyaching about it. All worried about Mr. Worth starting a town up here. Using the empty lots for stores and such. Never mind them and their worries, I want a store. Or at least a stand. We'll sell your freezer jam, too."

"Can I help?" Maggie comes out of her bedroom, where she's clearly been listening. "I'll work in your store."

"Perfect! A girl needs to know about business. Sit here." Mrs. Bell pats the cushion beside her.

I shake my head. "Maggie, you'll be long back home and in school before any store opens."

"No, she won't," Mrs. Bell disagrees. "I'm opening this Saturday. The men that take care of my lawn are coming to clear off the lot between your house and mine today. The bank told us months ago they couldn't take care of the empty lots, but we were free to maintain them. Free being the operative word." She pats Maggie's knee and winks. "We have to come up with an ad for the *Island Times* by three p.m. today to get it in tomorrow's paper."

Maggie jumps up. "I'll get a notebook!"

Mrs. Bell tilts her head and stares at me. "Are you going swimming?" Her eyes cut to my bikini top.

"I was. Guess I could put a shirt on over it until we're through." *Am I being dismissed?*

The sweet little old lady suddenly sounds mean. She's lowered her voice, but it's harder than I've ever heard. "Becca Sue,

I'm not sure what all you had to do with this plan, but it's a lifeline for you. You've sat in my kitchen more than once and wondered what to do, and every time I thought you were going to change things, I'd look over here to see Magnus in the pool or his car out front. I know you loved your Caleb, but Magnus? Are you in love with him? Is he worth investing your life into?"

Maggie plops down before I can say anything, so standing up, I mumble something about changing clothes or swimming or something.

In my bedroom, I hear the words again. "Is he worth investing your life into?"

"No" leaps to my lips, and although it only comes out as a whisper, in my brain it's shouted over and over.

Except... I lay on my bed where a rectangle of sunlight warms my quilt, and I close my eyes. Except... I'm afraid I might be pregnant. As I was throwing up this morning, I had the thought that I'd felt sick several mornings lately. And I can't remember when I had a period.

But I'm probably not. And Magnus says he wants a baby, but he probably doesn't. And I said I could move in with him, but I probably wouldn't. And besides, I'm probably not pregnant at all. Mostly I should put a shirt on and get back out there and help Mrs. Bell with her store idea. As crazy as all that sounds, it's easier to think about than being pregnant.

And there's no probably to that.

34

"What a fantastic idea, Becca Sue!" Mrs. Bell practically shouts. "A farmer's market."

Maggie squints at us. "What's a farmer's market?"

"Where farmers sell their stuff all together. My uncle takes stuff to the one in Piney, but I don't think that one is the same as the one here up in town."

Mrs. Bell raises her eyebrows. "Doubtful. This one has the farmers, but also has crafters, gourmet chefs with freezers, bakeries with tables of bread and cakes. There are pasta makers, just everything you can think of to sell."

Maggie asks, "What all would we have to sell?"

"Maybe that's what our ad should say. Not only getting people out here to buy, but to sell. We have your biscones, Mrs. Bell, and we can grow from there."

"But that sounds more like a flea market than a farmer's market. Not sure that's what we're going for, Becca Sue." Mrs. Bell rubs her hands and thinks. "I guess it could be some of both."

"Backwater Market," Maggie says as she draws on her notebook. "Then that way it can be both. Mrs. Bell leans over to see what she's drawing just as the doorbell rings.

Becca Sue walks to the door. "Hello?"

"Hi, I'm Sam Johnson. I'm looking for Rebecca Mason." The young man says as he sticks out his hand. "Are you Rebecca?"

She nods.

"Finally. This place is near impossible to find and the idea of a restaurant out here, especially the condition that road is in? Is this the right place? Is this Backwater?"

"Yeah, I guess it is. Restaurant?"

He looks at the paper in his hand. His hair is curly and almost black. His eyebrows are heavy, and they hide his eyes with his head bent toward the piece of paper. "1021 Oyster Bay." He looks up and smiles, and the brightness of his dark eyes make his eyebrows fade in importance. "Just how far are we from the beach here?"

"About fifteen minutes or so. Um, 1021 is right across the lake, I think. It's the empty house." She leans back and lifts her arm toward the back windows.

"Oh, so we'll be neighbors? Good to know. Thanks, Rebecca, but I better get to work. Nice to meet you." He waves and jogs back down the sidewalk to his truck.

Becca Sue closes the door and whispers. "Rebecca."

"So who was that?" Maggie asks.

"Sam, um, Sam Jones, maybe? Says he's here to work on, or at a restaurant in the abandoned house across the lake."

"Already?" Mrs. Bell beams. "We really are doing this. Look at our ad." She points to the notebook Maggie holds up.

Becca Sue reads out loud. "Backwater Market opening Saturday off Old McCaysville Road. Look for signs. Come to buy or sell fresh baked goods, fruits, vegetables, crafts, anything! Hey, that's my cell number on there for information."

"Of course. You're in charge," Maggie says with a shrug. "While you were talking to the restaurant guy, we called and got some sign prices, and they can be ready Thursday. Cab and I can put up signs on Friday all over."

"Don't get me involved in this mess," Cab shouts with the slam of the front door for emphasis. "I don't care what Grandfather says, this is a stupid idea."

Maggie visibly sinks back into the couch and lies her notebook down on her lap.

Becca Sue sighs. "Cab, some people are very excited, and

your grandfather hardly has stupid ideas. Come see what we're doing."

He stops beside the couch and looks down at his sister's ad. "I hate Piney. Why would I want to create another dump just like it? No, this one's worse. Its name is Backwater." He stalks off toward his room, lugging his duffle bag behind him. "I repeat, it's stupid."

Becca Sue takes a deep breath and shrugs as she looks down the hall after him. "Your grandfather said Cab was going to help with all this. I think he saw it as a way to see what Cab can do. He'll come around. He's a good kid." Becca Sue smiles and reaches out for the notebook. As she studies the ad, Maggie and Mrs. Bell meet eyes, roll them, and shake their heads.

Maggie jumps up when the doorbell rings again. In a moment she comes back, followed by a heavyset woman with a fluffy blonde ponytail. "There's Mrs. Bell."

The woman crosses to Mrs. Bell with her hand outstretched. "I'm sorry to track you down like this, but I'm Ashleigh Morrow from the *Island Times*. I tried calling your phone, but no one answered and I was out this way, so I thought I'd stop in to see about your ad."

Mrs. Bell shakes her hand. "Well, aren't you a go-getter!"

"Ma'am, you pert near have to be to sell ads in *this* economy, in *this* place, for *this* paper. Can I sit down?" She sits down and fans herself with the paper in her hand. "Lord, it is hot out there." She swipes across her forehead, and her full ponytail bounces with every movement. She looks at Becca Sue and tips her head. "Don't believe we've met. Are you from here? We look about the same age, but you don't look familiar. D'ya go to school here?"

"Uh, no. Hi. I'm Becca Sue, and this is Maggie."

"Well, nice to meet you both. I saw that young man getting dropped off here, so I thought I'd see if y'all knew where I could find Mrs. Bell, and here she is. Oh, let me see that." She reaches out to take the notebook lying in Maggie's lap. "Is that it? Your ad? Backwater Market. Oh, I can do some really cool stuff with that. How big should we make it?"

Mrs. Bell beams. "Well, I've got more money than time, so let's do it big."

The ponytail bobs. "Oh, you are my kind of woman. So, I want to know all about this market. What is Backwater? Can I get myself a drink?"

The speed with which Ashleigh zips from question to question is dizzying, but still, Becca Sue jumps up. "Oh, I'm sorry. Let me get you one."

"No, no problem at all." Both stand up, the stranger getting a jump on Becca Sue, and actually beating her into the kitchen. "So, where are you from, Becca Sue?"

From Piney, Georgia. It's a little town."

"How long have you been here?"

"Just a month or so. My husband, well, ex-husband, kinda left me with this house and all."

"Oh my goodness! Left you this house? It's beautiful. You must be some kind of happy."

Becca Sue hands the glass to Ashleigh, but doesn't answer. Doesn't mean the conversation lagged.

"How did this Backwater thing come about? Here, let's go back in the living room. I want to hear what all of you think." As they sit down, Ashleigh explains. "I not only do the ads for the paper, but I'm a reporter. Journalism is what I went to school for, grad school even, but we all know how bad newspapers are doing right now. So, I'm back home. Woohoo! Not. And, yes, before you ask, my father is the Dan Morrow who owns the paper. Not only am I back home, I got my high school job back." She takes a long drink of water, sits her glass down on the coffee table, and clicks her pen. "Okay, Mrs. Bell, since you're the one that called me. What in the world are you doing and what is Blackwater?"

"Guess no one ever lived here." Sam walks into the empty, unfinished house, followed by six workmen, two of whom immediately walk past him into the kitchen area while the others spread out exploring. "She said the kitchen backs up to the garage so we would open that up for the expanded kitchen."

"Turn the bedrooms into bathrooms?" a worker asks from the hallway.

"That's the idea, and good," Sam opens the back doors. "Patio is much closer to the lake than the houses on that side. Perfect for outdoor seating."

"Didn't I tell you?" Sybil says, coming in the front door. "Hi there. I saw you pull up."

Sam steps toward her and pushes his hand out. "Good to see you, again." The other men stand behind him, but she walks around him to shake their hands also. "Glad you were available to start on such a short time frame."

Sam shrugs. "A job's a job. Besides, isn't that what you pay us for? To come when you call?"

Sybil presses her lips together and folds her arms. "Exactly, that, and being the best in the business. So, show me how good you are and tell me when I can open."

Sam laughs, shaking his head, and turns around to face the lake. "Give us an hour to work it up."

Sybil nods. "An hour. I'll be back."

She exits the way she came in. As she closes the front door behind her, she looks up to see George in his wheelchair at the end of the driveway. "Great," she mutters through clinched teeth. Then, out loud, with a big smile, "George! Good to see you."

He waits for her to walk up next to him. "You're mixed up in this Roger Worth plan, aren't you? Trying to work your way back into Magnus' life by moving practically next door?"

She crosses her arms and looks down at him. "It's business. Magnus and I are done. Surely even you can see that if Roger Worth is involved there's money to be made."

"You've checked to make sure this is all legal? You're not going to invest in this and then be left hanging?"

"Oh, I no longer get left hanging for *anything*. I learned that lesson a long time ago. Roger has every i dotted and every t crossed. This is purely business. I wanted a restaurant in Florida, and now I'll have one."

George rolls back a few inches. "Let's head back to the house. Too hot out here for me, Pearl will want to give you the twenty questions about the restaurant, you know."

She looks back at the house and then walks into the road. "Okay, I do have an hour to kill."

"So, from what you're saying, fighting this thing doesn't stand a good chance to stop it. Roger has it all wrapped up?"

"Yeah, he's wanted to try this for some time. The idea that this property comes around, connected to his grandkids, with a town council desperate for some cash, was just too good to pass up."

"Sure screws us who thought we were buying a nice, quiet, gated, adults-only retirement."

"Who knows, George, you might like it. Might suit you. Pearl, now, she'll hate it." They laugh and turn into the Manninghams' driveway.

George slows and asks. "What do you think Magnus will think?"

"I think he's so happy getting drunk and banging that hillbilly across the lake he won't give a rat's ass."

In the silence, the bugs hum louder for a moment before stopping completely. George leads up the sidewalk and at the door turns to look at her. "So, nothing changes with Magnus. You're not—"

"I'm not." She pulls open the front door, and a wave of air conditioning greets them. "I'm not," she says again, and this time it sounds like she might mean it.

35

I could just dart into the aisle, pick one up, and tuck it into my cart. No one would notice. But then we move on past the aisle with the pregnancy tests. *Next time. I'll get one next time.*

Ashleigh slows down pushing her cart and asks me over her shoulder, "What else is on the list?"

In the past week since we met, I've discovered Ashleigh is a great believer in lists. I scan the one I've been put in charge of. "Just something for dinner. Maybe chicken from the deli?"

"Ugh. I hate buying my dinner where I buy my lawn chairs." She turns her full cart into the center of the main aisle. "But it would mean one less stop."

At the deli, I try to make room in my cart for the food. "Ashleigh, thank goodness you came with me. There's no way all this stuff would fit in one cart. You've done magic with our market idea."

She leans on her cart, pulls her hair out of its rubber band, and lets it fall around her face. It's full and thick and such a rich, sunny color. I'd never put it back, if my hair looked like that, but she immediately begins doing just that. Holding her rubber band in her teeth, she needs both hands to corral the mass of hair, then with a quick flip or two, it's all back and neat again.

"Why don't you ever wear your hair down?"

"Oh, I wear it down, but you've only seen me when I'm

working. We'll go out sometime and you'll see my secret weapon in all its glory." She winks and smiles.

Maybe we will go out together sometime? This week it's been like I have a friend. A girl friend who's not related to me. Ashleigh's been out to Backwater every day this week and worked just as hard as the rest of us to get the market ready for tomorrow morning. We have farmers, crafters, and junk people all coming tomorrow. Don't know what Roger did at his golf outing with the town council people, but crews were out Tuesday afternoon paving Old McCaysville Road, and although there aren't any yellow or white lines painted yet, it's smooth as melted chocolate.

Although Esmeralda hates the very idea of Backwater, Patrick is driving Cab and Maggie around to put up signs this afternoon. He says he loves the idea of "free enterprise", or people selling stuff, as I call it. What I really think he loves the idea of is Ashleigh with her hair down. Funny, but except for a bunch of years and a bunch of weight, Ashleigh and Esmeralda are a lot alike. Both can work me into the ground and still be humming like a June bug. As I've always suspected, I'm not all that partial to work, but this project is kind of fun.

Esmeralda is still cleaning my house, and that gives her reason to hang around. She says living in Backwater will be as bad as living back in the city where they sell stuff right on your doorstep. However, she has given us some good ideas from when her grandfather used to sell food in the Italian market back in the city. Mrs. Bell says she'll come around to supporting Backwater pretty soon, she guesses.

A couple of folks are already supporting us. There's Patrick and Sybil. Sybil actually owns the restaurant that cute guy Sam was talking about. She's only talked to Mrs. Bell, but apparently she's good friends with Roger.

Yeah, I started calling him Roger. We talk on the phone all the time. A big surprise has been Dr. King; he wants to plant a big ol' community garden. He's already had the lot on the other side of their house cleared, and a guy was out there yesterday tilling up all the ground. It's too hot to plant anything right now, he says, but he's getting the ground ready. His wife is not happy about it at all. She and Pearl are right upset.

My arm gets slapped, and I hear my name. My eyes blink and I come around. "Huh? You talking to me?"

Ashleigh grins. "Yes. After dinner, let's swim in your pool. I brought my bathing suit and fixings for margaritas. Oh, wait, I didn't bring any limes. You wait on the food and I'll meet you at the check-out counter." She pushes her cart around me. I cross my arms on the handles of my cart and lean on them. My phone rings, and with just a quick glance at it lying in the seat of the cart, I see that it's Magnus. Again.

The lady behind the counter sets two big bags up on top. "Here ya go, hon. You can get your phone first."

I take the bags and shrug. "It's okay. I wasn't answering it." Seriously, why start now? I haven't answered his calls since he left. Maybe his aunt left him a bunch of money and a big house and he's staying up there. Never coming back to Florida. Maybe.

We check out, and the whole time Ashleigh is loudly telling the folks in line with us, in line near us, or those working, about Backwater Market. The smell of that fried chicken has my stomach growling, but it's going to be cold by time we get out of here with all these folk's questions. Finally at the car we unload the carts, and I snag a wing out of the box. She's driving her mother's van, so we could fit everything in, which means I can eat while she drives.

"Why do you want to go swimming at my place? Don't you have plans for Friday night?"

She turns the air conditioner fan up high and pulls the front of her shirt in and out to get some air moving. "Same damn plans I've had since junior high. Go somewhere and drink and then go somewhere near the water - marsh, lake, beach, or pool, and drink some more. Except my crowd is kinda dwindling down. Now I know how my girlfriends felt when I went off to college. They said I abandoned them." We stop at the red light, and she looks for traffic so she can make our right-hand turn. "Now they're all abandoning me for husbands and babies."

She turns, and as our speed picks up on the highway she looks at me. "You never had any kids? Don't you want kids?"

There's nothing in my mouth, but I close it real quick and act like I'm chewing. I overplay the swallow, but I'm not a real actress, you know. "Me? Well, I did. Caleb, my husband..."

"Your ex?"

"Yeah, my ex-husband, well, apparently didn't want kids with me 'cause he had a vasectomy. I didn't know about it, just him and his momma knew. Then he had it reversed."

"So you two could have kids?"

"Um, no, so he could have them with this girl he was sleeping with. Audrey's daddy had some land Caleb's mother wanted." I wipe my fingers on a Kleenex lying in the center console and look up to see Ashleigh's eyes wide, staring straight down the highway.

"No wonder he gave you a house, hell, a whole subdivision."

"Yeah." Chicken must've been greasy, my stomach is kinda upset.

Ashleigh maneuvers the van up to the mailbox, then reaches in for the stack of mail. She hands most of it to me, but pulls the newspaper from the bottom. She shakes it open. "There you go. Look at that." "Backwater - Florida's Newest Small Town" in thick black letters on one side. There are pictures and a map. She shoves the paper into her lap, then backs the car into the driveway. "That should secure a big crowd for tomorrow."

We saw the signs Cab and Maggie and Patrick had set up all the way in, and the lot for the market next door looks ready for everyone. We open at 7:30 a.m. for customers, so the vendors will be getting here really early. Roger is actually paying a coffee shop from down near the mall to come set up each Saturday. He's paying all their overhead 'cause he said without coffee for folks we'd be in trouble.

"We're starving," Maggie and Cab say as we park. I'd texted them to tell them to be outside to help unload the van.

"Well, take a load in and then we'll eat. Most of this stuff we won't need until tomorrow." We set everything out on the table and eat while we go over everything we've done.

Maggie butters a roll and asks, "Did y'all see the fair signs? It's at the beach tonight and Patrick and Esme want to know if we can go with them."

Cab shakes his head. "Not me. Well, they would drive me, but I'd be meeting some of my friends there."

Maggie takes a bite of her roll but still talks, "Please, Esme needs someone to ride the roller coaster and fun stuff with. She says Patrick doesn't like them. Please."

"Of course, I guess," I say. "Cab, no drinking."

He salutes and gets up from the table.

Ashleigh is tapping her phone but talking to us. "Maggie, my niece is your age, and she's working at the raffle ticket booth for the volleyball team fundraiser. I just texted Cara and told her you'd stop by and say 'Hi'."

"Okay, sure. Her name's Cara?" Maggie doesn't look too sure, but she shrugs and keeps eating.

When both kids are gone, Ashleigh elbows me. "Pool party is looking better by the minute. Kids will be gone, and maybe we can those guys working on the restaurant to come swimming." She jogs out to the living room, and then is out the back door before I can say anything.

I finish cleaning the table and take another look at our list of things left to do. It's all crossed off, so I start another one for the morning. Leaning on the counter, I flip back a couple pages and see everything we've written down and then crossed off.

This is good. Real good. I can't believe what all we've done. What all we've put together. As I examine the pages I see where the lists started out in Maggie or Ashleigh's handwriting, but then how by the end of the week everything is in my handwriting. My lists. My to-do lists. My stomach feels funny again, but not in an upset kinda way, in a happy way. A bubbly way.

What do you know? I like lists.

"Glad I bought extra limes," Ashleigh says as she slams the

back door. "Where are you? Oh, you got everything cleaned up. You're getting fast at that. So, the guys are coming over for a margarita. Some of them are going to the fair or to the beach, but a couple said they just wanted to hang out and swim." She holds her hand up in the air at me. "It's a party, girl!"

I high five her and show her our crossed-off lists. "Look at all this."

"We are a good team. Now, let's get in our bathing suits and get in that pool."

"I just don't like lime." While we were changing, I came up with a way to avoid drinking tonight. I sat out some vodka, and I'll pretend I'm drinking mixed drinks.

"But you might like my margaritas. Well, the guys, especially that Sam guy said he loved margaritas." At the pool Ashleigh has set up her iPhone in a player and has a blender plugged in by the back door. Her hair is down.

She's larger than I ever was, I think, but she still has on a bathing suit, like she doesn't even care. It's a dark-red one piece with only one strap. She has a skirt thing wrapped around her, and its dark blue and green and red. She looks beautiful, and I wonder if I ever looked like that when I was heavy. No, I didn't. I look down at my bikini. Shoot, I don't look like that even now. I don't get it.

"Hey, you back here?" a voice calls from the side of the house.

Ashleigh shouts. "Perfect timing. Just finished the first batch. Salt or no salt?"

Sam comes in the gate, and he's with three other guys. "Salt for me." Another guy holds up a beer to say he's good, and the other two stop to talk to her. Sam walks over to where I'm getting ready to walk into the pool.

"Rebecca, right?"

"Right, yeah, Rebecca. And you're Sam."

"Thanks for inviting us over. We'd all talked about going into town, but I'm worn out. Be good to just relax. You guys have a big day tomorrow."

"Yes, we do." Wow, do I want a drink. His eyes are so dark and his hair so curly and his voice is so not southern. Wow, do I want a drink.

"Sam, here's your margarita," Ashleigh announces.

"Just sit it down there. I've got to get in the pool first." He smiles at me and then takes off his shirt. "Excuse me, but that water just looks too good." He tosses his shirt to the side then runs around the edge to the deep end and leaps up to do a cannonball. The other guys join him and Ashleigh digs a nerf football out of her bag. She throws it into the pool, and then jumps in. Beautiful hair and all.

As I walk down the steps I'm confused. Is this really what people do? I thought those beer and soft drink commercials were made up. But here in front of me is a pool full of people laughing and splashing. A laugh climbs up my throat. Wait, there are laughing, splashing young people in *my* pool. *My* pool.

I dive in and plan to come up right in the middle of it.

36

"Listen," Sam says from the deep end of the pool. "TJ's snoring."

In the quiet, soft snores come from the lounge chair next to the house. The sun stayed high and hot then, wrapped in blazing orange and pink, it gave way to summer twilight. Finally the only lights in the sky were the endless stars. Only TJ had left the pool, claiming exhaustion from the hard-fought game of keep away.

"Boss man here," Carlos throws the wet nerf football at Sam, "has been working us hard."

Ashleigh is seated in the pool on a built-in seat, nursing another margarita, and she asks, "So what all are you doing over there?"

Sam is swimming back and forth, but he stops to tread water. "Making a restaurant. Owner wants a small place, limited menu, but a place to hang out. We're also making a designated area for takeout service, which the more I'm here, the more I think that's the real ticket."

"You know a lot about restaurants?" she asks.

Carlos answers, "Try everything. We're the go-to guys in the industry right now. Sam was all over the economy falling apart. Restaurants went from always full, turning away customers and expanding like crazy, to barely making a profit. Sam here knew how to scale back, build smaller, capitalize on doing less, but still make money."

Sam squeezes water out of his hair and sits on the under-water bench near Ashleigh. "I kinda grew up in the business." He reaches out for the bottle of water he left on the edge of the pool, then takes a drink of it.

Ashleigh looks down at her feet in the blue lit water and kicks them. "Do you cook, too?" She looks up to see him nod. "Which do you prefer?"

"Hard to say. I'd like to find a place small enough that I could cook and still do some consulting." He grins. "And con-struction is just fun."

As a float meanders up to him, he pushes it a bit. "Think she's asleep, too?" he whispers. Ashleigh and he lean over, but can't see Becca Sue's face.

Carlos grins, his teeth glowing in the pool light. "We could make sure." He dives under and then explodes up, taking one side of the float with him.

Becca Sue screams as she's dumped in the water. Everyone laughs, but Carlos' laugh is cut short when he's jerked under the water. Becca Sue comes up holding his foot high. She lets it go and then splashes Ashleigh and Sam. "That's for laugh-ing."

"Is this a private party, or can anyone crash?" The voice from the darkness by the house makes all four look that way.

"Magnus! You're back." Becca Sue treads water, but doesn't move to get out.

He looks around and nods. "Guess I see why you were too busy to answer my calls."

Becca Sue looks back at Ashleigh and Sam, then turns to Magnus. "Do you want to, ah, swim?" He waits, but that's all she offers.

His face sets hard and his voice deepens. "No, think I'll just go to bed."

The words "goodbye" fade on Becca Sue's lips as he opens the back door and walks inside. At the door, he turns back. "Have fun, sweetie. Wake me up when you come to bed."

As the door shuts, Sam drops quietly into the water. Car-los throws the football up in the air and catches it. Becca Sue turns to see Ashleigh's eyes wide as golf balls. "What the hell? Who is that?" she asks.

Sam comes up near the steps. "This has been great. Thanks, but TJ's not the only one tired. Think we should call it a night."

Carlos agrees and lifts himself up to sit on the edge of the pool. He throws the wet football at TJ, who wakes up with a shout. He stretches and stands up.

"You want us to help clean up?" Sam asks. "Although guess there's not that much." He looks towards the house, and his desire to not follow the older man into the house, helping clean or not, shows all over his face.

"No, we'll get it. We're going to swim for a little bit," Ashleigh answers. "Glad y'all came over. We'll do it again."

Becca Sue, hanging on the side of the float, doesn't say a word. Even as everyone says goodbye, she keeps her face down.

Ashleigh reaches out with her foot and pokes the float. "They're gone. Who in the world is that old man, and tell me he was joking about waiting for you in bed."

"He never looked that old before."

The silence stretches on and on. Ashleigh usually peppered questions, but like a good journalist she knew sometimes the best answers come to questions not asked.

Becca Sue pushes away from the float, dives under, then comes up next to where Ashleigh is seated in the water. "His name is Magnus Llord, and he's a lawyer. That's his house over there." She points to where an interior light dimly illuminates Magnus' screened porch.

"Oh, so it was a power play. He didn't have to sleep here. He could've easily gone home, he just wanted the good-looking young men in the pool to know he had first claim to you. Sounds like a lawyer." She rolls her eyes and drops her voice in a deeper range. "Oh, no, you're not married to him or anything, right?"

"No. Not at all." Becca Sue pulls up to sit next to Ashleigh. "He did ask me to move in with him before he left. When I thought I was going to go bankrupt."

Ashleigh finishes her margarita and pulls out the lime. "Knowing you, you weren't even actually using him, were you? You just were rolling along and he was the next safe port. Thank God you told him no, that you were going with Roger's plan and Backwater."

"Well, I didn't actually tell him any of that. He left before... before."

"You going to go crawl in bed with him, now?"

"What else can I do?"

"What's he going to think in the morning when you jump out of bed at 5:30 to set up Backwater Market, which he's never even heard of?" Ashleigh sticks the lime in her mouth and bites off the pulp. "You are crazy." She tosses the lime rind into the dark of the yard and then eases into the water. "I'm cleaning all this up. You need to go tell the old lawyer what's been going on here this past week. By time I come into the house to say goodbye, he should be on his way to his own house and his own bed."

"But what if I want to be with him? What if I love him?" Becca Sue demands from her corner seat.

Ashleigh doesn't even turn around to answer. "Then you would have leapt out of this pool and welcomed him home. Introduced him to us."

Becca Sue twists her mouth. "Oh yeah."

37

"Guess I showed up just in time to ruin your party."

In the kitchen, wrapped in one beach towel and using another towel to dry my hair, I lean against the counter and watch Magnus pace. Each time he comes near the kitchen table, which is loaded down with Backwater stuff, I think he'll stop and look at it. So I wait for the questions.

He turns again at the table. "Any wine? Or have you and your friends finished it all off?" He jerks open the refrigerator and grabs the first bottle he finds. "There was only one car in the drive, local tag. I guess, like Cab, you found some local yokels to hang out with. I hate that my attending my aunt's *funeral* caused you to be so lonely."

He pulls the cork out of the bottle and looks up at me. "Oh, and I'm fine, by the way. Got old auntie buried, my last living relative. Thanks for checking on me. You Southerners are all warm and sweet on the outside, but colder than the Statue of Liberty's tit in January on the inside, aren't you?" He walks into the living room to the rack of nice wine glasses.

"I should've called you back, but things have been kind of crazy here. And really busy. And I just don't know..." I wad the damp towel from my hair up and hold it against my stomach.

"Here." Magnus says as he holds out a full glass of wine to me.

The tension in my face melts, and I can feel my eyes widen. My mouth drops open with a soft "No." First he tightens, like he's mad, then he tilts his head and when his eyes drop to where I hold the wadded up towel, I close my eyes because I know what's next.

"You're pregnant."

After a lifetime living around clueless men, I had to go and find myself a smart one. "Maybe. I don't know." He sits down both glasses on the counter and opens his arms. He wraps me up and gently sways with me, pats my back and murmurs that it's all going to be okay.

This. This is what I needed. As my body warms and my shoulders relax, I let his words seep in. "A baby. My baby. This is the greatest. I'll take such good care of you both. You don't have anything to worry about. Nothing at all." He steps back so he can look in my face. "And you come with me to my house tonight and let the rest of them worry about that silly market in the morning."

I pause. "What?"

He grins and pulls me tight. "You really think I didn't know about this Backwater rigmarole? I've talked to folks here, and even had lunch with Roger this week in the city. I wasn't sure how I felt about it, but now I do. No way is my baby growing up in a place called Backwater. Hell, I'll take a loss on the house here. My aunt left me two houses of hers. You are going to love her place in Vermont." He squeezes me. "Let's go now." He drops his arms from around me to step back and lift his glass of wine.

"But what if I'm not pregnant?"

He toasts me. "Then here's to making it happen."

"Making what happen?" Ashleigh asks from the doorway.

Magnus turns. "A family. Our family. And who are you?"

I step between them. "This is my new friend, Ashleigh. She's leaving. Can you also leave, Magnus?"

"Ashleigh, nice to meet you. Here, would you like Becca Sue's glass of wine, since she can no longer drink?" He hands her my glass, and I watch Ashleigh putting pieces together.

She looks at me, looks at Magnus, then back at me. With each change of eye direction, her mouth turns farther down.

"No way."

Magnus moves beside her and puts his arm around her shoulder. "Yes way. My girl there is having my baby. A toast to Becca Sue."

Ashleigh shakes her head at me. "I have to go home. I'll be back in the morning, and we can talk. Or not. You don't seem to understand what being a friend is." She pulls her bag strap up further onto her shoulder and pulls away from Magnus.

She pushes by me, and my stomach falls as I turn to watch her leave. I don't reach out to her or call to her. Magnus comes up behind me and pulls off my towel. He puts his arms around my waist and starts kissing my neck. When the door closes behind Ashleigh, Magnus squeezes me. "No worries, sweetheart. She's just a redneck Florida girl. Let's get you out of this wet bathing suit and go to bed, here or my place. We'll just ignore them in the morning if we stay here."

Looking down at all the Backwater papers on the table, my notepad with my list for the morning is on top. Nowhere on it do I see anything about going to bed with Magnus. Of course I didn't write "get pregnant" down on no list and that happened anyway. But, no. No.

"Magnus, can you please just go home tonight? I have to help in the morning, and the kids will be coming home soon. I, I want to stay here."

Hurt causes his face to look even older. The exhaustion and sadness from his trip add more years, and my heart aches at what I've done. To him. To me.

He kisses me on the top of my head and lets me go. "Sure. I am really tired and have no interest in being in the middle of all the mess tomorrow morning. Monday morning, though, I'm taking you to the doctor."

I nod, and he moves around me to the front door. He smiles at me from around the opened door and then leaves.

Air-conditioned chill sweeps over me, and I wrap the towel back around my body. Guess I don't need a pregnancy test now. Monday I'll know for sure, and life will roll on. In the bedroom, I drop the towel, take off my bathing suit, and crawl into the made-up bed. Deep tiredness pulls at me like spring-time mud, bathing me, then thickening and sucking me under. Going down, two visions battle in my head. Roger's vision of Backwater and Magnus' vision of a family.

Must be nice to have a vision.

38

The doorbell rings just as alarms in Maggie, Cab, and Becca Sue's rooms ring out. Even as one by one the phone alarms quiet, the doorbell keeps ringing, over and over.

Cab jerks open the front door, dressed only in his boxers. "What?"

Mrs. Bell barges in with her arms piled high. "Your doorbell must be broken. I've been out there pushing it for ages. My hands were too full to knock. Take this before I drop it."

Cab takes the box out of the old woman's hands. "No, the doorbell works fine. It's just that it's the middle of the night."

"Glad you're all up. Maggie, there you are! Turn on the oven. I'm going to use it for a warmer. Folks already want my biscones." She giggles and claps her hands. "Cab, you'll need to run between the houses this morning as I take out fresh batches and bring them over here to stay warm."

"What folks?" Becca Sue asks. She has Magnus' silky blue robe pulled around her. "Who already wants your biscones?"

"The people out there setting up. Lucky I'm an old woman and didn't need to set an alarm clock to get up at the crack of dawn," she yells as she heads back out the front door. "Although, I guess dawn hasn't actually cracked yet."

Becca Sue rushes to the door and catches it before it closes. She follows Mrs. Bell onto the front patio. Soft, gray air meets her and lays warm droplets in her hair and on her skin. They evaporate almost as quickly as they land, leaving a sheen on her skin.

On everything. The grass and bushes are bathed in the moisture, soaking wet. Even in the pre-dawn gray, the sky is smooth and cloudless. At its edge, across the field and road, the sky is yellow with beams shooting out here and there. Voices next door in the usually empty lot cause her to turn and see people working on putting up canopies or unloading the backs of trucks and mini vans. The saturated air muffles the sounds, but carries freshness. New corn, ripe tomatoes, tinged with truck exhaust. The sulfur smell of Florida groundwater is laced with the smell of coffee brewing.

"The coffee guys are already here?"

Mrs. Bell hooks her arm through Becca Sue's and leans on her a bit. "We did this. We made this happen, Rebecca. People started getting here about thirty minutes ago. No idea how far some of them came. When I saw all them, that's when I started making more biscones. Isn't it exciting?"

Becca Sue smiles and nods. "Yes, it is. I need to get dressed." When she pulls her arm away from Mrs. Bell, the woman sways. Becca Sue grabs her. "You need to come in and rest for a minute, okay?"

Mrs. Bell blinks a couple times and then nods her head as she turns around, never losing contact with Becca Sue's arm. As they enter the house, Becca Sue calls for Maggie.

"Can you go over to Mrs. Bell's house and keep an eye on the biscones in her oven?"

The older lady adds, "I have another sheet of them ready to go in. They cook for about fifteen minutes." She lowers herself onto the couch, finally releasing Becca Sue's arm. "I'll just sit and rest a minute."

"I'm here, and I brought lots of help!" Ashleigh shouts entering the standing open front door.

Becca Sue makes sure Mrs. Bell has her feet up on a footstool, then turns. "Mrs. Bell is just going to rest ... oh. Sam. Oh, hi." Becca Sue pulls on the short robe first in the front, then at the hem. Ashleigh, Sam, and the two men behind them all look her over.

"Did we get you out of bed?" Ashleigh is no longer looking her over, but staring her down.

"No, I mean, I was just helping Mrs. Bell in, so she can rest a bit. Maggie, aren't you supposed to be over there watching the oven?"

"Oh, yeah. Guess I'll do the rest of the signs later, okay, Cab?"

Cab mumbles about having to do everything himself and heads to the garage.

Sam backs toward the door. "Let me. I'm a cook. It's the biscuit scone things, right?"

Becca Sue looks down to see Mrs. Bell has fallen asleep. "Yeah, she said they cook about fifteen minutes, and she has at least one more tray ready. Thanks."

He pulls on his friends to come outside with him, but they grin and raise their eyebrows at him, motioning that they'll stay inside where the tall, half-dressed girl keeps leaning over.

Ashleigh listens to their whispered comments and asks, "Shouldn't you get dressed? The rest of us all have clothes on." With the head jerks and clipped words, she leaves no doubt of how she's feeling after last night's betrayal.

Cab sticks his head out of the garage door. "Mags, are you coming or not? Signs need to be up."

When everyone looks toward his shout, Becca Sue pads quietly on her bare feet to her bedroom, then shuts herself in the dark room. "No wonder they were all staring," she says looking in the bathroom mirror. Her hair, wet when she went to bed, had taken on a life of its own as it dried.

She pulls it into a quick ponytail and runs a washcloth over her face. Wearing a pair of jean shorts and a sleeveless pink T-shirt she starts to the door without a bra, then stops with her hand on the door knob. She asks out loud, "Shouldn't a mother wear a bra? My mother didn't, but she didn't really need one." She turns around and rips off her t-shirt. She fishes out a bra from the stack of clothes on the foot of her bed and puts it on. She puts on her shirt and looks in the mirror. "Yep, this is more like it." She leaves the bedroom and turns into the kitchen, where Ashleigh leans on the counter.

Ashleigh is eating a tangerine, and as she throws away the handful of peel she asks, "Is he here?"

"Who? Sam? Didn't he go to Mrs. Bell's?

Ashleigh rolls her big blue eyes. "Not Sam, the old lawyer guy."

"Oh, Magnus. No, he went home last night." She says while grabbing a bottle of water out of the refrigerator.

"Lord, your hair. Sit down." Ashleigh pulls out a kitchen chair and motions for Becca Sue to sit.

Becca Sue sits down and sips on her water. Ashleigh pulls the ponytail elastic out of her hair and smoothes the muddy brown hair down. "So, are you really pregnant?"

"Could be. But maybe not. Just always thought I couldn't be, so I haven't thought about it much."

"But your period?"

"I've never been real regular. Another reason I thought I couldn't get pregnant. My cousin Jen said not being regular makes it harder to get pregnant."

"Your cousin Jen? What about a doctor? Didn't you go to a doctor when you didn't get pregnant when you were married?"

Becca Sue laughs. "Go to a doctor because I wasn't getting knocked up? Yeah, that's not how it is in Piney. Girls there sneeze, and out comes a baby. Besides, Caleb's momma said God knew I didn't need a baby since I could hardly take care of myself."

"Wait." Ashleigh steps from around where she was fixing Becca Sue's hair and looks at her. "His momma was telling you that, when she knew all along you weren't getting pregnant because she'd had her boy fixed?"

Becca Sue's eyes and mouth open wide. "That's right. See I just found that out, but hey, that's right."

Ashleigh makes a disgusted sound and goes back to Becca Sue's hair. "That woman is the very last person on earth who should be speaking for God."

For a few minutes they sit in silence, and then Ashleigh pats Becca Sue's shoulder. "There you go. Much better. Go look at it in the hall mirror."

In the mirror, Becca Sue tries to see what her hair looks like in the back. "Is that a French braid?" she calls to Ashleigh still in the kitchen.

"Yep! Looks good, doesn't it? Your hair is perfect for it, all the little pieces that come out curl so cute. When pieces of my hair fall out of a braid, it's like a stick. I'd love to have hair like yours."

"No way does anyone want my hair," Becca Sue says to herself and then she looks more fully at her face. Louder she says, "It does look good. Thanks."

Ashleigh comes to the doorway and leans against it. "You have no idea how good-looking you are, do you? No idea that Sam and his guys all loved seeing you with those long tanned legs this morning, hair all over the place, and that scrap of a silk robe laying on every curve."

"Me? I'm chunky and slump over and my hair is a mess."

Ashleigh waves her hands down her body. "Now, *this* is chunky, and as for slumping over, I've not noticed that. And hair is hair, but when it looks like you just crawled out of bed, guys love it, short or long, blonde or brown, curly or straight. And I may hate the idea of you being with that old man, but I figure he's had his share of beautiful women. He doesn't strike me as someone who goes slumming. He was pleased as punch last night to think you were carrying his baby."

They move to the kitchen to pick up their notebooks and lists.

Her arms full, Becca Sue says, "No, he just wants a baby. He always worked and never had any kids, that's what he's so pleased about. You go on out there, and I'll check one more time on Mrs. Bell."

Ashleigh leaves and Becca Sue tiptoes into the living room. She waits to listen to Mrs. Bells' smooth breathing, then tiptoes to the front door and outside.

She closes the front door behind her and as the sound of the click echoes in the house, Mrs. Bell opens her eyes and sighs.

197

39

By seven o'clock sunshine filled the eastern sky, broken only by the large oak trees across the street. Within minutes the droplets of dew and morning mist disappeared. Where the sun peaked under canopies or through tree branches, it roused and stirred with its first touch of heat. That early heat was why they'd decided to start the market at eight a.m. And by ten a.m., they were glad of that decision.

Steady streams of people shopped in the open lot. Parking was full along the road and in the two driveways, Becca Sue's and Mrs. Bell's. Most everyone left with bags of produce, a biscone or two, and a coffee.

"We need some picnic tables for folks to eat on next week," Sam says from behind the table of biscones and jams and butter.

"I agree. And my biscones are better if they are hot," Mrs. Bell says from her chair in the shade. "We could even have a sign like Krispy Kreme that lets folks know when we take a new batch out of the oven. Or maybe just a bullhorn, and we could shout it out."

Sam laughs. "Mrs. Bell, you and I could make a killing with these in New York. These are truly an original idea. Next week we should make some breakfast sandwiches, with ham and sausage?"

"Son, you read my mind. And I must say, that batch you mixed up are almost as good as mine."

"I used your recipe, didn't change a thing." He sits on a corner of the table and looks around the lot. "So this was all your idea?"

"Guess it was. However, I needed Ashleigh and, of course, Becca Sue to make it happen. And, oh yes, Roger Worth's money for the whole Backwater thing. How's your restaurant going?"

"Oh, it's not mine. I'm just working for the client, but it seems to be coming along."

"How do you know Sybil?"

"We're both from New York. In the restaurant business."

He stops talking, and Mrs. Bell follows his eyes. "That Ashleigh is something else, isn't she?"

Sam stands up and folds his arms. "Yes, she is."

"But you weren't looking at her, were you?"

He chuckles and drops his arms as he looks at Mrs. Bell. "What do you think I was looking at?"

Mrs. Bell shakes her head. "Not what, who."

"Okay, who?" His dark eyes dare her to say it.

She just shakes her head again. "I think breakfast sandwiches would be a great idea. Picnic tables, too." She looks up and smiles. "Eason, Ruth! Welcome to our market."

Ruth has her arms tucked in tight to her body, her lips tucked tight to each other, and her words come out tucked tightly together. "More like a junk yard, if you ask me."

Mrs. Bell catches her breath. "Oh, Ruth, you aren't like that! You love new things. You love people being happy, and look how happy this makes me."

Eason laughs and pulls his wife to him with one long arm around her squared, taut shoulders. "She'll come around as soon as she's eating some of the fresh vegetables I'm going to grow next door in the Backwater Garden. Extension agent is coming out this week to give me some ideas."

"Maybe we ought to look into having a section there for fresh veggies, and maybe some strawberries, for the restaurant." Sam steps toward the couple. "Hi, I'm Sam Jones."

"Oh, so you're the young man Sybil hired to renovate her

restaurant." Eason shakes Sam's hand. "Eason and Ruth King."

"Sam is also a cook. He made my last batch of biscones. Try one." Mrs. Bell points to the sample basket of biscone pieces in front of her.

Ruth looks at Sam and reaches for a bite of Mrs. Bell's invention. "Aren't you also going to stay and help run the restaurant for Sybil?"

Sam shoves his hands in his jean pockets. "No. I'm not, and she knows that. I better get to work." He nods at all three, but never takes his hands out of his pockets to wave. He strides across the field and heads down the road which will take him to the restaurant.

"Well, he doesn't seem very friendly," Ruth says. "Sounds like he's from home, New York accent along with New York bluntness. Wonder why Sybil hired a work crew from back there?"

Mrs. Bell shakes her head. "I don't know, but I do know Sam has been extra friendly when I've talked to him, and he was a lifesaver this morning." She drops her eyes to her lap. "Have either of you seen Magnus this morning?"

Eason brushes his hands to get rid of crumbs. "Oh, he's back? His aunt's estate is huge, so I wasn't sure how long it would take him to get things settled. Although with her being sick for so long, they probably had it squared away."

Ruth looking through the bags of biscones sighs. "And him all alone, wonder what he'll do with all those houses?"

Mrs. Bell shrugs and looks away, but rubs her lips together, in and out. Like she has something to say, but can't let it come out.

Eason tips his head to the side and watches her. "Ruth, I'll pay for these." He takes the bag in her hand. "Why don't you go pick out some corn for me to grill tonight? Also, look for some other vegetables."

Ruth's earlier tightness is gone, and she heads to the nearby stands in a relaxed walk.

When Eason turns back to Mrs. Bell, he's anything but relaxed. "What is it you know? Something about Magnus not being all alone, right?"

Mrs. Bell doesn't look up, but finally words come out of her overworking lips. "I don't know what you're talking about."

"You won't meet my eyes for some reason. You know, don't you?"

She looks up at him, her head tilted back and to the side. "What do I know?"

He leans toward her and whispers, "His son. Did Sybil tell you?"

"You don't know it's going to be a boy. She's not even showing."

"Sybil's not showing? Showing what?"

"Although you *are* a doctor, maybe you can tell things others can't so early in a pregnancy." Mrs. Bell shrugs. "And I didn't even know Sybil and Becca Sue knew each other."

Eason stands completely still and suddenly pulls out his wallet. "How much do I owe you? I have to, uh, I have to go."

"Five dollars." Mrs. Bell purses her lips. "I'm glad others know. I was afraid maybe I was letting the cat out of the bag. Just think, the first baby in Backwater! Won't it be exciting?"

"Oh, yes, it should be exciting."

With his bag clutched in his hand, Eason walks away from Mrs. Bell's canopy and hurries up to his wife. "Honey, you about ready to go?"

"Almost. Look at all these lettuces! I want to get some of all of them to try this week."

The doctor, biscone bag still clutched in his hand, looks around. He steps a little away from his wife to watch Becca Sue talk with the big blonde girl from the newspaper and a man he doesn't recognize. With her hair pulled back and standing up straight she looks like she could pull off being Mrs. Magnus Llord, mother-to-be.

Why not? According to George, their friend will never know about his grown son. Sybil is more determined than ever to keep it a secret. She'd told George about her son being Magnus' years ago when they had a fling before George married

Pearl. George had only told Eason one afternoon when the two drank too much bourbon, and they neither one had any idea Sybil would be moving to Florida and in with Magnus. After Magnus had gone to New York to put his aunt into a convalescent home, he showed back up in Florida with Sybil and her stuff. She moved in and stayed for six months before they had a huge fight and she left. Now she was back, but avoiding Magnus, from what Eason could tell. He'd begun wondering if she was after George. He also wondered if George might be interested in Sybil. Pearl could be a real pain.

"Or maybe Sybil just wants to open her restaurant," he said with a sigh. "Magnus deserves to be happy, and I wish he and Becca Sue all the luck in the world."

Ruth comes up to her husband's elbow. "What did you say?"

"Nothing. Don't you think Becca Sue looks good today?"

"I have to admit, she does. And pulling this whole market thing off is remarkable. Maybe she'll discover she has more to offer than just a warm bed, and she'll kick Magnus to the curb. Not that I think Magnus would mind all that much. Surely that whole thing has about run its course, don't you think?"

He takes the sacks of produce from her and raises an eyebrow at her. "From what I hear, it's just got a whole new life. Literally."

Forty years of communicating mean nothing more needed to be said for his wife to understand. Her eyes dart to Becca Sue, and her nose wrinkles. "Really? Well, I hope they don't expect a baby shower." They walk towards the street. "Maybe we can just take up money to start a therapy savings fund. God knows the kid will need it."

"What about a double date?" Walking up behind Sam on the back patio of the restaurant, Carlos asks his question, then nudges his boss in the shoulder with a cold bottle of water. "Here. Want this?"

Sam twists the cap off and takes a drink. "Double date? With who?"

"Who else? The girl you stare at every day. You watch her swim, wait for her to come out of the house, perk up when you hear her laugh float across the lake. My mother told me we needed to be careful coming down here, that these Southern girls know how to get in your blood." Carlos squats down and takes a drink from his water bottle. "The blonde chick isn't in my blood, but I think she and I could have some fun. I dig that accent, and she's all up in everyone's business like my sisters. Plus, that hair is crazy. Let's see if they want to go out tonight."

Sam swats away a mosquito. "Didn't you see that old man last night? Guess he and Rebecca are together."

"No way that old guy can handle what I saw in that blue robe this morning! You need to save him from himself. She could probably give an old dude like that a heart attack."

Sam takes a deep breath and then a long drink.

Carlos stands back up. "Besides, he wasn't there this morning. I asked Ashleigh when we were setting stuff up."

"Oh, you do know her name? Not just 'that blonde chick'?"

Carlos stands up and punches his friends arm. "Just 'cause I know her name don't mean nothing. She's fun." They turn to walk back up to the house. "Tell you what, let's just invite them over to try out the new oven. To check out the place, then we can see where things go. We'll see what kind of vibes you get from your girl. I already know the vibes I'm getting from the blonde. We *are* going out tonight, just need to see if we'll have company."

Carlos pulls his phone from his pocket and dials. When Sam tries to tell him to wait a minute, he says, "Hello," grins, shrugs, and turns away to talk.

Sam throws up a hand in surrender, turns and enters the house. He surveys how much they'd done in only a week. Bumping the kitchen into the garage was the biggest job, but it was practically done. The open wall allows the front part of the kitchen to be seen from the living room. The huge oven takes up lots of space, and he immediately starts thinking about what to cook for Rebecca and Ashleigh tonight. Something light, fresh. Bruschetta with tomatoes and avocado. Lime shrimp scampi and a good white wine blend.

"They'll come by around eight. Ashleigh and I are going out afterwards, and she said it would be up to you to talk Becca Sue into it. Or Rebecca, as you call her." Carlos stops at the door. "See, just the fact that you have a different name for her means something."

"Yeah, it means her name is too hick for words. We've got work to do if I'm going to cook tonight."

Carlos pulls his work gloves on. "Then let's get to it."

40

Mrs. Bell lays her head back against her couch back. "I love air conditioning."

Maggie flops beside her. "I've never been that hot in my whole life. Next week we should only go until noon."

My foot won't stop jiggling, and while they both look like they're trying to catch flies with their drooped mouths, my bottom sits right on the edge of my chair.

If I was a runner, I could run all the way around the lake, I think. I'd swear I'm drunk, but I haven't had a thing all day. My brain feels full of fizz, like a shook-up Coke. "Only 'til noon? I was thinking we should go all day. Were you two really ready to stop at one, when we did?"

Mrs. Bell lifts her white head, closes her mouth, and looks at me. "You're crazy. I've never been so tired in my life. I'd go get in bed, except it's all the way in there."

"We could just sleep here," Maggie says without moving a muscle or opening her eyes.

I jump up. "Well, I'll leave you two to take a nap and go see what Ashleigh is doing. Cab went back to the house, didn't he?"

Maggie nods without opening her eyes or lifting her head. "Yes, and then he's going fishing or crabbing or something with those guys who were selling watermelons."

That slows me down. Cab Mason hanging out with real Florida guys? Good Florida guys, from what I could see. Their family has a farm not far from here, and the boys sell whatever is in season. They were some of the first people to sign up for the market today. "Well, anything that gets him away from those stuck-up kids at the beach."

A soft snore from Mrs. Bell makes me shut up and tiptoe to the front door. These two are fine.

As I quietly pull the door closed behind me, I look around for Ashleigh. The lot next door looks strangely empty. The canopies are gone, along with the cars and people. A few scrubby bushes and several pin oaks are all that's left. Heat makes the air shine and almost takes my breath away. It bakes down into my bones and sweat coats my skin, especially my scalp. The French braid kept my hair back, and I squint as I wonder where I left my sunglasses. Probably at Mrs. Bell's, but I don't want to wake them up, so I'll get them later. As I walk across the empty lot, the grass crinkles under my flip flops. A splash causes me to veer toward the back gate and the pool.

"So there you are." Ashleigh is swimming along the edge of the pool. "I was going to wait on you, but thought maybe y'all fell asleep over there. Mrs. Bell looked worn out." She's swimming on her back and talking to me.

"They did. Maggie's on one end of the couch, and Mrs. Bell on the other. I'll go put on a suit and join you. Pool looks awesome." I enter the darkened living room. "Cab? You still here?" I walk down the hall and knock on his door.

"Yeah?"

"Can I come in?"

"Yeah."

"So I hear you're going fishing?" He's sitting on his bed with his laptop in front of him.

"Yeah, with those guys from Peterman's farm."

"Sounds like fun." He doesn't look up, just scans the computer screen. "Okay, well, thanks for all your help today." But I don't get the door closed before he stops me.

"Becca Sue, do you know what all we, I mean Mason Farms, grows? Like anything other than the pecans?"

"No. I mean, I don't know, not really. Why?"

Then he looks up from the screen and at me. "No reason. Just thought I should know."

"You're right. Give your grandfather a call. He always handled the farm stuff. It never really interested your dad or uncle."

He goes back to the screen. "Maybe I will. Thanks."

Walking back down the hall I remember how folks in Piney, my father especially, talked down Caleb and Jameson about not caring about what got them all their money in the first place. But folks didn't know how Mrs. Mason talked down to their daddy, about him being dirty and sweaty and stinking all the time. She had no intention of her sons knowing anything about the farm except how to spend the money made on it. She always said, "Mason Farms grows money. Only crop worth growing." Maybe I should warn Cab. I stop in the living room and turn to go back to his room, but wait. I laugh a bit, and turn back how I was going. Cab knows his grandmother. He knows better than to be honest with her. Another laugh, stronger this time, leaves me with a big smile. Cab might actually be exactly what Mrs. Mason deserves.

In my swimsuit, I grab two bottles of iced tea and go to the pool. Ashleigh has moved onto a float, lying on her stomach. I sit the bottles on the side and walk in down the steps to keep from making a bunch of waves. I swim back and forth and can't believe how good the water feels. Guess I still prefer lake water to pool water, but today it feels like silk on my arms and legs.

"We have a date tonight," Ashleigh says from her float. "Over at Sam's restaurant."

I stop and tread water. "You and Sam have a date?"

"Oh, wait a minute, do I hear concern?" She lifts her head, then folds her arms on the headrest and lays her chin on them. "Me and Sam having a date cause a problem for you?"

Swishing in the water, I turn from her stare. "No, I just thought. Well, that you kinda had a thing for Carlos. But Sam's cute, too."

"Which one do you think is cuter?"

"I don't know."

"Baloney. You think Sam is hot, I can tell. And that's good."

That stops me before I go underwater. "What? Why is that good?"

She lays her head down, face away from me. "Because you have a date with him tonight."

Under the water, I try to keep from smiling and succeed in looking stern when I come up on the other side of her float. "Why do you think I have a date with Sam?"

"Because I made it for you. And you're right. I do have a thing for Carlos. We apparently have a thing for each other, which works out nicely. They are making dinner for us at eight over at the house." She points across the lake. "Then Carlos and I are going out, up in town. Sam is going to try and talk you into going with him."

"No, he's not. You're making this up."

My stomach is doing flippy things and I remember. "But I might be pregnant. With Magnus' baby. He'll probably think me having a date is a bad idea."

She suddenly flips her head to look at me. "I didn't ask about what Magnus thinks. Do you want to go out with Sam?"

Our eyes meet, and I let myself slip under the water. I dive down to the bottom of the pool and then push back up at the other end. I rest my folded arms on the edge of the pool facing the lake. Water runs down my face, and the drops on my arms reflect the high sun in each one. From my eye level the grass and lake seem endless until I lift my eyes a bit and see the houses on the other side. Eenie Meenie Miney Mo.

My Grandma had a way she made decisions. She'd say to live with a decision for a bit. Act like you made the decision and see how it felt. So I close my eyes, rest my chin on my arms, and picture this afternoon on Magnus' porch. Just for fun I give myself a belly full of baby. He's grilling something, and then we go in for a romantic dinner. Lots of candles, the jeweled-colored couches, soft music and...

My legs itch. Like crawlin' with chiggers itching. I push away from the wall, turn over and swim. Back and forth I swim, lap after lap. I swim like I've seen Magnus swim, face in the water half the time, only lifting out as that arm goes up and then I grab a mouthful of air. At the ends, I turn without looking up. I swim until my legs stop itching and I turn over to float on my back. My ears are just below the surface of the water, and I can hear Ashleigh talking to me, but not her words. My head hits the shallow side of the pool so I put my feet down on the bottom, stand and say, "I can't do it."

Ashleigh has flipped onto her back on the float. Sunglasses shield her eyes from the sun. "Okay. But can you at least go have dinner with us? Just friends?"

When I don't answer for a while she lifts her head, pushes her sunglasses up and looks at me. "Hey you. Dinner?"

Climbing out of the pool, I answer, "Sure."

Although my ears are no longer underwater, I act like they are and ignore her questions as I wrap in a towel and enter the house.

I just can't do it.

41

"I can't believe you went over there and bought stuff!" Pearl exclaims looking at the haul of vegetables laid out on Ruth and Eason's kitchen table. "Aren't we supposed to be fighting this whole ridiculous idea?"

Ruth sits down in the chair next to the one she pulled out for Pearl. "Sit down, Pearl. I only meant to check things out, but everything was so fresh. And Mrs. Bell was so happy."

Pearl slumps into the high back, woven sawgrass chair. "George tells me we don't stand a chance fighting this. We're stuck living in an experiment. If you think Mrs. Bell is happy, you should hear Sybil talk about her restaurant. She says it's not all about getting Magnus back, but I don't believe her."

"Oh, I met the young man who's doing the work over there. He seems nice. Very good-looking, and he seems to have an eye for Becca Sue. Of course, that's not going to work now."

"Maybe that's why Sybil had him come down here, to distract Becca Sue so she could get back with Magnus." Pearl smiles as she picks up a bunch of radishes and smells them. "That could explain why Sybil's so happy."

"But that's not going to work now. I told you." Ruth emphasizes her last three words and tilts her head, eyes wide, peering at her friend.

Balancing the fire engine-red radishes in her palm, Pearl looks closely at Ruth. "You told me what? Why won't it work?"

Ruth picks up an ear of corn and lays it in front of her. She lays another beside it and then another. When the line of corn is six ears long, she places her hands in her lap and looks at the corn. "I can't say."

Pearl drops the bunch of radishes and leans toward her friend. "It's a secret?"

Ruth nods. "A big secret. But not one you can keep forever."

"Why can't you keep it forever? It's too juicy?"

"Well, yes, but it has a time limit built in to it."

"A time limit? Like a statute of limitations. Like something is going to happen so everyone knows. Right?" Pearl stares at the table of vegetables and thinks. "Is someone going to be arrested?"

"No." Ruth's eyebrows hunch in frustration. "Nothing illegal. Very natural. Very. Between a man and a woman." She widens her eyes. "*With* a time limit."

"Oh! Someone's pregnant!"

"Shh, Eason is here. I can't tell you this."

"Okay, okay," Pearl whispers. Then her face falls. "The hillbilly is pregnant."

Ruth nods, looking around the corner to make sure her husband isn't in sight.

"Poor, poor Sybil. Here she brings in a boy toy for the hick, and it's too late. Hick lost her last sugar daddy in Caleb Mason, probably realized her mistake in not getting pregnant with a Mason kid, so this time she knew better." She stands up. "Does Magnus know?"

Ruth stands also, but doesn't answer right away. "You know, I'm not sure. But you can't tell him. Matter of fact, you can't tell anyone. I'm not even sure how Eason knows, people just tell him things. Must be that he's a doctor."

"Must be. I have to go. Poor, poor Sybil. Wait until she finds out." She lays a hand on her friends arm. "But don't worry. She won't hear it from me."

Pearl walks around the lake and talks to herself to work up a sweat. "Whew, I have to slow down." She fluffs the front of her blouse to fan up a breeze and adjusts her visor to block the late afternoon sun. "Becca Sue is pregnant. Serves Magnus right. Playing around like he's a teenager."

"Hello."

Pearl staggers a bit as a young voice speaks up from behind her. "Oh, hello."

The young man lifts his hands, holding full bags. "Just ran over to the market to pick up the veggies I bought this morning. I'm Carlos."

"I'm Mrs. Manningham. So, do you live here? I don't remember seeing you."

"No, I'm working on the restaurant. We're at a hotel near the highway."

Pearl blinks and thinks, 'He sure would work to distract the hillbilly if it weren't too late.' "How are things coming with it? The owner is my good friend."

"We're making fantastic progress. 'Course that's easier when someone is greasing the wheels with permits and such." He lifts the bags again. "We're actually trying out the new oven for the first time tonight for a couple of ladies."

Pearl slows as they approach her driveway. "Oh, you've already met some, uh, friends?"

He points across the lake. "Well, one of them lives here. Becca Sue? Do you know her?"

Pearl tightly nods. "How convenient for all of you. Well, this is my house. Nice to meet you, Carlos."

"Good to meet you, too," he says with a wave. He resumes his jogging.

She stomps up her driveway, a fresh layer of sweat popping out. "I knew it. Knew this is what would happen when we turned into a... whatever it is we are now. Young people having parties, getting pregnant, jogging around like they own the place."

She's barely in the house before she yells for her husband, "George! George, you are not going to believe what's going on." She pauses for a moment to lay her hand on the cold granite of the bar between the kitchen and living room.

The house is all gray and white with accents of green. A

huge live palm tree fills one corner and leans to fill the space of the high ceiling. Through the bank of windows, the sun reflecting off the lake fills the space with sunlight. Before the sun dips behind the pines on the far end of the lake, it turns the Manninghams' home into a study of light and shadows. The main reason they chose such simple colors, so the light could be seen more clearly.

Pearl takes in the sunshine... and curses it. "We need shades. I'm sick of all this light," she says, as she does every day about this time. It only took a year of year-round sunshine for Pearl to realize she missed fog, clouds, dreary-rainy days, and cold, in other words, variety in her weather. "George!"

"In here."

She leaves the brightness behind her and strides into George's office. It also faces the lake, but the smaller windows are covered with custom-made shades. "George, you're not going to... oh, hi Magnus."

George and Magnus are leaned back in leather easy chairs watching a ball game on the big screen TV and smoking cigars. "What am I not going to believe?"

She sinks onto an ottoman near his desk. "Just, well, Ruth went to that farmer's market this morning and bought a whole table full of stuff."

"Was it a success?" Magnus asks.

"What? Oh, yes, I guess so. Didn't you go over to see what, uh, what Becca Sue was up to?"

He grins. "Naw, figured I'd give her a little space. A little space to get tired and frustrated in. Find out starting something like this isn't all fun and games. She's probably taking a nap about now." He lifts his cigar towards George. "Pregnant women do that a lot, don't they?"

As both men look at her, Pearl remembers to react in fake surprise. "What? Pregnant? Becca Sue is pregnant?"

"Yep, I'm going to be a father. Never realized what I missed. Just talking over plans with George here. Figure I'll put the house here on the market soon as possible. Not trusting some beach boy doctor to take care of my heir. Nope, we'll be moving home soon as we can."

George shakes his head. "New York isn't Becca Sue's home, I keep telling you."

Magnus laughs. "Pearl, what do you think? Becca Sue will love living in a mansion in upstate New York, won't she? And there's also an apartment in the city. What woman wouldn't want all that to raise her baby? And of course, we'll get a nanny."

Pearl can't control her eyebrows as they leap up her forehead. "Becca Sue in New York City? Magnus, you can't be serious. And what about the little fact you've already had a heart attack? Aren't you supposed to be relaxing?"

"But that was from working too hard. This will be all fun. All relaxing. We all know she's not exactly my type of woman, but she's carrying my heir, and she's a good one for adapting. She knows how to play the game. Look at all the crap she took from the Masons. And sooner I get her north of the Mason Dixon line, sooner she'll see I'm right."

Pearl licks her lips and turns to her husband. "You're being awfully quiet."

His eyes never leave the television. "I'm watching the game."

After a pause, she pushes her husband a bit. "You think Becca Sue will fall into line as easily as Magnus seems to think?"

George's chin digs deeper into his chest, and his lips stay closed. Pearl stands up and waves her hands at the men. "Well, I'll leave you two to your game." Shouts from the TV erupt, and the men turn up the volume to hear what happened. They miss Pearl shaking her head as she leaves the room.

In the living room, pink air fills the open space. The white walls reflect the beginning of another brilliant Florida sunset. The sunshine on the lake is deep gold. Pearl closes her eyes and shudders. "Just go down already!" she exclaims. "These god-forsaken sunsets take way too long."

42

"What the hell is going on here?" Sybil stands in the open doorway from the house. The four sitting at the wrought-iron table on the patio stop mid-bite, mid-story, mid-laugh, and focus on her.

Sam tips back in his chair. "We're having dinner."

Carlos frowns and stands up. "Can we help you? We were just trying out the new ovens." He motions at Sam, but his friend looks back at his plate and lifts a shrimp into his mouth. Carlos smiles and takes a step toward their boss. "Would you like a glass of wine?"

Sybil walks to the table. "Welcome, ladies to my restaurant. Apparently we're having an early open no one informed me of." She holds her hand out to Ashleigh. "And you would be...?"

Ashleigh's eyelashes flutter up and down as she takes her hand off her wine glass and takes Sybil's hand. "Ashleigh Morrow. I write for the *Island Times*. In town."

Sybil adds her other hand to the handshake. "Well, Ms. Morrow, we hope you only have good things to say about our place. Have these two treated you right?"

Ashleigh nods. "Oh, yes. You definitely have the right people doing the job here. But I'm not here to review the restaurant or anything, I'm just..." She looks at Carlos and shrugs.

Carlos lays his hands on the back of his chair, and after a hesitating look at Sam, whose focus stays on his shrimp, speaks up. "We just wanted to get together and try the ovens. A date night, I guess." He and Ashleigh laugh, and Sybil backs away. She smiles like she's about to join the laughter, but her mouth never opens.

"Then I'll leave you to it. Have a good evening. Sam? Could I have a moment?"

He puts his napkin beside his plate. "I'll be right back. Boss needs to see me." He follows Sybil into the house and pulls the door closed behind him. He leads her into the kitchen.

Once they are both inside and the door is closed, he spins around to face her.

"What? What do you need to tell me so badly you come around after working hours on a Saturday? You told me and the guys to feel free to use the kitchen, since we are in that decrepit hotel until this job is done."

She folds her arms and leans back against the counter. "That hotel is your choice, not mine."

He turns away from her and mumbles. "It's cheap, and I want to make as much money as possible so I can pay off my debts."

"What did you say?"

"I said, I want to pay off my debts so you can't pull my strings and tell me which jobs I have to do. So I don't have to drop everything at home and rush down here to do your bidding. The sooner I pay you back, the sooner I get my life back."

The toss of her hair and firm set of her jaw almost, but not quite, hide the sheen of tears in her eyes. "Fine. I'll release you from your debt and you can go back to New York."

"What?"

"This was a bad idea for you to come here. I'll pay you for what you've done, and you can go back."

"Oh, and everyone will know I failed at another job for you? You don't think that hurts my reputation that I can't seem to satisfy someone of your stature, your reputation?" He shakes his head. "Thanks, but no thanks."

She slaps her hand onto the counter. "If you just weren't so adamant about keeping our relationship secret, it wouldn't matter!"

"Maybe not to you, but it would change everything for me. Maybe when I pay you off, we can try to fix things. I'm going back outside." He pushes through the swinging door but stops halfway. "Oh, and I'm not quitting. We have a deal, and I'm seeing it through."

Sybil waits for the door to stop swinging, and then she pushes it open enough to see the back patio. In the soft lighting she sees the table as Sam approaches it. He doesn't look back, but she knows he knows she's watching as he goes to the darker-haired girl, that Becca Sue, and places his hands on her shoulders. He leans down and kisses her cheek, and although the girl pulls away, it's obvious who he's interested in.

Sybil slips out the front door after a bit and walks down the street toward Pearl and George's house, where she's staying.

"Hi there," Pearl calls out from the other side of the road. In the deepening shadows, she's walking Freddie and Scooby.

"Hi," Sybil says as she gets to their driveway, where she waits for Pearl.

Pearl exclaims, "I'm trying to walk off some of my frustration with those men in my house."

Sybil looks toward the house. "George and Magnus?"

"Yes, they're, well, oh, never mind. What are you doing tonight?"

Sybil never looks at the other woman, but continues to stare at the house. Then suddenly she turns, takes Pearl's arm, and pulls her toward the front door. "Why don't we all take a walk down to the restaurant? I, uh, I want to get your opinions on something."

Pearl moves along, pulled by her friend on one side, and the dogs on the other. "But you might want to know, well, Magnus and, well..."

"Pshaw, I don't care what Magnus is going on about now. I'm concerned with the restaurant, and I need your opinions quick. Now."

She bustles Pearl, Freddie, and Scooby into the house, and in only minutes is bustling Pearl, George, and Magnus out.

Sybil is pushing George's wheelchair and outpacing Pearl. Pearl stops at the end of her driveway. "What is the hurry? It's still over eighty out here!"

"You're right. I'm just excited to show you, to show you the restaurant. And even though it's hot, it's a beautiful evening. We should enjoy the walk." The cars in the drive up ahead tells her the young people are still there, so she slows down.

"Man, you've got to quit being so rude to her. She's the boss," Carlos says as Sam comes out of the house.

Sam shrugs and walks up behind Becca Sue's chair. "I'm sorry for that. She acts like she owns the place. Oh wait, she does."

He laughs and lays his hands on Becca Sue's bare shoulders. Her sleeveless sun dress has a ruffle top and was something Ashleigh had shown up with for her to wear tonight. Ashleigh said it was from some of her skinny clothes, but she'd given up ever being skinny enough to wear it again. Then Ashleigh had braided Becca Sue's hair, this time tucking it up to make a bun. This should have meant that her neck, shoulders, and upper chest were bare and open for caressing, but the Georgia girl jumped like Sam had dumped a handful of spiders down her top when he laid his calloused hands on her.

"What are you doing?"

"Just giving you a little neck massage and apologizing for my boss disrupting our evening." Sam picks up his wine glass and finishes it. "Who wants another drink?"

Becca Sue slides out from under his hands and walks to the edge of the patio. "Not me. I probably should be going home."

Carlos stands up, too, and picks up the empty wine bottle. "I'll get another bottle. You sure you don't want another glass of water, Becca Sue?"

She shakes her head and continues looking out at the lake,

at her house across the way. Sam follows Carlos, saying, "I'll cut some more bread."

"Sure looks different from over here, doesn't it?" Ashleigh says as she comes to stand by her friend. "So, that Sybil lady. Why did she ignore you?"

Becca Sue shrugs a bare shoulder. "She and Magnus had a thing going a while back, I guess."

Ashleigh smooths down her short jean skirt and then sits on the bench beside Becca Sue. "Oh. Well, she looks more his age. Are you having any fun at all tonight?"

The other woman ignores the question. "Can you believe I own that house over there? That's where I live? When you put up my hair tonight and I saw myself in this dress, I felt like Cinderella. To see someone like Sam looking at me like he was," she leaves off with a deep sigh. "I don't know who I am."

"Exactly why you aren't ready to be a mother."

"But that's something I should've thought about before. I could never end a pregnancy after, well, my momma had several abortions when I was growing up 'cause she said she wasn't cut out to be a momma. I'm only around because she didn't know she was pregnant until everyone else did, too. Believe me, she told me that often enough."

"Girl," Ashleigh stands up and puts her arm around Becca Sue. "You don't have to think about any of that tonight." She leads her back to the table. "You change seats with me, that way I can more easily make eyes at Carlos, and you won't have to worry about Sam touching you. We'll finish eating, and then I'll take you home. Sam Jones is a big boy, he can handle a night on his own, I promise."

Just as the girls sit in their new seats, the guys come back out. "Changed seats?" Carlos asks.

Ashleigh does her best Scarlett O'Hara imitation, "Oh fiddle-dee-dee, who cares where we sit. Just pour me some more wine and pass the bread."

Sam sets the new basket of bread on the table. Just as Carlos is opening the new bottle of wine and filling three glasses, the doors fly open again. Magnus comes through, followed by

Pearl and then George. Sybil stays just inside, as if the wheel-chair blocks her.

Magnus walks to the table. "Good evening. Looks like I'm making a habit of interrupting this intimate group. First, last night in the pool, and now a nice lakeside dinner."

Pearl has put two and two together, and her smile grows. This is why Sybil was in such a hurry to get them, Magnus in-cluded, down here. *So she* does *still have feelings for Magnus.* "This does look rather intimate, doesn't it? Wait, Becca Sue, is that wine? You're drinking?"

Becca Sue looks at the table and Ashleigh's dishes and wine glass. "Oh, this isn't..."

Sam hadn't sat yet, so he moves around behind Becca Sue, whose back is to the lake. Sam bristles. "Excuse me, these are my guests. You can't just barge in here asking what they are drinking or doing."

Pearl stutters. "But she's shouldn't be drinking."

Ashleigh stands up. "Okay, we need to just slow down here. It's time for us to leave." She lays her napkin on the table. "Thanks guys, but maybe another time. Becca Sue, let's go."

George has wheeled himself onto the patio, leaving Sybil exposed in the doorway where Sam sees her.

"Of course!" he says. "That explains everything. You couldn't wait to interrupt our dates again..."

Magnus interjects with his courtroom voice. "Dates? Becca Sue, are you on a date?"

Sam lays his hand again on Becca Sue's bare shoulder and keeps her from getting up. "So, what if she is? What if she has a drink? What is wrong with you people down here?"

Sybil groans and comes closer to the table, just as Mag-nus leans over and picks up Ashleigh's wine glass, now sitting in front of Becca Sue. Sybil puts her hand to her throat and groans again, staring at the brown-haired girl across from her. "You're pregnant."

Magnus lifts the glass. "Or are you lying? Seems you'd know better than to be drinking if you actually were carrying my child." He downs the rest of the glass and shrugs. "But then you are an uneducated girl from the backwoods of Georgia so maybe *y'aaaalllll* haven't heard alcohol isn't good for a baby."

Sam's hand leaps off the bare shoulder like Becca Sue's braid conceals a coiled-up rattle snake. "Pregnant?"

Pearl raises her hands in front of her in offering. "Oh my, maybe it's his baby. Or his?" She says this first looking at Sam, and then at Carlos. Carlos just shakes his head and steps out of the way.

Becca Sue stands up, no caressing hand to stop her this time. "I have to go home."

Only Ashleigh moves, to open and close the door behind them. Magnus pours a fresh glass of wine from the bottle Carlos had just opened and downs it.

Sybil steps to the table, picks up a full water glass, and throws the water onto the lawn. She holds the glass out to Magnus. "Fill it up."

Magnus does, and Sybil sits down where Sam had sat earlier. She opens up the cloth in the basket in front of her. "Mmm, bread. Anyone want to join me?"

Sam looks at everyone in turn and then fills up his own glass with wine. "So. Is she really pregnant?"

Magnus reaches for the bottle. "We'll know Monday morning."

"And then it got ugly. Fast." Carlos is filling Ashleigh in. Their table overlooks the marina where still, warm water reflects lights from the anchored boats, the dock, and the small restaurant situated between the road and the water.

"The old guy, not the one in the wheel chair, lost it on Sam. Wanting to know how long he'd been seeing Rebecca, and every time Sam called her Rebecca someone would correct him and say, 'Don't you mean Becca Sue?' Then he got all defensive about that, and that woman Pearl kept insinuating he was sleeping with Becca Sue. Then Ms. Johnson, Sybil, stepped in on Sam's part, saying she'd been working him too hard for him to be seeing Becca Sue even though she *had* been chasing him..."

"What? Becca Sue chasing Sam? No way!" Ashleigh exclaims.

"Exactly! But that's what she said, of course, that sent Sam really over the edge and he started telling off the old guy, not the one in the wheel chair—did you know he's an author? I've read some of his books even, the military thriller ones."

"Really? I need to interview him for the paper." She gets them back on track. "So, Sam and Magnus got into it?"

Carlos leans forward. "It was *epic*. Sam threw him out of the house. If you'd been outside at Becca Sue's, you would've heard it across the lake. By time they were through, they were both yelling. Sam's got a temper, and apparently the old guy does, too. And the author's wife, she egged it on something fierce. She was having a blast." He sits back and picks up his beer. "So anyway, everyone left, Sam and I cleaned up the kitchen and went back to the hotel, and that's when I called you."

Ashleigh lifts her bottle of beer in the air to clink with Carlos'. "And I'm so glad you did. Becca Sue is kind of in a fog. Until she finds out if she's pregnant, she can't make any decisions."

"About keeping the pregnancy?"

"Naw, she says abortion isn't an option for her. But just about what to do."

"Well, if she is pregnant, we both know it's not Sam's, so I'm assuming it's the old guy's. I bet he has everything all planned out. He said they were moving to New York."

Ashleigh wrinkles her nose. "New York? No way. Can you even imagine Becca Sue in New York?"

"Not really, but then the author's wife kept talking about how she hooks up with rich guys? That she owns the whole subdivision?"

Ashleigh sighs and looks out at the water. "That's kind of

true, I guess, but she's paid dearly for it. It's pretty much like that saying, 'If you marry for money, you earn every cent.'"

Carlos flags down the waitress. "Want another beer? We are all caught up on those people, so now we can concentrate on us."

Ashleigh smiles and looks at the little beer left in her bottle. "Sure, another one would be good."

"Two more. Thanks," Carlos says to the waitress as she nears the table.

Ashleigh reaches back and releases the barrette holding her hair. She shakes her head and blond hair falls around her shoulders. "There, that's better."

Carlos nods and grins. "I so agree."

43

"Shhh," I whisper as I crack open the front door early Monday morning. "Oh. Magnus."

"These are for you." He holds out a huge bouquet of flowers, hot pink and orange. "I'm so sorry about Saturday night." He looks around. "Can I come in?"

How can I turn him away when he looks so sorry? "Sure, just be quiet."

"Okay. Kids asleep?"

"Sure, something like that." We go through the kitchen so I can put the flowers in some water. I fill a pitcher and stick the bouquet in it, wrapping and all. "I haven't made coffee yet. I guess I'm sorry for not answering your calls and texts yesterday." I lead him through to the living room where I shove blankets and my pillow to the side, so we can sit on the couch.

"Well, we both needed some time to think and like I said, I'm so sorry. I know the baby's mine. It was just jealousy." He looks down at his hands for a moment.

I know that he's waiting for me to say it's all right, but all that comes out is a yawn. "Sorry, I didn't sleep too much last night..."

He immediately grabs for my hands. "I know it was my fault, but that boy got under my skin. He's so arrogant, so full of himself and thinks he knows what's best for you. Listen, I'll take care of everything. I should've come to apologize yesterday morning, but I was busy all day. For you. For us.

I've already talked to Roger about hiring someone to manage Backwater, and he'll find just the right person, so no worries there. We can keep this house so we have a base in Florida. A realtor is coming out to my house this afternoon, and it'll be on the market tomorrow morning."

"Our base? Do you still want to move to the beach? And what if I'm not even pregnant?"

"Oh, I forgot we talked about the beach, but no, New York. My aunt's properties, remember?"

I hold my breath for a moment. "But I can't live in New York."

Magnus grins and pats my hand. "You'll love it. We have tickets to fly up there this weekend. You won't believe how much you're going to love our house on the lake in upstate New York. Makes this place look like a dump."

When I look around the room, my eyes fall to the folder of information Roger left for me to go through. I'd only made it through a couple pages before I lost hope. There's no way I can do everything he wants me to do with Backwater. I'm so tired, and thinking about what happened over at Sam's Saturday night makes me sigh. Not to even mention last night. "Might as well tell you," I start, "Cab came home late last night, half-drunk, and Maggie called Jameson who yelled at me on the phone."

Magnus pulls a sympathetic face. "All the more reason to move to New York. Leave that family alone. They don't deserve you. They should take care of their own kids. Like we'll take care of our kids."

"Our kids? We don't even have *a* kid yet. Magnus, I'm just too sleepy to think about all this."

He slides closer and puts his arm around me. "I know, poor thing, having to deal with teenagers that aren't even yours. Believe me, our kids won't be like that."

I lay my head on his shoulder. "And this couch may be expensive, but it sure isn't comfortable to sleep on." We snuggle for a bit and then I feel his head lift off mine.

"Oh, the blankets and pillow. Why did you sleep out here?"

Maybe if I don't move, breath nice and even, he'll think I'm asleep.

"Wait, who's sleeping in your bedroom? Becca Sue?"

And then my eyes open just enough to see my bedroom door cracking open. So I close them back. Tight.

"Good morning! I heard you asking who was in here, so I thought I'd give you a look see! It's us!" I hear, as Magnus struggles up from the couch, letting me fall to the side. "Aren't you handsome?"

Oh lord, Momma's using her waitress voice.

Yep. Momma's here. Daddy, too.

"Susan, honey, get up off that there couch and introduce us to your good looking friend."

"Susan?" Magnus asks.

"Oh, what does she have y'all here to call her? I named her Susan after my favorite movie, *Desperately Seeking Susan*. I love Madonna, folks think we look alike."

"Isn't that the stupidest thing you've ever heard?" comes from the bedroom. Daddy's up. "Everyone knows you name young'uns after family. Rebecca was my mother's name. Susan is just common." He comes out of the bedroom with his jeans on, barefoot, and no shirt. He holds his thick, muscular arm out. "Rick Cousins, and from what I heard you saying out here, you're the man that finally knocked up my girl here." He stands in front of Magnus with his hand out stretched and a huge grin on his face. "You're a good bit older than her last husband."

Daddy is good-looking and about twenty years younger than Magnus. He works hard and his chest is muscled, explaining the no-shirt look.

Momma comes up and stands beside him. She pulls his right arm over her head and he settles it around her. She nestles into his muscles and asks Magnus, "You two married?" Momma is petite, tiny. People do say she looks like Madonna because she works real hard at it. Her hair is jet black, she has a painted-on mole and dark, dark eyebrows. If there's an 80's Madonna in a wax museum, my momma looks just like it. I only wish she was wax and couldn't talk.

Pretty much like how Magnus can't seem to find his tongue. Guess I have to talk for him, so I sit up. "No, we're not married. Momma and Daddy meet Magnus Llord."

"Well, now, I've not ever heard a name like that. Real pretty," Momma says as she holds out a gloved hand. Fingerless glove, of course.

"Magnum? Like the gun?" Daddy asks.

Magnus clears his throat. "Um, no, Magnus. Good to meet you both." He shakes Daddy's hand again, and when he reaches out for Momma's, she bats it away.

"We're practically family," she says with open arms for a hug. "However, I don't think I'll be calling you son, now will I?"

Daddy stretches and then heads toward the kitchen. "Faye, get in here and make some coffee for everybody. I don't have an idea how this fancy pot works. We eating breakfast here?"

Momma lets go of Magnus as she yells, "Rick, don't touch that machine. You can't make decent coffee, no ways. Be right back, sugar," she says to Magnus.

I groan and collapse back onto the couch. "They showed up last night right around the time Cab was throwing up."

"Did you know they were coming?" Magnus asks. He hasn't moved an inch.

"Are you kidding? Like I'd still be here." I lean up with my elbows on my knees and bury my face in my hands. "Apparently word got around in Piney about the house here. Maggie put stuff last week about the Backwater market on Facebook, along with pictures of the house and the pool. Momma and Daddy put two and two together, and here they are."

"For how long?"

"Not sure. Momma says she's never going back to the diner, but she says that a lot. Daddy says there's not much to do on the farm in the heat of summer."

We can hear them arguing in the kitchen, and Magnus goes from stone still to a blur. "I've got to get back to the house. Um, the realtor is coming. Doctor appointment is at 11, so see you then. I'll leave you to visit with your parents, and we'll talk later, okay?" By this time, he's closing the back doors and headed for the side gate.

Funny, wonder what in the world set him off like that?

Maggie comes out of her bedroom, peeking around to check for who's up. I hold up an arm for her to snuggle under, and she slides onto the couch next to me.

"So I didn't dream your mother and father came here last night?" she asks.

We listen to them argue over everything from how many scoops of coffee to use, to how Daddy is making the water come out of the faucet too strong, to Daddy saying Momma could make better coffee if she didn't have those Madonna gloves without fingers on. After a while, we start giggling at them.

Momma pops her head into the living room. "Me and your daddy are going to step out front. Hey, Miss Maggie."

Maggie says, "Hey," but Momma's head is gone, and we hear them heading out the front door.

"Oh crying angels, you know they are out there smoking on the front lawn," I say.

Maggie nods with a growing grin. "Wish Miss Pearl would see them, don't you?" We giggle again. "Are you really going to have a baby?"

"No."

"But everyone says you are."

"I thought I was, but found out this morning I'm not."

"I heard Magnus here, did you tell him?"

Here I should say, "No," and then she can ask, "Why?" Then I would say, "That's a good question." Instead I just bury my face in the blanket.

Why didn't I tell him?

I don't know.

I can't figure out how I ended up in the middle of things. More importantly, I can't figure out how to get back on the sidelines, where I watch other people live out their lives, but no one even notices me.

When I feel Maggie stroking my head, I lift my head. "Oh, honey, don't feel sorry for me. This whole mess is my own doing, and I'm going to talk to Magnus in just a bit. But until I do, don't say anything, okay? I'm just sick of people talking about me."

"Sure thing. I'm going to go get a shower." She stands up. "Oh, you do know Aunt Helen is coming over, right? She said she was going to call you."

Leaning over, I grab my phone off the end table and turn the ringer back on. "Oh no, she left a message." I struggle out of the blanket and off the couch. "I'll get dressed while Momma and Daddy are outside." First, I dart into the kitchen for a cup of coffee, and then I hear them outside just as Momma creeps in the front door.

"There's some woman out there with like white hair saying she's related to the Masons somehow. She threatened to call the cops on us, but your daddy is talking to her. Helen's her name, I think she said. She likes your daddy, I can tell." Momma pours a cup of coffee and sits down at the kitchen table. "She looks like your daddy's type."

"I'm getting dressed." In my bedroom, with the door closed, I sit on the bed. Lord, my Momma and Daddy have slept with everyone available in Piney, and now they've moved on to the next state. And Momma's right, rich women go for Daddy. Rich women are used to strings attached to everything in their lives: their men, their children, their pocketbooks, everything. Daddy ain't never seen a string, and they love that. Love it.

I put on the blue sundress I had on Saturday night 'cause it's easy to find, and it was really cute on me. I think I might need to feel cute today. My hair is still kind of braided from Saturday night, and with a pat or two from wet hands, it looks okay. I clean the mascara smudges from under my eyes and feel pretty good. "I'm not pregnant," I say out loud to the mirror.

Now what? For a start, let's go see what Helen wants.

"Momma? Are you smoking in the house?" I round the corner into the kitchen to see Momma waving her hand around in the smoke from the cigarette lying on the saucer in front of her.

"No."

"I can see it. You're lying."

"Oh, okay. What's for breakfast?"

"Daddy still outside with Helen? I need to talk to her about Cab?"

"Whoo boy, that Cab sure takes after his daddy, don't he?"

I ignore her and go out the front door. And then in the front door. "There's no one out there."

Momma takes a sip of coffee. "Told you Daddy and that woman were hitting it off. You didn't plan on them hooking up right there on your front lawn, did ya?"

"He left with her? He didn't even have a shirt on."

"Sweetie, we're just lucky she still had *her* shirt on."

"Her daddy is my boss. And Maggie and Cab's grandfather."

"Then good for you. She didn't look too easy to work with when she got here. Your Daddy will fix that. Get some coffee and sit down here."

I pour a cup of coffee and sit across from her.

"So, you're not pregnant?"

"How do you know?" *Can't I even have a sip of coffee?*

"Just a mother's intuition." Then she starts laughing. "That's a joke, isn't it? Me having mother's intuition. Bathroom garbage can. Some people like to snoop in medicine cabinets, but I think a garbage can tells you more. Don't worry, I won't tell that Magnum guy. He looks like a good catch." She flips back her jet black hair. "Not sure how you keep hooking these rich guys."

"I'm not hooking anyone. I just, I mean, I'm going to tell him. I just found out this morning."

"Before he came over?"

"Well, yes, but..."

"See? Not a problem. He believes you."

"But I don't want to have his baby." *Wait, that feels true. Okay, I really don't want to have Magnus' baby.* I take a deep breath and a long drink of coffee. *I don't want to have Magnus' baby and I'm not. Whew.*

Momma lights another cigarette. "See, I knew you'd figure things out. Girl, you're doing right well for yourself down here. And the old guy mentioned hiring a caretaker for all this. Well, your Daddy and I accept the job. We've got nothing holding us in Piney. Then you can decide what you want to do about the old guy. His houses sound pretty impressive. You wanna get right on locking this down."

My brain freezes thinking of Momma and Daddy moving in here, and before I can say anything Cab comes storming into the living room. I jump up to meet him.

"Where the hell is Aunt Helen? Do you know what time it is?" He's shoving his feet in shoes and smoothing his hair down with his hand. His shirt is unbuttoned and untucked, and his khaki shorts aren't buttoned. "We're supposed to be at the courthouse this morning at 9 o'clock for that hearing or something."

"Your Aunt Helen was here, but she had to leave," I say. You have a hearing this morning?"

"Yeah, something from that thing a couple months ago where the idiots arrested a bunch of us. I missed the last one and so Grandfather said he was sending Aunt Helen to make sure I got there."

Momma walks into the room. "Son, you look better than you did last night."

Cab snarls. "Well, lady, you don't. Who are you?"

I step between them. "Cab, I'll take you. Meet me in the car. I'll get some shoes."

Sliding my flip flops on, I go to Maggie's door. "Aunt Helen got, she ah, got distracted so I'm taking Cab to the courthouse. You want to go with us, or stay here?"

Loud, strangled sounds of "Like a Virgin" coming from the kitchen might have had something to do with the speed at which she got off her bed and started throwing on clothes. "I'll go with you."

Cab is sitting in the passenger's seat when we get to the

car. "Hurry up. I don't even know who I'm supposed to be meeting. Aunt Helen's not answering her phone." I slide in the driver's seat, and Maggie jumps in the back. As we back out of the garage, Cab gets a text.

"She texted me the lawyer's name. He's going to meet us outside the courthouse. Says to tell you thanks and that your daddy says 'HI' and there's a bunch of smiley faces. What?"

"She ran into my father this morning." We pull out onto the smooth, newly paved road. "So where's the courthouse?"

"Downtown across from the ice cream shop."

Maggie catches my eyes in the rearview mirror. She gives me a smile and a thumbs up. She is way too sweet for all of the kooks she's surrounded by. Myself included.

A spot opens up on the side street beside the courthouse, and we pull right in. Cab is barely out of the car before he's met by a young man in a dark suit. "Cab Mason? I'm Tim Rogers. Let's get inside." He bends down to talk to me in the car. "Ma'am, we're going to head on in since we're running late. You can meet us outside courtroom C, on the 2nd floor, but no hurry. We're just going to check in, but won't be called for a bit and then wait in the hallway. You can take your time. C'mon, Cab."

Maggie leans up through the front seats. "Wonder what time the ice cream shop opens?"

"Probably not until ten or so." Paused after the rush of getting out of the house, I let out a long sigh.

"Oh, Becca Sue, don't worry. I don't really want any ice cream this early. We can just sit here in the car."

"Maggie, honey, how did you ever get so sweet? Thanks, but believe it or not I don't have enough room in my head for worrying about all that now. Seems kinda silly how I acted about an ice cream shop, doesn't it?"

And as I look down the street, I see little has changed since the days when it looked like a horror show to me. People just walking around. And they might be judging me on the way I talk and the way I look, or they may be like Ashleigh and ready to make a new friend. Maybe while I was worrying about everyone judging me, I was busy judging them.

"Isn't there a bookstore down closer to the marina? Let's take a quick walk and see what time it opens." With a grin at Maggie, I pull open my car door.

Maggie scurries out, and we cross the street in the warm sunshine. The ice cream shop is still closed, but we can see workers inside making fudge. As we pass stores, owners sweeping off mats or setting up displays speak to us. Invite us to take a look inside. At the bookstore, we find the doors closed and lights off, but the display makes my fingers itch. I've not read at all this summer. Usually that's all I do.

"We are coming back here later," I say to Maggie. "Let's go check on Cab first."

Folks around us walk slow, most have cups of coffee and a pet and look like they live here. The shoppers and ice cream eaters are probably still in bed. Nobody is dressed fancy, and the women don't have on makeup. No one seems to pay any attention to me and Maggie, and by time we get back to the courthouse I'm smiling. We enter, and the random morning sounds fade away with the slow closing of the heavy, centered doors. A grand staircase greets us, and we start up it towards the second floor.

When our flip flops flip and make loud, echoing sounds, we both giggle. Maggie bites her lip, then whispers, "Feels weird to be wearing flip flops here, doesn't it?"

At the top of the stairs, we see a sign for the courtrooms, and as we walk down the huge hall, a door opens beside us and a man hustles out.

"Oh, excuse me," he says as he steps to the side. "Miss Mason?"

"Yes? Oh, hi. Mr., um..." The large man who had all the paperwork for me and Mr. Worth to sign at my house holds his hand out to me.

"Jim. Jim Caldwell."

"Yeah, Jim. This is Maggie Mason."

"Oh, your stepdaughter. Nice to meet you, Miss Mason." He shakes Maggie's hand and then looks at me. "How are things in Backwater? What I've heard about your market this weekend was all very positive. And, just between us, there have already been three building permits authorized. You all might have just figured out how to get things moving around here." He laughs and winks. "Like we didn't already know it was just having enough money to spend and the right people on your side. But whatever works to get things going, right?"

This time his wink doesn't feel as friendly, and he turns so it doesn't include Maggie. What's he thinking?

"Can I help y'all find where you're going?"

Why does such an innocent question make me want to pull the neck of my dress up several inches? "Thanks, but we're good. Courtroom C should be down here, right?"

"Yes, ma'am. Third door on your right. Good to meet you," he says to Maggie. Then he turns to me and adds, "Good to see you again, too." He winks one last time, and then hurries back down the hall toward the stairs.

"Did you hear what he said?" Maggie asks.

Just as I try to figure out how to say there is nothing going on between me and her grandfather, she adds, "He called me your stepdaughter."

My brain trips and backs up. "What? Yeah, I guess that's right."

She slows down and then stops to look up at me. "But no one's ever called me that. I don't think I ever really thought of us being related. You know, officially."

She's right. Even in my head I never thought of her and Cab actually having ties to me. I was more like their nanny than a relative. "Wait, that's right. I was married to your father, so you and Cab are my stepchildren." Now, that word may not be a good one in the storybooks and such, but it feels like gold right now.

Maggie and I stare at each other and barely above a whisper, at the same time say, "We're family." Like how the evil queen dissolves in the Disney movies is how I picture Maggie's grandmother right now. Melting into a puddle of water at the mention of the F word. "I have a daughter. The best daughter in the world," I say as I wrap my arms around Maggie. "Oh, and a son. Cab is my stepson! What am I doing out here? He needs me." We rush to the door and pull the big heavy thing open.

And on the same day I find out I'm not a mother, I find I've been a mother all along.

44

"Hey, what are you doing here?" Ashleigh asks as she walks up to Becca Sue, Maggie, and Cab. They are sitting underneath the looping arms of a massive tree, eating a late breakfast of pastries, fish nuggets, hush puppies, and real ice cream shakes.

"Just eating breakfast slash lunch. Sit down." Becca Sue pulls over a metal chair from the next table.

"For a minute. Can I have a hush puppy?" Ashleigh asks with her fingers poised over the paper basket next to Cam. He nods, and she takes one off the top of the pile.

"We got an extra order. Tara's makes the best hush puppies on the island, well, at least that's what the sign said, so eat up. And the ice cream shakes are amazing! Try this." Becca Sue strips the paper from an extra straw and sticks it in her cup.

"I thought you didn't like being downtown," Ashleigh says, unconvinced, before she takes a hard pull on the straw.

"She likes it now," Maggie offers with a big smile and a mouth full of flaky pastry. "Want to try my shake? It's bubble-gum and mint."

Cab makes a bit of a gagging sound, and Ashleigh laughs, "Okay, that's rude, but I think I agree with your brother." He doesn't look up, but shoves another hush puppy in his mouth.

"He *is* rude, and he's also hungover, so he probably won't join you in laughing. I think it's all he can do to keep from throwing up, but the carbs should be helping. Cab, apologize to Ashleigh."

The boy lifts his head, nods, and mumbles. "I'm sorry."

Ashleigh furrows her eyebrows and looks from the pale young man to her friend. They meet eyes, and Ashleigh's questioning look is met with a smile, a shrug, and change of subject. "So, how was your date with Carlos Saturday night? Yesterday kind of passed in a fog, so I forgot to call you." Becca Sue leans back and relaxes her bare shoulders in the morning sunlight.

"You couldn't have reached me yesterday anyway. Spent the day on the beach with Carlos, and then we went out again last night."

"Really? You had fun?"

"We had a blast! My folks even liked him."

"What? He met your parents?"

"Right here. We walked down here for ice cream after supper, and my family was sitting over there. Listen, bound to happen in a place this small. He was cool with it. Said it made him miss his family back in New York."

"That's great. Hey kids, why don't you throw this stuff away if you're done, and start back to the car. I'll meet you there in a minute."

Ashleigh holds her hand out over the table. "Wait, take the leftovers down to the dock and feed the pelicans lined up outside the fish tables. They'll love it."

"Cool! Can we?" Maggie says.

"Cab, will you go with your sister?"

"Sure," he sighs as he stands up. He takes a deep breath. "I feel a lot better. Thanks for the food."

As they walk away with their bag of scraps and their milkshakes, Ashleigh watches them and asks, "Okay, where did the kinder, gentler Cab come from?"

"You mean my stepson?" Becca Sue grins. "We just came from court, and the judge told him the only thing keeping him out of juvenile detention was me. His stepmother."

"Well, about time."

"Not just for him, for me, too. I haven't been acting like a stepmother. I've been acting like a teenage housekeeper, but not anymore."

"This have anything to do with being pregnant?"

"Oh, wait, I'm not. Found out this morning."

"You've already been to the doctor?" Ashleigh asks.

"Oh, the doctor. That's why Magnus keeps calling me. I turned off my ringer to ignore him," Becca Sue says as she punches buttons on her phone. "Okay, there. Texted him to cancel doctor. So, no, we didn't go to the doctor. I got my period this morning. Whew." She takes another drink of her shake and closes her eyes. "Thank God. I never knew how much I didn't want to be pregnant with Magnus' baby until I wasn't. So, Carlos?"

"Wait, this is huge. So Magnus doesn't know yet?"

"No, he came by this morning, but well, my parents are here and it was kind of a mess. Then Cab needed to come to court, but his Aunt Helen, who was supposed to be his ride, ran off with Daddy."

Ashleigh's mouth had fallen open at some point and hung there as the flood of information filtered behind her wide eyes. "What? *Your* dad?"

"Yeah, while you were off laying around on the beach and strolling downtown sharing ice cream cones with your dream man, all hell was breaking loose in Backwater. Wait 'til you meet my folks. But first, what did Carlos say about Sam?"

"What would he say about Sam?"

"You know, like, did he have a good time the other night?"

Ashleigh's mouth not only closes, but she presses her lips together as she looks toward the marina where the kids are walking back with empty hands. She stands up. "Here come the kids. You probably need to go, and I definitely need to get to work."

Becca Sue only tilts her head back to better see her friend. She squints in the bright sunshine. "So, Sam is done with me? Can't blame him."

Ashleigh looks down and sighs. "He's involved with Sybil. Carlos caught them at the restaurant late Saturday night. He went back over there to make sure it was all locked up after he dropped me off, and they didn't see him. They were out on the back patio, so he just backed out of the front door and left."

"What? They were kissing?"

She shakes her head. "He didn't say, just that they were together, alone, late at night, and that he knew something was up between them, he just couldn't figure it out before. He said it explained a lot."

"Oh. Okay." Becca Sue stands up and turns as the kids reach them. "Well, it was fun for a bit, wasn't it? See you later. Let's go, kids."

Ashleigh waves at them then turns down the street to the newspaper office. "Maybe her being pregnant wouldn't have been that bad. Maybe her being with Magnus wouldn't be so bad." She sighs, and as she pulls open the front door, she says to her reflection. "And if her hillbilly survival skills kick in, that's just where she's headed. Back to big daddy Magnus."

45

Eason pulls open the door to Magnus' screened porch and steps in. "Isn't it a little hot to be sitting out here?"

Magnus grunts and picks up his bottle of water, which trails a stream of condensation across his lap and shirt. "I'm waiting."

The doctor sits down in the chair next to his friend and studies the direction Magnus is staring in. "Becca Sue?"

"Yeah, she cancelled her doctor appointment with a text earlier. Won't take my calls."

A shrill whine fills the air as the cicadas kick up in the noonday heat. The whine stops abruptly, just as the air conditioning unit buried in the bushes cycles on. Eason takes off his straw hat and fans himself with it. "Who are those people in Becca Sue's pool?"

"Her folks."

"Becca Sue's? No, they look too young."

"Nope, I met 'em. Can't tell you their names, but they are definitely her parents. Real works of art."

"Guess that's why you're not waiting for her over there, then?"

"You got it. They were plum tickled that I'd knocked up their little girl. Even though I'm so much older than they would *eeevvveeerrr* imagined. They're the kind that say whatever pops into their empty little heads."

Eason grins. "In-laws straight from heaven, you say?"

Magnus grunts again and takes another drink of water.

"So, quite a scene over at Sybil's restaurant Saturday night, I heard."

Magnus adds a dismissive hand wave to his grunt.

"Pearl says if we'd been out on our porch, we could've heard you and the boy going at it."

"*Boy* is about right. Didn't have a clue what he was talking about. Making moves on Becca Sue, calling her Rebecca, and he didn't even know she was carrying my child."

"Why do you think she went over there?"

"She was with her friend. Eating dinner. That's all. He just needed to be put in place, so I did."

"Well, seems he got over her pretty quick." He waits for a follow-up question, but Magnus just sits and stares.

The bugs raise a chorus again, and when they stop, the air holds the void of sound, trapped in humidity and light. Both men sit motionless for a moment more, then Eason stands. "Well, guess I should get back home. Ruth will want to know about Becca Sue's folks. She wanted me to check on you, although I told her you were well over Sybil. On to new things with Becca Sue." He steps to the door.

"Wait. Why is she worried about me? What's going on with Sybil?"

"Oh, just while we missed the big scene over at the restaurant, Ruth did see Sybil and the boy over there on the patio later that night. Moon's almost full, so she said she could see them pretty clearly. Not that she was watching them, you know." Eason smiles and winks. "Good luck on your waiting. Let me know what Becca Sue's explanation for canceling the appointment is. You know, maybe something with the kids. She did head out of here this morning with both kids in the car."

"Yeah, maybe."

Eason closes the door behind him and walks through the thick grass around the lake. Magnus watches him, his eyes leaving his focus point. A loud laugh pulls him back to the pool where Becca Sue's mother is running around the pool with her hands clutched over her chest, bathing suit top nowhere in sight. He sighs and shakes his head. "Rednecks," he mumbles but then a grin creeps across his face. "Although, guess me and Becca Sue provided quite a show ourselves at times."

He rises from his chair, stretches, and looks across the backyards to his left. The patio of Sybil's restaurant sticks out closer to the lake than the others, and he stares at the chairs sitting close together at the edge. Perfect spot to be seen from across the lake.

So Sybil and that boy.

Once again, he sighs and shakes his head as he turns to go inside. "Poor thing, makes her look like an old fool."

"Did you see the woman running around the pool over there without a top?" Sam asks, coming into the kitchen. The three guys working there all step into the large dining room to look out the windows. He adds, "She covered herself up with her hands, but what kind of crazy place is this?"

Carlos hops up on the granite counter between the kitchen and living room. "I don't know, but I'm loving it. Crazy people just crawling out of the woodwork. Reminds me of home, except instead of traffic and winter, there's summer and beach."

"You're awfully happy. Banging the blonde?"

Carlos jumps down and punches his friend in the arm. "No. Jerk. You know me better than that.

"You're right. I'm sorry. Glad you're liking it, but I just want to get out of here." He pulls a tape measure out of his shirt pocket and squats down to measure the bottom of the counter.

"You seemed pretty happy Saturday night."

"Saturday night?" Sam rolls his eyes. "Are you joking? That was a disaster."

"I meant, later. You know, after we left. I came back to

check on things. *Later.*"

Sam stands up and turns around. "What are you talking about?" The men face each other, both pairs of dark brown eyes searching the other.

Carlos drops his eyes and holds up his hands. "Nothing. My bad. So, you know what you want to do with the facing here?"

Sam shrugs. "Yeah, then once the painters come back, we should be done with the dining room and just have the kitchen to wrap up. And none too soon." He stares out the back doors and Carlos comes up behind him.

"The topless woman back?"

"Who? Oh, no. I don't think so."

Carlos backs off and walks into the kitchen to pick up the truck keys off the counter. "I'll make that run to the hardware store and bring back some lunch, okay?" A look through the pass-through tells him not to expect an answer as his friend is still staring across the lake. He quietly closes the outside door and walks down the driveway. "Poor fool, stuck on a pregnant girl from the South." In the truck he holds his phone in his hand and punches a button.

"Hey, you!" Ashleigh's voice bounces from the phone.

"Hey yourself. You at work?"

"Yep, getting ready to head over to the school offices to work on a back-to-school story. Can't believe the summer is already winding down. Where are you?"

"Heading to Home Depot and then picking up lunch. I had fun yesterday. Want to go to the beach tonight?"

"How about a private beach?"

"Private beach? Sounds, uh, interesting."

"Well, it's just that the tourists don't really go there because they don't know how to get through the parking lot of the Pirate Booty Bar."

Carlos laughs. "I'd ask if you were joking, but I've figured out by now you're not. This place is crazy."

"Crazy in a good way?"

"Oh, yes, most definitely a good way. How about I come pick you up around seven, and we'll get sandwiches to take with us."

"Perfect. So, you by yourself?"

"Yep, why?"

"Guess who's not pregnant?"

"No way! That's great. Isn't it?"

"I guess, but she was asking all about Sam this morning, and I had to tell her about him and Sybil. Sam could definitely get her away from the old guy, but now I don't know if he wants to. Sounds like he's tied in tight with his boss."

"I tried to get Sam to talk about that earlier, but he wouldn't. Maybe it's just something like 'boss with benefits'? Maybe we just ignore it. No one else knows, right?"

"Yeah, I guess. Hey, I've got to go, the principal is here. Talk to you later."

As the phone goes dark, he tosses it in the seat beside him. He turns into the Home Depot parking lot with a scowl on his face that a deep breath erases as he parks and turns off the truck. "Hope Ashleigh still wants to go to her private beach after I tell her." He slams the truck door. "I have to tell her tonight."

"Oh, hey there. Your momma is taking a nap." Rick raises his eyebrows, grins, then adds a wink for his daughter as he shuts her bedroom door behind him.

"Daddy! In *my* bed?" Becca Sue groans, but reaches out and grabs his arm, pulling him toward the pool door. "Come out here for a minute."

"Sure, sugar. And your momma and I were talking about how good you're looking. That man is taking right good care of you, isn't he? You never lost weight for Caleb, so you must really like this one. Your momma also told me you want us to stay here and take care of this place for you, so we need to talk about how much that would pay."

She pushes through the doors and pulls them shut behind her father. "Pay?" she spits. "There is no pay. There is no job. Now, about Helen."

"Who?"

"The woman with the convertible this morning."

"Oh, Helen. That's right. Good-looking woman, there."

"She's Cab and Maggie's aunt, and her father is my, well, my boss here at Backwater. What happened with you two?"

Rick grins and rocks back and forth on his bare feet, his hands stuck down deep in the front pockets of his blue jeans. "We went for a ride."

"And? Nothing else?"

"Of course there was some talking and stuff."

Becca Sue waves her hands. "I don't want details. I just want you to leave her alone."

"Hon, you know how the ladies are about me. I make them happy. And Lord knows that Helen is one unhappy lady. We have a date tonight."

"No." Becca Sue closes her eyes and leans against the house. "Daddy, it was different in Piney. Everyone there knows about you and Momma, and well, it just is what it is. But this is my new home."

"And maybe it'll be our new home, too. Piney with a beach and all new people." He winks and pulls open the door. "Hon, you worry too much. Ain't nothing different, people are all the same everywhere. Now, I'm going to take a shower for my date. There's shampoo and soap in your shower, right?"

Becca Sue nods, and he reaches over and kisses her cheek. He walks inside, while Becca Sue kicks off her flip flops and walks to the pool. She steps down onto the first step and pulls her dress up a bit, so she can step down another step. A door slamming across the lake causes her to look up and see Magnus standing outside his screened porch.

She holds her bunched-up dress in one hand, so she can wave with the other. Magnus starts walking around the lake, and Becca Sue steps out of the pool. She walks along the side, through the lanai, and out to the lake. At its edge, she stops and looks at the reflections of the tall, skinny pines against the deep blue sky. The still, orangish-black water reflects every weed, every hovering bug, every tiny cloud. Magnus has reached the end of the lake and will be with her soon. She lifts her eyes from the water to look straight across. The windows reflect almost as well as the lake, so she can't see if Sam is there, watching her.

"Sam," she whispers. Then her voice hardens. "Sam and Sybil." She peers at, and tries to peer into, the windows, then can hear Magnus approaching from her left. She turns to face him, eyes still wide-open and intense.

"Magnus, there is no baby."

46

"I was afraid you were going to say that," Magnus says, once he reaches her. He holds out his arms and pulls her to him. "But it doesn't change anything for me."

"What?" I pull back. "It changes everything."

"No, ma'am. I've decided you make me happy. I've been sitting over there this afternoon waiting on you, and I watched your parents. Why, they're like a couple teenagers, and that's how you make me feel. I've not had as much fun in a long time, and who better to help me spend my aunt's money and live in all her houses than you?" He grabs me again and this time rocks me back and forth. "If we don't have any kids, fine, and if we do, that's fine, too."

"But, this, this, thinking I was pregnant made me know that I do want to have kids," I say.

"Great! Then let's have a bunch of kids." He steps back, but keeps hold of my hands. "Life goes by too fast to not enjoy it and guess what?"

My head is spinning, and the energy jumping off him is making me dizzy. I pull my hands out of his and fold them across my chest. "What?"

He grins and lifts his eyebrows. "I have an offer on my house."

"Your house? *That* house?" I point without fully unfolding my arms from each other.

"Yep. Backwater is hot property, with the low taxes and everyone knowing Roger Worth is backing it. So, we're practical-ly out of here!" he shouts, then laughs out loud.

His joy spills over to me, and I laugh, while reaching out a hand to him. "You still want to be with me?"

He grabs my hand. "Shocking, isn't it?"

"Yes, it is. I thought if you were stuck, maybe, but..." I shrug, I can't talk. People always get stuck with me. My parents, Ca-leb, Caleb's family, even Cab and Maggie had no choice. No-body ever *chooses* to be with me, so how could someone like Magnus Llord choose to be with me? Stuck, I could under-stand. Being someone's choice, I don't understand at all.

His voice lowers and is serious. "Becca Sue, I don't get stuck. That's just not who I am. A baby wouldn't make me stay with you if I didn't want to. I might be stuck paying for it, but that's about it." He moves in and wraps me in his arms again. "I'm choosing you. I'm asking you to be with me. Who knows how many good years I have left, and I want to laugh. You make me laugh."

He puts one hand into my hair and pulls me into a deep kiss. On the edge of the black lake, with pines towering over us, and also staring up at us from the water, we kiss. He lights up the fire in me he's stirred from the beginning. Knowing he wants me, and not just for sex, makes me even hotter. When he pulls away from me, I can see the heat in his eyes, too.

"We should head toward my house while I can still walk," he says with a grin.

Holding hands we start walking, and I wrap my other arm around our twined hands. It's harder to walk this way, but I really want to show him how I feel about him choosing me. Wanting me. With his free hand, he pulls out his phone and pushes at it with his thumb. I lay my head on his shoulder, which is hard to do as I'm as tall as he is, but I'm just so happy.

"Roger? Magnus here. Yeah, it's a deal. We're out of here. Talk to you later." Then he hangs up and drops the phone in his pocket.

"Wait. Was that Roger Worth? Was that about me? Us?"

He drops my hand and puts his arm around my waist.

"Yep. You no longer have any worries with Backwater. It's all taken care of. All you have to do is pack up whatever you want from your house, preferably some time when your parents aren't there, and our flight is Friday afternoon. No need to come back here until we're sick of winter, and by that time your folks will be out of the house. The Masons will have figured out how to survive without their babysitter. And Backwater will be running like Roger has in mind. All you have to do it make me laugh, oh, and maybe get pregnant." He squeezes my waist. As we continue walking, his hand drops to my behind, and he settles it there with a pat. "I like this dress. Reminds me of you sitting there with that boy the other night. Guess we know who won that, don't we?"

No answer was needed.

His hand said it loud and clear.

47

"And he's not a religious guy? It's about his sisters, he says?" Becca Sue leans her elbows on the table between her and Ashleigh as she asks her questions.

"Yeah, well, he goes to church, but he said it's not just that." Ashleigh chews the side of her mouth for a minute, shrugs, and picks up her cup of coffee. Still behind the trees to her back, the sun shoots the morning sky full of peach and orange rays. "Look at that, bet it's a beautiful sunrise at the beach. Guess I'll have to go home and get ready for work soon, but I'm glad we got to have coffee together."

"Yeah, when I got your text, I'd been awake for an hour. That couch is awful, plus, well, I took a little nap at Magnus' yesterday afternoon." She buries her gaze into the black of her coffee and waits.

"Did you tell him you're not pregnant?"

That causes Becca Sue's head to pop up. "Of course. And, well, here's the thing. He still wants to be with me. To take me to New York. For us to be together, married probably at some point, but who cares? He still wants me."

Ashleigh sits back in her chair. "So, you're going to just leave Backwater?"

Becca Sue shrugs. "Roger knows. He's handling it all. It'll all move right along."

"But you won't. Isn't this too much like what you did with the Mason guy? Ignore your life and just jump into his? For crying out loud, have you ever even been north of Atlanta? You have no idea what you're doing. Where you're going."

"But wouldn't this be my chance to get to see the world? To do something new?"

"As long as it's what Magnus wants to do, right?" Ashleigh snorts in disgust.

"No! He went with me to the fish camps, and he likes me for who I am. He chose me. He wants me, Becca Sue Mason. Not some *Rebecca* who doesn't even exist. And I didn't get all bent out of joint when you told me your boyfriend won't have sex, so lay off."

"That's true. Okay, sorry, but I'll miss you being here."

They sip their coffee and watch the sun come over the trees, running the morning shadows away.

Becca Sue asks, "So just how many sisters does Carlos have?"

"Four, and he's the baby of the family. The oldest one is married now, but she had a baby before she got married. The guy ran out on her, and he said he saw what it did to her. Then the sister closest to him was date raped by a friend of their family, but the guy never got in trouble over it. Police, and their neighborhood, believed they were 'consenting adults,' but he says she's not been the same since. Real guarded. Scared. He said he just doesn't think sex has to be such a big part of a relationship until there's a real, long-term commitment."

"Sounds reasonable, I guess, just not normal. But if it's what he wants, and you're okay with it. So, why the early morning text? Are you not okay with it? Besides, he'll be leaving soon, and you won't have to think about it anymore."

"But, well, yeah. But sex, I mean, do you think that it's even possible that he's right? I mean, my mother kinda talked like this to me in high school, and I bought it, but then at college. Well, it just seems like, like you have to do it. Is it possible for sex to *add* to a relationship later instead of start the relationship? And then what if you really like each other, but sex isn't any good when you do do it?"

Becca Sue grins and tosses the bit of coffee left in her mug onto the ground near the patio. "Apparently not something I have any experience with. I honestly think I wouldn't have gotten together with Caleb or Magnus if they hadn't liked going to bed with me. Don't think they would've given me a second glance. My grandmother used to say a man won't buy the cow if they can get the milk for free. Guess I'm proof they will if the milk is good enough."

Ashleigh stares at her friend. "But if they're only in it for the milk... never mind, I don't know what to think. What if I do agree to not have sex, buy into what he's saying, and then he leaves? What if I decide it's a good way to have a relationship? I'll be spoiled because, if there are any guys in Florida that think like him, I sure haven't met them."

"Me either. So no action on the beach last night, then?"

"Oh, we kissed and made out and all, but then we'd talk and walk instead of finishing things." She smiles and stretches her arms above her head. "Gotta admit, it was kinda nice."

"Morning, girls. Mind if I join you?" Rick Cousins steps out from behind the row of bushes to the side of the lanai.

"Daddy!" Becca Sue jumps up as Ashleigh pulls her arms down out of their stretch. "Ashleigh, this is my dad."

"Why hello, Ashleigh. Look at all that hair you have there. Bet when you let it down the boys go crazy."

The women look at each other, and Ashleigh starts to stand up. "Nice to meet you, but..."

"No, you girls sit back down. I need to talk to you a minute." He pulls over another metal patio chair and sits down. He taps an unlit cigarette on the table for a minute, than puts it in the pocket on his short-sleeved shirt which hangs untucked over his jeans. Once his hand is empty, he pushes it through his thick, dark hair. "I heard y'all talking. Been there in the side yard having a smoke. I know you might be uncomfortable, but you don't have to say a word, neither of you." He raises an eyebrow at his daughter. "Y'all talking about men folks and sex, and both of them are subjects I know way more about than either of you."

Becca Sue tries to smile, and nods at her friend, whose eyes are stretched wide in semi-horror. She sits down and holds her hand out flat towards Ashleigh. "It'll be okay. Let him talk, but just for a minute, Daddy. Ashleigh has to go to work."

"Good enough. Now here you two girls sit, early in the morning, talking. You think two men would do that? Call up another guy and say, let's get up early and talk?" He looks at Ashleigh. "And why'd you call my Rebecca here? You must've passed up houses of dozens of other girl friends on your way here. Weren't you raised here?"

"He calls you Rebecca?"

Becca Sue rolls her eyes. "I'll tell you later."

Ashleigh nods, then agrees with Rick. "Sure."

He continues. "But for some reason you two have clicked in the bit of time Rebecca's been here. She's the one you wanted to talk to, and she was ready to talk to you. It was early, she could've turned over and gone back to sleep, right? But she didn't. Well, girls, sex is the same way."

He sits back, and then leans forward suddenly. "You girls mind if I smoke?"

They shake their heads, now too interested in what he's going to say to interrupt. He pulls out his cigarette from his shirt and wrangles a yellow lighter out of his jeans pocket. He lights it and takes a long draw. He blows the smoke off over his left shoulder.

"See, everybody's different. Me and Rebecca's momma like sex and don't give it any more meaning than smoking this here cigarette. We fought about it something fierce when we was younger. Rebecca can tell you, she had to put up with it all, then we came to understand it's just something we both like to do, with each other and with other folks. And as long as you make sure the other people understand it's nothing more than fun, then everything is good. Honestly, darling," he bends his head towards Becca Sue, "that's why we didn't want to have any kids. Not because you weren't just about perfect, but this isn't good for kids to have to deal with. Just isn't. They don't understand."

Ashleigh had gone from horrified to stunned. Her mouth

hangs open, and she looks back and forth from Becca Sue to the table. She shakes her head a bit. "I don't know what to say. You're, like, Georgia swingers?"

Rick laughs. "Yeah, that's it. And we're happy, glad we're together. Probably won't change until we can't find anyone that wants to have sex with us."

Becca Sue lifts her head, eyes closed. "Okay, Daddy, what does this have to do with us?"

Rick taps ashes off to his side and takes another draw. "First, darling, you are *not* like me and your momma. You think you might be, but you're not. You need to figure out how you feel about sex and then live that out, quit thinking there's only one way to act. If I could, would I just love your momma? Would I want her to just be with me? Of course, and we've both tried. Lord knows we tried."

Ashleigh leans forward, her eyebrows pushed together. "So you heard about my boyfriend, and you think, you think what?"

"That he's doing the right thing. He's thinking about it. Not just acting on what his pants tell him. You feel vibes from him? Like he wants to do more than kiss and stuff, right?"

"Yeah."

"See, he's making a decision. A hard one, no pun intended. And you girls need to do the same. Think about sex. Don't just do it because everyone else is or some guy wants to or," he turns to his daughter and lays his hand on top of hers, his smoking cigarette sticking between his fingers. "Or because you want some guy. If you're not just doing it for fun, planning to just walk away, then you need to know why you are doing it." He pats her hand, then lifts his cigarette to his lips, and stands up.

He talks out one side of his mouth, and the cigarette bounces. "Sorry to crash your little hen party, but figure no one else is going to talk to girls like you this way. You're both too good, too pretty, to be confused about sex. You know how you like your coffee, you know who you like to talk to, you know what you like to wear and eat and smell like, so you know what you think about sex, if you'd just think about it." He takes a couple steps away and turns as he smiles, "Nice to meet you, Miss Ashleigh, and I do bet that hair of yours drives men crazy."

Both women sit while he disappears around the side of the house.

"Guess I oughta apologize for him, but I think he means well," Becca Sue finally says.

Ashleigh sits up straight and pulls the rubber band off her pony tail, then smooths her hair back with both hands. "Naw, its okay. And you know, he's right. Think about it. I'm such a thinker and yet I haven't spent much time thinking about sex. Well, okay, I think about sex, but not like how it fits in my life and stuff. Gives me something to think about on the way home." She stands up and shakes her head. She steps away from the table and gets to the edge of the pool before she turns back around.

With her hands on her hips she rolls her eyes and laughs. "And now I can't *wait* to meet your mother."

48

Before the sun got up much at all, it was met with some fast-moving clouds I could see coming in from the horizon. I watched it from on top of my crossed arms, on the table in the lanai. My hair felt like a horse blanket laying across my neck and shoulders, so I sat up and wrapped it into a ponytail. Without a rubber band, I had to just hold it up. The breeze felt good for a minute, then it didn't. It felt like someone's hot breath on my neck, then the sky opened up.

Home we'd call this a "gully washer" 'cause it would cause little ditches, gullies, in the clay. Here, though, there ain't no hills to rush down, and it just seeps into the ground. "Shoot," I say and look down. Rain bouncing up on the patio is hitting my legs, so I move over to stand next to the wall of the lanai. No worries about getting back in the house, another thing about Florida rain, it don't usually last too long. Leaning against the stone wall, the air is cooler now. Through the sheets of rain, everything is gray and green. The lake is just a blur with the rain hitting it so hard the splashes make it hard to tell whether more water is going up or down.

I heard Ashleigh's car leave, so I know she at least got to her car before this started. My shoulders fall, and I let out a long breath. Alone. Totally alone. Through the rain I can see Magnus' house and Sam's restaurant— *no, Becca Sue*, Sybil's restaurant.

"Guess Sybil don't agree with Carlos' ideas on sex. Shame,

I think Sam could do better."

Okay, I can admit it out here surrounded by the rain: I kinda like Sam. And I think he kinda liked me. But he liked me when at the same time he was sleeping with Sybil? That don't seem right. I mean, like Daddy was saying. That's just not thinking about things at all. But it sure helped me out with my decision to stay with Magnus. Baby or no baby.

I bend my right leg to rest my foot on the wall at my back and look down at my other bare foot. Daddy's cigarette butt is lying there beside it. He's so country, doesn't throw it in the yard, just drops it where he's at.

He said I'm not like him and Momma.

Maybe he's right, because if I thought the only other person I'd ever have sex with is Magnus, I'd be fine with that. Something red across the lake cuts through the rain, and I squint to see Sam has walked out on the back patio, staying underneath the overhang from the house. I don't think he can see me, I'm kinda hidden in the lanai.

If I was over there, I bet we'd go out into the rain. Not worry a bit about getting wet. We'd be warm and wet and then we'd—wait. I turn away from the lake. What is wrong with me? I was just saying I could be happy with Magnus, and in less than a minute I'm daydreaming about another man? Maybe Daddy's wrong.

Stupid rain. I'm tired of being out here alone, thinking. Daddy's wrong about that, too. No need to think about everything. It'll all work out. It'll be exciting going to New York.

The rain begins to slow. Everything in me says to turn and see if Sam is still outside, but no. I'm done thinking about this. Magnus wants me. As light peeks through the clouds and soothes the ruffled surface of the pool, I run alongside it and dart in the back doors.

"There you are!" Momma exclaims. "Your daddy said you were out there just waiting out the storm. Maggie's making breakfast."

Momma has on my—well, actually Magnus's—blue silk robe. She has her dark hair up in a black bandana and full makeup on. She's painting her toenails, and I'm hoping she has underwear on because the way she has her knee bent if she don't, everyone's going to get a peep show.

"Momma, put your leg down. No need to show everyone your panties."

"Panties?"

"I don't want to know. Just put your leg down. This isn't the trailer, this is, well, this is my home. At least for now, but the kids are here."

She drops her foot to the floor and twists the cap back on the pink polish. "We missed seeing you last night 'cause we went out to that place down under the bridge. You been there?"

"No, its kinda rough, isn't it?" I move through the room, straightening the end tables, collecting trash, putting pillows back in their places.

"Not if you know how to make friends with the locals. It was just like home. That Helen girl made lots of new friends, if you know what I mean."

"Helen? Helen Worth went there with y'all?" I sit down on the chair, pillow in one hand, wadded-up candy and chip wrappers in the other. "Do I even want to know about her making new friends?"

Momma's thin, plucked-to within-an inch-of-their-life, dyed-black-to-match-her-hair eyebrows jump high. "Oh, not friends like that! That's just something with her and your daddy. She was buying for everyone. Everyone all night. She could run for mayor this morning and win in a landslide."

"Helen, as in my *Aunt* Helen?" Cab is standing across the living room in his boxers and socks, razor in hand. "My Aunt Helen buying for the crowd at the Down Under? And what do you mean she's *friends* with your daddy?"

"Cab, honey, we didn't know you were up." I drop the pillow and start towards him.

"I was in the bathroom shaving, and your mother's voice carries like crow cawing. Is she talking about Aunt Helen?"

I push him back towards the bathroom. "I don't think so.

You know how it is when you're new somewhere, you get names confused and stuff. You finish shaving, Maggie is making us pancakes," I say as I close the bathroom door behind me, wadding the trash in my hand even tighter.

Momma is waiting at the end of the hall for me. She begins to whisper, as I pull her with me towards my bedroom. "Susan, maybe it will help him to know he comes by drinking and partying honest. Between what we know of his father, and now his aunt, well, honestly, he should feel good about how together he is."

"Momma, shut up," I say when we get to my room. For a minute I'm thrown by the apparent fact that a hurricane came through here. Dishes, Coke cans, clothes everywhere, sheets everywhere but on the bed, and the glimpse I get of the bathroom causes my mouth to fall open. I pick up a glass off the night stand and see its left a ring.

"This furniture is brand new. Look at it!" I rub at the water ring, but the wood is warped a bit under it. I can see where one of the little baskets from the dresser is completely out and on the floor where it's been stepped on, or fallen on, and one corner is bent under. I go to pick it up and momma passes behind, dropping her, my, Magnus', robe on her way.

"I'm taking a shower. Tell Maggie I'll eat later. I'll let her know when I'm ready for some of those pancakes."

This. This is what I'm leaving. I'll be out of here in a couple days. The furniture I loved so much is just furniture. A mistake by Mrs. Mason.

Magnus will buy me whatever I like.

And even as I think that, I know it's not true. Ashleigh's right. Everything will be what Magnus likes, but that's okay. That's okay. I don't even pick up the bent basket or check for more water rings under the other dishes as I walk back around the bed. All this is no longer my problem. I step over Momma's robe on my way out. She can have it. She can have it all.

Carrying a stack of dishes from the dining room after breakfast, I can hear Jameson shouting through the phone. Maggie follows me into the kitchen.

"I'm trying to put her on the phone, Uncle J, but she won't take it. Becca Sue, he wants to talk to you. Please..."

I put the dishes in the sink and ignore her, but she just stands there holding the phone at my back. Finally I agree. "Okay, for just a minute."

With the phone in my hand, but nowhere near my mouth, I walk out the front door. After a deep breath, I lift it and talk. "Okay, Jameson, what?"

"Maggie says you are moving to New York with Magnus Llord. Have you lost your mind?"

"No."

He waits for more, but there isn't more. Then he explodes again. "No? That's it? I give you a house, furnish it, hell, give you a whole subdivision, let Roger Worth play around and experiment on our property, which is turning into a gold mine, and you're going to just drop it all? Including Maggie and Cab?"

"Maggie and Cab are leaving this week anyway, right? I figured you'd be sending someone to pick them up for your wedding on Saturday and then they start school next week. Like usual, I'm not leaving them, they're leaving me. Remember what you said about your family, all of your family, being done with me?"

And I burst into tears. I manage to push the end button before either of us says anything, and I shove the phone in my pocket.

Sobs rack me, and with my face in my hands, I turn to the wall beside the front door. My last time to take care of them, and I blew it. Kept thinking I'd fix everything before they had to go back, and yet it's worse now than ever. I literally moved them into the mess I grew up in. Even Daddy said this morning that it wasn't a good way to raise kids, and here they are. This summer was my last chance, and it's over.

The sobs ease off, but threaten to start again when I realize Jameson didn't even call back. No. I'm done crying. I'm done trying to run my own life. I'm no good at it. Everything has to be Magnus' way? Good.

Might not work for Ashleigh, but it's the only hope I have.

49

"It started raining Monday night and hasn't stopped," Eason explains as he looks around the Ocean Club Cafe. "There's not a happy man on the island. Or any women not sick of hearing us grump around."

Patrick lifts up his Irish coffee in a salute. "Drinking and praying for sun are the only hope we have. Esme threatened me with shoving my golf clubs somewhere they don't belong, if I didn't get them out of her living room today. So, here we are. Well, the clubs are in my car."

"We sailed in nothing but rain all the way down." Roger sits back and crosses his legs. "No storms, so nothing even exciting, just constant heavy rain. Stopped out in Backwater this morning, and it's as soggy as everything else. Lake is high, but no danger of flooding."

"Boy, Magnus stealing that girl out from under you and taking her to New York sure threw a wrench in the works, didn't it?" Patrick says with a laugh.

Roger uncrosses his legs and leans up as he nods. "Yeah. Well, we'll see how that all works out."

"Esme says there'll be a murder-suicide down the road, but she can't figure out which one will do it."

Eason holds up a hand. "Now, wait a minute. That's a little farfetched, isn't it?"

"Just telling you what Esme said. Of course, she is Italian, so she tends to think things have to end with bloodshed."

"Then guess you better watch your step there, Patrick," Roger says as he stands up. "See you both tonight at the party? You can see the plans for remaking Becca Sue's house into the clubhouse. I have the work crew starting on renovating it next week."

Both men nod, then Eason tilts his head at Roger. "Then I guess its good Becca Sue and Magnus leave tomorrow. Nice of you to throw them a going-away party before you tear her house apart." He tilts his head back a little further. "Just why *are* you throwing a party for them?"

"Oh, well, why not?" After a shrug and small smile, he walks away from the table. The men watch him walk through the room speaking to someone at virtually every table to the door.

Patrick squints as he takes another drink. "So, did ya hear Worth's daughter is screwing the hillbilly's father?"

A moment of disgust crosses Eason's face, but with a sigh, his face falls. "Yes. Yes, we did." He picks at the tablecloth as if there are crumbs to be picked up, then he takes a deep breath and brushes the imaginary crumbs off his hands. "Wicked business for our little neighborhood."

"Esme says the wife doesn't seem to mind, but once again, my little woman makes it clear she believes some bloodshed is in order. Think they'll all be at the party tonight?"

Eason sighs. "Yes. I do believe so. Should be interesting. Ah, well, Ruth asked me to pick up some things at the market on my way home. Hopefully the rain will stop by this evening for the party. Might be tight quarters if we can't spill outside onto the pool area." He stands and puts on his windbreaker jacket.

With a wave to the waitress, Patrick orders another Irish coffee. Staring at the rain-washed window beside him, he grins. "Maybe this Helen would like a little Irish action herself. The hillbilly has to be getting tiresome, *and* he's on his way back to the woods."

"Worse idea ever, catering this party when we're trying to open the restaurant this weekend," Sam says as he slides a plastic wrapped tray into the rack of similar trays. Some empty, some also full, and wrapped in plastic. Bright lights fill the kitchen, and the dark skies outside make it look like night. Music on the intercom system fills the house, now fully a restaurant, with country music. With the last tray in place, Sam puts one empty hand on his hip and waves the other in the air. "And this noise is driving me crazy. It's awful."

Carlos closes the oven he was looking into and grins. "It's actually kinda growing on me. 'Course it helps when ya got a blonde in your arms teaching you about it. She loves her some country music, so I told her I'd try getting used to it. That's her CD in the system."

Sam squints at Carlos. "You've kinda fallen for this one, haven't you? Your mother will kill me, and then kill you, if you fall for a girl down here and don't come home."

Carlos throws the oven mitt down and then leans against the dark granite counter. "I'm really feeling this place, too. It's not just Ashleigh either. The heat, the slow pace, the water everywhere—" He looks out the window. "Okay, maybe this is a bit more water than necessary, but the lakes and beach and marshes."

Sam shakes his head. "Okay, so your mother *will* kill you, after she kills me. But I know what you're saying about liking it here." He pauses, listens for a minute to the song about a redneck bonfire. "I'm kinda missing the city, though. The busyness, all the people."

A buzzer sounds, and both turn to the ovens to remove trays of empty crusts. "We'll fill these at the party tonight," Sam says. "Hey, and thanks for helping with all this. Sybil is insane for insisting we cater this. But you know how she is."

"I think you might know her better than I do. What's up

with you two?" Carlos turns to face his friend and watch his expressions.

Sam never blinks or looks away from his work. "She's my boss. That's it. She's just not reasonable making us do this party and the opening tomorrow. It's a mistake, but she's the boss."

Carlos waits for more, but all he sees is a tightening of Sam's jaw. He crosses his arms and tries something else. "So, not the boss causing your mood. Could it be you don't want to see Becca Sue before she leaves?"

Sam continues taking off the crusts and placing them on wire racks, but doesn't answer. Finally he turns and stares at his friend. "Who?"

"Its nerves, that's all. He's just scared about taking such a big step."

"Maybe he'll change his mind, not go. Stay here."

Sybil shakes her head, and her smooth, dark hair moves across her face. She leaves it there and continues to stare at the floor. Dark on a bright day, George's den is like a cave with dim, gray light coming through the skinny openings in the thick, wooden blinds. A small light on the bookshelf offers a bit of brightness, but it's soon swallowed up in the shadows. George looks at the windows and wonders about opening the shutters, but no, it's best to leave the room dark. "Pearl will be home soon."

Sybil coughs a small laugh. "Is that a warning for me to leave, or a hope for you to get out of this conversation?"

"Neither. Though I do wonder why you've come to me. You know Pearl is already suspicious about us."

"Can't say that doesn't help me. If she were less worried about me and you, she might figure things out."

"Plus, you love yanking her chain."

Sybil pulls her hair behind her right ear and looks up smiling. "And there is that. You really love her, don't you?"

George moves his wheelchair to sit beside the window and pulls the cord to let more light in. "Yes, and she really loves me. Never thought this kind of thing truly existed. She and I know, know without a doubt, we are better together than apart. We're on the same page." He pauses and drops the cord. "Except I've kept her in the dark too long with all this. No more sharing your secrets with me, friend. This was the last time, and tonight's the last night for you to stay here with us. I thought I could help you out, but it's only become a bigger mess."

Sybil stands and goes to his side. "You're right. I'll pack up now." She bends down and hugs him, but he doesn't lift his arms toward her. She straightens up. "You know, we could've been together, then maybe I wouldn't have messed up with Magnus. I mean, Pearl already suspected." She smiles. George looks to see if she's joking, and when he sees she's not, his face becomes like stone.

"No, you don't understand. Go on and pack now, and close the door when you leave. I need to do some work."

Sybil closes the door behind her and walks out into the living room, which is even more beautiful with streaks of rain falling down the large windows. Far over the marsh, the sky seems brighter, and it shoots a glimmer into every drop rolling down the expanses of glass.

"So you're leaving?" a voice says from the chair in the corner.

Sybil starts. "Oh, Pearl, you're home."

"Yes, I came through the garage, a bit ago. I went to tell George I'm home, but I heard you and him talking. So nice of you to offer to sleep with my husband, just to give ground to my suspicions."

Sybil turns and laughs. "Oh, that was a joke."

Pearl shakes her head. "Let me know if you need any help when you pack. So..." She sighs, shakes her head, and folds her legs up under her in the chair. "I was going to ask where you'll stay now, but then I realized I don't care." She lays her head back on the chair and watches the rain. "Looks like the sky is clearing inland. Maybe the rain is moving out to sea."

"Yes, I'll go pack, but then need to get to the restaurant to see what's left to do for tonight." She turns and heads down the hall, but she's only gone a few steps when she's called back into the living room.

"Yes?"

Pearl leans forward, elbows on her knees and fingertips together. "George is right. We do love each other."

"Good. Is that all?"

Pearl sighs again and closes her eyes. "Yes."

Maggie knocks on Cab's door. "Can I come in?"

"Yeah."

She closes the door and sits in his computer chair. Cab is lying on his bed. "Whatcha doing?"

"Just thinking. I need to pack. You packed?"

She shakes her head. "How are we getting home?"

Cab holds his phone up and looks at it. "Uncle J says he's sending a car for us tomorrow. We'll get home in time for the rehearsal dinner. He says Cecelia has your dresses ready for the rehearsal and for the wedding."

"I don't want to go home," she whispers.

"You don't have a choice. There's the wedding, and Becca Sue's leaving tomorrow."

Maggie pushes herself around in his chair to face his open laptop. "What's all this?"

Cab sits up. "Farm stuff. I'm going to find out about our farm when we get home. My friends here know more about what we do and own than I do."

"Grandmother will be pissed."

Cab looks up from his phone, and his grin grows wide.

"Yeah, I'm sure she will."

"Where's Mother? She still in China?"

Her brother's grin fades. "Guess so. You miss her, don't you?"

Maggie shrugs. "Not when I have Becca Sue, but going home feels, well, I don't know."

"Yeah, I know. I don't want to live with Audrey since Dad's not there. Do you?"

"No, but the baby *is* our little brother."

"I don't care. I'm going to live at the farm with Grandfather. You and me will be good there. I won't let Grandmother bother you too much."

Her voice is even more of a whisper. "You don't want to go up north with the Worths?"

"Naw. Thought I did, but those girls are weird. It got kinda creepy being around them. Plus, they all look alike." He stretches back out on the bed. "Honestly, Mags, I can't wait to get back home, get on a four wheeler, and go all over our land, like the guys here do. And not just for fun, you know?"

Maggie nods. "Guess I should go pack." At the door, she leans her forehead against the door jamb and looks at him. "The summer's been all right, hasn't it?"

Cab laughs. "Yeah, you're not the one that went to jail."

Tears spring to his sister's eyes, and he sits up on the bed. "I'm sorry, Mags. That's over. Won't happen anymore, okay? I, uh..." His eyes get shiny, but he keeps eye contact with her. "I want to be a good big brother to you, okay?"

She smiles. "I'd like that," she says and then turns to leave his room.

"This is the plan for the new house, drawing of it on the other side. I know the plan doesn't make a lot of sense to you, but look at the picture." Roger hands the paper to her. "What do you think?"

Becca Sue looks at the picture, then looks up at the palm tree leaning over the land right where it meets the water. "Rain's stopped."

She pulls open the door of Roger's jeep and steps out. Thick brush prevents much walking, but she moves around the edge, her tennis shoes quickly drenched from the water on the grass and the drops rolling down from every branch, twig, and leaf. Shafts of sun push through the lavender clouds and wake up the bugs hidden from the constant rain. Sound rises with the steam from the wet ground and then as the sun light falls just right, it ignites every drop. Like twinkle lights at Christmas, the thicket surrounding her comes to life. Becca Sue takes a deep breath and wonders, "This smells nothing like Georgia. It smells, it smells like..."

She turns around to see Roger standing beside his car, and she makes her way back to him. "Real nice, but no. This is done. Time to move on. We're having a party and everything."

In the car she looks out at the woods and the lone palm tree stretching high against the rapidly bluing sky. Then she snaps her eyes closed. *No, Magnus is my future. My only future.*

50

"**B**e honest, sugar," Faye says as she puts another layer of mascara on her false lashes. "You're not just running off with this Llord fella to get away from me and your daddy, are ya?"

Becca Sue lowers the toilet lid and sits down. "No, Momma." She smooths out the skirt of her dress. With a soft background of dusty pink and stripes of blue, green, and yellow, it's fresh and young. Another dress from Ashleigh's college closet. She catches a glimpse of herself with her thick braid and simple dress and smiles. She looks just like one of those people in the downtown ice cream parlor that she used to be so scared of.

"'Cause we've 'bout had our fill of this place. We're ready to head back to Piney. Diner opens back up on Monday, and I've decided I'm ready to get back to work. Plus, the new owner is quite a looker, if you know what I mean." She winks in the mirror at her daughter. "Your daddy says he talked to you some about how it is with us. You know that's not how it is for most people, right? I mean, me and him have tried and tried to not cheat, but we just can't do it." She stands up and looks in the mirror, adjusting the little cleavage she has to be on as much display as possible. "'Course, doesn't help that everyone knows about us and expects us to, well, be available."

She turns around to look at Becca Sue. "Sugar, I thought being here where people don't know us might help, but you can see it didn't. Your daddy, well, he's just who he's always been. Most people are like that. What they are is what they are."

Becca Sue picks up a lipstick case lying on the counter. "Like me. I'm a mess and always have been. Just been lucky to find some men who'll put up with me."

Faye bursts out laughing. "What?! You, a mess? No, honey. Your mess is the men you keep picking."

Becca Sue's mouth twists into a frown. Then she jumps up from her perch and pushes past her mother into the bedroom, still clutching the lipstick in her fist. "But you always said Caleb was such a catch and we didn't belong together."

"Exactly. He was a catch. He was rich. *And* you didn't belong together." Faye stands in the bathroom door.

"But we didn't belong together because of me. I was the problem, right?"

"Of course."

Becca Sue relaxes her shoulders. "See, my fault."

"'Cause you couldn't see. Always been your main fault. You trust people. You don't trust yourself. You think everyone is as straight shooting as me and your daddy. We didn't always talk honest with each other. Lord, you remember all the sneaking and fighting and..." Faye stares at her daughter who stands wide-eyed, only two feet away from her, shaking her head.

"Really, you don't remember all that? Guess you were pretty young. A lot of that fighting took place when you were living with your grandmother." Faye steps to Becca Sue and gently leads her back into the bathroom. She stands her in the light from the mirror, then takes the lipstick from her daughter's sweaty palm. "Open your lips a bit. You know, like when you were little." She begins dabbing the thick pink onto Becca Sue's bottom lip. "This was easier when you weren't so much taller than me, wasn't it?"

"Yeah, here, let me bend down some."

"Better. Susan, I never wanted you to be like me, and I never thought you would be. First of all, you never were that cute, more like your daddy's side. Being cute can be a real curse.

But never mind all that. There's reasons me and your daddy are like we are, and we stopped fighting it and fighting each other a long time ago. And you seemed to be doing okay until you got mixed up with Caleb and all. Law, you pretty near worshipped that bum."

"Momma, he wasn't no bum. He loved me. He..."

"I know, he loved you and you loved him. But he sure found lots of other girls to love while you were still loving him, didn't he? And he didn't want *you* having his babies, did he?"

In the mirror, their eyes meet. "How did you know?"

"Honey, everybody knew. You could've known, too, if you'd wanted to."

Becca Sue's eyes fill with quick tears, but with a deep breath and fast blinking, they disappear. "Well, see Magnus wants to have a baby, lots of babies, with me, so that's good."

"Rub your lips together. There." Faye puts the cap on the tube of lipstick and sits it on the counter. "That's a good color on you. You're looking good, baby girl."

Becca Sue closes her eyes while still facing the mirror and says, "Magnus is good for me. We'll be happy. I think we'll be happy."

"Honey, being happy has never been your problem. You're happy with whatever scraps get left for you. What if you stopped settling for scraps? What if you decided to shoot the works and do what *you* want? Stop fitting into what other people want from you."

"But I *want* to be with Magnus." She opens her eyes and smiles at her mother. "I really do."

"Why?"

"He, um, he..."

Faye sighs and leaves the bathroom. "Try starting that sentence with 'I.' But I don't think it will get any easier to answer me." She opens the bedroom door at the same time someone knocks on it. "Speak of the devil. Hey there."

Magnus scoots in the door as Faye leaves, and he closes the door behind him. "Well, hello, gorgeous. You getting dressed soon? Folks are showing up out there."

"Oh, I am dressed." Becca Sue looks down at the patterned sundress with the full skirt, then points at his dark brown slacks, collared shirt, and beige jacket. "You look great."

"And since you'll be on my arm for our going away party, maybe we should match better."

"You're right, I guess, but what?" She opens her closet as he sits on the bed.

He says, "That green dress I bought you at the salon."

"Oh no, that's too fancy, and too..." She lifts her eyebrows at him and grins. "And too revealing."

"Exactly. Show everyone just what I'm taking off their hands. Make every man here jealous." He stands up and pushes her up against the closet door. "You've not been around all week. I couldn't keep my mind off you." He pushes one of the straps off her shoulder and kisses her while he fumbles with her strapless bra. "A bra? I liked you better before you got all caught up in wearing these things. But I know you've got to wear them with the fancy dresses. There, that's better." The dress slides down, and Becca Sue pushes into him, wanting to push everything her mother had said away, but a knock at the door and the door starting to open makes them pull apart and her dart into the walk-in closet.

"Becca Sue?"

"She's getting changed, Ashleigh. We'll be right out."

"Okay, I was just looking for her." Ashleigh waits a moment, but when her friend doesn't appear, or say anything, she slowly closes the bedroom door. Magnus turns back toward the closet and takes a step in.

Becca Sue is arranging the tight green dress as he steps up behind her. "So, where were we?"

"I was getting dressed. You sure this isn't too fancy?"

Magnus grins. "Who cares? It's what I've been dreaming of seeing you in all week. My girl, in the dress I bought her." He sidles up behind her, and his hands examine the dress and all the curves it wraps tight. Into her neck he whispers, "And at some point we can sneak away from the party and come in here for a little party all our own. Finish what we started. You make me feel like I'm on fire."

"Okay, you go on out. I need to change my lipstick." She slaps at his hands and pushes him ahead of her, then toward the bedroom door while she goes into the bathroom.

In the mirror, Becca Sue rubs off the pink lipstick. Subtle and dusky, it doesn't go with the shiny satin and beads of the green dress. "This braid doesn't go with this dress either, but it's too late to change it." She looks through her mother's make up scattered all over the counter for a brighter color. Putting on the orangey-red, she hears her mother's question in her head, "Why?"

She rubs her lips together and stands straight. "I want to be with Magnus because I... well, I can't think *now* with people here and all." She turns off the bathroom light. "I need to get to the party."

51

I knew it. Knew this dress wasn't right. Too late now.
"Well, here you are waiting right outside my bedroom door,"
I whisper to Magnus.

He grins, looks at my overly exposed breasts, and winks. "I
can't help what people think we were doing in there. You look
magnificent." His arm around my waist is too tight, so I pull
away to step into the kitchen.

"Oops, sorry." I'm almost run over by a guy carrying a tray,
but I'm not only sorry for that. This is not a good place to be.
The four waiters here have no shame at all about staring at
my boobs. At least in the living room half the people, women
mainly, will pretend they don't notice.

"Now *that's* a dress," Sam says as Carlos whistles.

"Just want to get some water," I say and jerk open the refrigerator door. Standing in the sudden coolness and brightness, I take a deep breath. Oh, yeah, my refrigerator. I was so
happy to have my own refrigerator. A little ripple of sadness
runs through my stomach, so with another deep breath, a big
smile, and a bottle of water in hand, I let the door close.

Sam is standing behind the door, and our eyes meet when
there's nothing blocking us.

"Haven't seen you all week," he says.

"Been busy, with packing and all, but I meant to call you
and say thanks for dinner. Hard to believe that was less than
a week ago."

"Yeah, it is." He shakes his head, and his black curls bounce. It is *so* not fair Sybil gets to be with him. He's just too young, too cute. "Hey, so, you and Sybil are together? Is it serious?"

Now there's no bounce in his hair, or his eyes. They are hard and black. "Why would that matter to you? To anyone?"

"She's just so old, and you have so much, so much life." And I see it in his eyes. That's what he thinks about me and Magnus. "No, it's not the same with me. It's just not."

He leans close to me, and his lips are next to mine. I draw in a breath, but I don't move away, and the sound all around us fades as my eyes start to close.

"Are you really that stupid?"

My eyes flutter and I step back. He also steps back and turns back to work.

Stupid? What's he think I'm stupid about? Magnus? Sybil? Him kissing me?

"Hon, come on." Magnus places both hands on my hips and pulls me out of the kitchen. I wish I knew if Sam was watching, but I couldn't make myself look up as I turned and followed Magnus.

"Sure, just wanted a drink of water." When I do look up Momma is standing in front of me, staring right into my chest. "Momma, you having fun?"

"You changed dresses."

"Yeah, we thought this one was better for a party."

"We?" Momma has a bottle of beer that she lifts high to take a swallow.

Magnus grins, not a happy grin, but a let-me-explain-things grin. "Doesn't your daughter look lovely?"

"D'ya buy that dress?"

He tilts his head, and bows just enough to hide the tightness of his mouth.

"Thought so. Guess I better get some of that shrimp before it runs out." As she passes me, she looks down at the dress, then back at me. "Scraps."

Magnus leans in. "What did she say?"

"Nothing." I step out of Magnus' crooked arm, and through

the people near the couch and chair, I see my neighbors standing beside the back doors. Pearl and Ruth and their husbands stand, well, George is sitting, with little plates of food and glasses of wine.

I speak up before I get to them. "Remember that first morning when y'all were banging on this door, demanding to be let in to your clubhouse?" They open up their little circle to give me entrance.

Pearl clears her throat. "And you looked lost. Wearing that skimpy dress and trying to keep us from seeing there was nothing on underneath it."

"You could tell I was naked?"

"We couldn't see anything," Eason explains. "It was just the way you were holding it that made it obvious what was going on."

"Guess y'all will get your club house now."

Ruth points toward the dining room. "Did you see the plans? Up on the tripods there."

I look behind me and shake my head. My throat is dry and thick.

Mrs. Bell comes into the circle and stands next to George. "Screw the clubhouse, Becca Sue. If you'll stay, we don't care about a clubhouse."

George shakes his head. "Speak for yourself. Becca Sue, has Magnus shown you any pictures of your new home? Or guess I should say homes."

"Not really, I've been real busy this week, with my folks here and all." I motion behind me with my head, and then I notice everyone is looking behind me. Daddy is in the corner with Momma, and they are making out like a couple teenagers. Magnus catches my eye and winks at me while nodding at them.

"They're going home real soon," I say. I grab a glass of wine from the waiter walking by. Don't know who he was taking it to, but when a young guy like that gets boobs like mine stuck in his face, he goes with the flow.

Mrs. Bell, eyes never leaving the show in the corner, says,

"Your father and I had some very interesting talks this week. He's quite the philosopher, isn't he?"

Ruth, Pearl, and I all now stare at her like we were staring at my folks. "What?"

Mrs. Bell laughs her tiny, rich older lady laugh. "Oh, he is very country, but he has some interesting ideas..." She pauses, but not long enough for me to interrupt. "About sex."

Eason takes a deep breath, and his eyes go clear and wide. "Oh, my, well, Mrs. Bell, are you looking forward to the market this week?"

"Isn't that interesting? Rick said that the subject would immediately be changed if I brought up our talks. See how smart he is?" Her giggle sounds like a little girl's, and makes us all even more uncomfortable. Pearl downs her glass of wine and sighs.

Sybil joins us. "Lovely party, Becca Sue. Hope the food is satisfactory."

Her sheath dress is all black, the front is high, but the back is low cut. She's as tall as I am so our eyes meet, but all I can think about is her with Sam. "I've not had any, but I'm sure it's great. Sam is a..." My mouth is dry again.

"Sam is a what?" He speaks up behind me, and all I can do is shrug. Sam steps in front of Sybil. "Try these caprese bites. They'll be on Sybil's menu this weekend."

I shake my head, and don't look up when the tray comes to me.

George puts one into his mouth, then clears his throat. "Delicious, ah, just who we were missing. Magnus, have you tried Sam's caprese bites?"

"Yes, you must," Sybil purrs, and a gasp from Ruth and Mrs. Bell makes me look up. Sybil is putting one of the red, green, and white bites into Magnus's mouth, and her other hand is wrapped around his upper arm.

Now my mouth feels like red clay in a Georgia August—dry, cracked, and hard. Magnus closes his lips on her fingers, and then licks his lips. Oh, so that's where all the moisture in my body has gone to, his shiny lips.

Sam abruptly turns and heads to the kitchen.

Sybil moves away from Magnus and lets her hair fall across her face. When she pulls it back, she's looking at me. "I'm getting a drink. Can I get anything for anyone?" She looks around the group and dares anyone to say anything. She walks away, and Magnus steps closer to me. Eason and George are both looking at the ground, but Pearl and Ruth stare at me. And I don't disappoint.

I lean over and kiss Magnus' lips and move to put my breasts where he can't ignore them.

Nope, this isn't my first rodeo. Ya wanna ride the stallion, you gotta figure other riders are in line.

52

"**A**re you out of your mind? He is feeling Sybil up right in front of you." Ashleigh finally corrals her friend, and forces Becca Sue into her own bedroom after trying for the past hour. She's yelling, but in a whisper.

"So, stuff happens. He's leaving with *me* tomorrow. What do I care about tonight?"

"She's making a laughingstock out of you!"

"Haven't you noticed? Everybody's been laughing at me since I moved to Florida."

"Sam is in the kitchen ready to kill Magnus. Carlos, too. They aren't laughing at all."

"Oh, well, then let me put them out of their misery," More than a little wine, and the two shots of lemon vodka Patrick talked her into, give Becca Sue a head of steam as she storms out of the bedroom. Marching into the kitchen, she ignores Mrs. Bell's hand on her arm, and with a bit of a head shake warns off her Daddy bearing down on her.

Magnus grins from across the room where he stands with Roger. He only shrugs as his lips curl higher. He knows he has nothing to worry about.

"Sam. Carlos." The men look up from the counter. Another waiter leaves the kitchen in a trot, just as Rick steps in the door opposite his daughter.

Becca Sue puts her hands on her hips and stands tall. "Ashleigh is afraid y'all might try to step in and save my honor or something stupid like that. Magnus chose me, not Sybil, to go with him tomorrow. She can flirt all she wants, but it's all just a game."

Carlos shakes his head at her, then his eyes and quick shrug at Ashleigh says, "See what having sex does to people?"

Behind Becca Sue, Pearl speaks up, "A game Sybil is winning, Becca Sue." The older woman takes another swallow of wine, and as Becca Sue turns around, Pearl wobbles a bit. She leans against the doorway. "Becca Sue, she's been at Magnus' every afternoon this week, and they're not playing badminton. She's a witch. She even said today she wanted to sleep with George to throw us off her and Magnus' track." Tears fill Pearl's eyes and her speech. Ruth puts an arm around her.

Everything is quiet as George fights to maneuver his chair through the crowd. "Pearl, let's go home. I'll explain everything."

"But look at her," Pearl has turned at her husband's voice, and she falls back against the other side of the door opening. She stares at Sybil through tears, and her voice raises, "I let her stay in my house, and she's not ashamed at all. She slept with my husband in the past, she's slept with Magnus in the past, and now, and she's even sleeping with that poor boy in the kitchen." She looks up at Ruth, and her voice drops. "Has she slept with Eason?" Then she looks at Esme, speaking louder so Esme can hear her across the room, "And, Esme, she's not slept with Patrick because I was there when she told him no. Poor Patrick."

"Hey, don't bring me into this!" Patrick pulls his arm off the couch from behind Helen, as Helen slides a pillow from the couch between them.

"Patrick, remember coming to our house and trying to get me to leave you alone with her? But she told me not to. She said she'd made it very clear she wasn't interested." Pearl's eyes fill and tears run down her face. "And I listened to her because I thought she was my friend and I was protecting her."

Sybil rolls her eyes and shrugs at Patrick. He pushes up off the couch and goes to stand beside Esme. Mrs. Bell looks around Becca Sue, and asks loudly, "Which boy in the kitchen?"

Carlos and two of the waiters raise their palms and say, "Not me," staring daggers at Sam.

Sam explodes. "Me?! For God's sake, I'm not sleeping with her!" He pushes past Rick and the others in the hallway and enters the living room in full stride, headed for Sybil. "Tell them. Tell them I'm not sleeping with you."

Magnus grabs Sam's arm. "Watch it, boy. Go on back out to the kitchen and leave her alone. She's helped you and your little career enough; she's done playing with you."

Instead of pulling away from Magnus' grasp, Sam pushes into it, and his face is inches away as he spits, "Oh, and are you already through playing with *your* little toy? Rebecca ought to get a signed statement that you won't leave her up in New York when you're done playing with her. How soon will the Southern accent get old?"

"You son of –" Magnus yells and takes a swing at Sam. "You snot-nosed kid, you just want her, and you can't have her."

"But old man, you can have her *and* my mother?" Sam yells as he ducks and then pushes Magnus with both hands.

Magnus falls back onto the arm of the couch and holds up both hands. "Your mother?"

Eason's voice is incredulous. "Sybil's your mother?"

George groans, and Sybil steps forward to lay her hand on her son's arm. She pulls Sam's face towards hers with her other hand and then looks at Magnus. "Sam, meet your father."

53

"What are you doing?" Ashleigh asks as she walks into my bedroom.

"Packing. If I wait until tomorrow to see what Magnus wants to do, it'll be too late."

She sits on the bottom of my bed. "You'd still go with him?"

There's a crush in my chest, like someone squeezing the air out of me. It hurts. I stop folding clothes for a second and work to take a deep breath. "If he still wants me."

"Why?" she says, and I have to look up to make sure it's her and not Momma asking.

I still haven't figured that out, even though all I've done is think since Sam flew out of the house an hour ago and everyone realized we should've figured this out from the beginning. Sybil still oversaw the clean-up in the kitchen, while Magnus left with George. Ruth and Eason half-carried Pearl to the car. Now Cab and Maggie and the whole Worth clan are outside in the lanai talking with my parents. Candles lit in the living room were still burning when I moved into my bedroom.

Ashleigh grabs the tail of the shirt I'm folding and tugs on it. "Look at me. What do you want?"

"To be wanted." I pull the shirt out of her grasp and lay it in the suitcase.

She stands up and walks behind me to the door. She turns before she leaves. "That's not enough, you know? To just be wanted. It's nice, but it's not enough."

I wait until she's gone. Until the back door opens and closes and the house is empty again, then I let the tightness in my
chest have its way and I gasp for a breath. Then another. By
time I find a third breath I'm lying across my bed sobbing.

The exertion from crying like that should've made me fall
asleep. At least that was my plan. Wake up to a new day. Let
Magnus make his decision on what to do while I was out of it
all. Between the crying, the wine, the vodka, the busy week -
shouldn't I be asleep by now? But no.

I struggle up from the bed and into the bathroom, where
the harsh light makes things look way worse than they really
do. The green dress was awful before, but now it's creased and
has dark splotches all down the front. My hair is half out of
the braid and frizzed everywhere. My lips are huge and orangey-red like a clown, not to mention the mascara all over
my cheeks and around my eyes. One boob is out of the dress,
and I'm hoping that just happened crawling off the bed. But if
someone told me I'd walked around half the night at the party
like that, I wouldn't be surprised. The grip around my chest
has moved to my head, and my brain is trying to escape by
jumping out my eyes.

"Becca Sue?"

Of course I hadn't closed the bathroom door, so when my
bedroom door creeps open, my full glory is on display.

"Oh sorry," Jameson says as he pulls the door back.

"Give me a minute." I pull on the blue silk robe and walk
out to open the door again. "What are you doing here?"

His eyes are wide, and he blinks several times, taking in all
my loveliness. "I came to pick up the kids. Things were a mess
in Piney, so I thought I'd just head on down here tonight. Who
are all those people out at the pool? Is that your mother and
father talking to Roger and Kathleen Worth?"

His eyes are bugged out. I've never seen Jameson Mason
looks so confused. I laugh. And laugh more. And more, until I
have to sit down on the bed. Jameson closes the door behind
him as he starts laughing, too, and I point him to the pile of
clothes in the corner where a chair is hiding. At least there was

one there when my parents arrived. He unpiles the chair and sits down, now laughing as hard as I am. It takes a few minutes for us to settle down.

"Tonight was your going away party wasn't it? What happened?"

"Oh, I don't know. A lot. It was kind of a disaster."

He points to the suitcase. "You're still going tomorrow?"

I shrug. "Don't know. Did you see the kids?"

He nods. "They're in the pool. I just peeked back there and no one saw me."

Then it gets real awkward, and we both just sit and looked around the room. He finally says, "So, you never said if you liked the furniture."

"Oh, I didn't? Sorry, yeah, it was real nice of your mother to send all that. Real nice."

"I meant this, your bedroom furniture."

"This? Well, figured it was an accident since it's so not your mother's taste, but it's wonderful. I love it."

"Uncle J?" Maggie says from the doorway.

"Hey Mags, come give me a hug."

She scampers into the room, wrapped in a bright blue towel. "I didn't know you were coming to pick us up."

As Cab comes into the room, I get up. "Okay, before everyone is in here. We should go out there. Let me change real quick."

Maggie gets up and pulls her uncle up by both of his hands. "They said we had to get out of the pool since the adults are all going out."

That gets my attention. "Where are they all going?"

She shrugs as she and Jameson pass me. "Down under something."

"Oh, Lord, I better hurry. Tell them to wait on me," I yell as I dash into the bathroom.

54

"Kinda reminds me of the Dew Drop Inn," Jameson says as he pulls a barstool up beside Becca Sue.

"You ain't ever been in the Dew Drop Inn."

"Oh, sure I have. Caleb dragged me in there several times."

Becca Sue's eyes hold tears that reflect the neon signs from behind the bar. "Caleb didn't have no business being there. At least you were single."

"True, true, but you know nothing stopped Caleb from having what he wanted."

"I don't want to talk about this. Bet you never saw a table full of people like that one behind us in the Dew Drop." They both turn to see the group better.

"Never. But what's the deal with everyone knowing Helen Worth? She walked in here like she owns the place."

Becca Sue closes her eyes and takes a drink of her Diet Coke. "She and my folks partied rather hard here the other night."

"Cab said something to me about her hooking up with your father?"

"Yeah. It's been a busy week."

Helen was sitting on her husband's lap, and the way his hand was moving up her leg caught Becca Sue and Jameson's eyes at the same time. They turned back to face the bar, grinning.

"Can I get a bourbon? What about you two?" Roger asks

from the corner of the bar, where he leans after walking up.

Jameson slaps the bar. "Sure, I'll join you in a bourbon. Becca Sue?"

She shakes her head and points to her glass of Diet Coke. "I'm good."

Roger walks with both glasses down to the end of the bar where they are seated and sits on the stool on the other side of Becca Sue. He raises his glass toward Jameson. "To Becca Sue."

Jameson agrees, clinks glasses with the man, and takes a big swallow.

"Why? What did I do?" She pushes up the sleeves of her long black T-shirt. She'd scrubbed her face, pulled back her frizzed hair into a low ponytail, and taken off her bra. She had on an old pair of jeans and flip flops. No worries of upsetting either man she'd spent the last weeks worried about; they had bigger things to think about than her tonight.

 Roger tips his head to stare at her. "Remember when I came to you and we had lunch talking about Backwater? About small towns and how things didn't always have to turn out bad? That getting to know all kinds of people can really be something good, and that was what I had in mind for our little town?"

She chews the inside of her mouth. She'd let him down. She'd let everyone down. "Hey, can I have a bourbon?" She yells to the bartender at the other end. He nods and brings her a glass. After a big gulp she nods, then adds, "Yes, yes I do. Sorry I couldn't make all that come true. I know you counted on me and I let you, I let everybody down."

Roger stops his glass halfway to his mouth. "What?" He sets his drink down and pulls on Becca Sue's shoulder to turn her around to face the room of people. "Look. Just look."

Her eyes immediately go to see how far Helen's husband's hand has gotten and she sees both his hands in sight, his wife still on his lap—smiling. Kathleen Worth is talking to a man setting up a karaoke machine. Her white blazer has the sleeves pulled up, and she's lost the gold belt that held her silk dress tight to her waist. The dress is billowing in the breeze from the ceiling fan, and from somewhere in her car she'd found a pair of old boat shoes to replace the high heels she'd had on at the party. Her mother behind the bar talking to a woman in the kitchen through the filthy pass window and her daddy, well, he's nowhere to be seen, but then neither is the big blonde waitress. Speaking of blonde hair, when did Carlos get here? He has a head of blonde hair cornered in a back booth that Becca Sue hopes is Ashleigh.

"And this is just the folks with us! Pearl got drunk, Magnus was speechless and almost came to blows with his own son, whom he knew nothing about, and Sybil showed you just who you were about to run away with. Or maybe you're still planning on running away with him. But, honestly, hope you're not that stupid."

Becca Sue leans back on the bar. "What do I have to do with any of this?"

Jameson heaves an exasperated breath and turns back to his drink.

"What?" Becca Sue leans back to try and look in his face, but he turns away from her and scoots down a couple bar stools while lifting up his empty glass for a refill.

"I don't know what his problem is," she says to Roger Worth.

"I do. It's that you don't see that this is all your fault. Your wonderful fault. You wander through life collecting people, attracting people to you. They interact with each other and change things. Cab can't wait to get back home and pick up farming. That's all because of you. You don't judge people, or put boundaries on them, or even expectations." Roger grins. "Now that one tends to get you in some trouble on the man front, but you allow people to be who they really are, and that's a gift."

She spends a few moments looking around her. The smell of marshland mixed with old beer took a bit of getting used to, but now she finds herself breathing deep. "Can I ask you something?"

"Sure," Roger says.

"Why do you think I want to be with Magnus?"

"I'm sure I don't know."

"I was afraid of that."

"But I do know why Magnus wants to be with you."

She turns all the way around on her stool, leans on the counter towards him, and asks, "Why?"

"You make him happy."

"Well, that's good, isn't it?"

"I guess, as long as you don't ever expect him to worry about *you* being happy."

She shrugs. "But he might..." She stops as Roger shakes his head.

"Nope. Not his nature and not the way you have things set up with him."

From two stools away Jameson asks loudly, "Doesn't that sound familiar? Like with my brother?" He stands up and asks the bartender. "Where's the bathroom?"

"Out the front door and to the right. Women's to the left."

"For God's sake, outdoor bathrooms. God love Florida," Jameson says as he lumbers toward the front door.

Rick nods at his daughter from across the room as he follows Jameson. "I'll follow him and make sure he's okay."

Roger pushes away from the bar. "Guess I better go help my wife pick out a song to sing, or we'll be here all night. She always ends up singing something by ABBA. Probably won't go over too well in a place like this."

Becca Sue puts her elbows on the bar and her chin in her hands, then stares in the mirror at the people behind her. They are only wavy figures, so she closes her eyes and breathes deep. After a few minutes she turns around, leaves her half-full bourbon and takes her Diet Coke with her across the room. She slides into the booth across from Ashleigh and Carlos, who are still sitting close, but only talking. "Okay, so what's Sam been doing since y'all left the party at my place?"

"A lot of yelling," Carlos admits.

Ashleigh shakes her head. "How did we not see how much

they are alike?"

"Who? Sam and Sybil or Sam and Magnus?"

Carlos and Ashleigh answer together. "Both."

Carlos adds, "He looks so much like her, but it never crossed my mind. He told me his mother lived overseas and never mentioned her. He said she wouldn't tell him about his father, so he had left her and didn't speak to her. My mother asked about his mother, but he told her the same story. And some of it was kind of true. Tonight he explained that when she came back to New York, he borrowed a bunch of money from her for chef school, but it didn't work out, and he couldn't pay her back. She hired him to work in her restaurants, and he developed a name as a developer. She pays him really great, too. He said he'd only work for her if she told no one that she's his mother."

"And to find out like that that Magnus is his father." Ashleigh wrinkles her nose at Becca Sue. "And apparently it's true she's been, uh, with Magnus this week. Sam knew, and it was driving him crazy that his rival, which is how he saw Magnus, was sleeping with his mother. Yuck. Did that sound as awful as it felt?"

Becca Sue nods. "Sam has a lot to figure out." She lets her statement hang in mid-air as the other two stare at her.

Finally Carlos can't help it. "And you? Don't you have some things to figure out?"

She takes a deep breath and then a long draw on her straw. "You two have no idea how bad I want this to not have happened. To still be leaving with Magnus tomorrow. Everything in me wants that to still be my plan."

Ashleigh shakes her head, and her voice is hard. "But it's not. And you know that it's not. And you know it's good that it's not. Grow up."

"Hey, don't be so hard on her," Carlos urges.

Ashleigh's voice is no longer only hard, it's loud. "I've not been hard on her because I wanted her to figure things out on her own. Backwater needs you. I need you. Mrs. Bell needs you. Maggie and Cab need you. Stay here and grow up. Let's go." She scoots out, pulling Carlos by the hand behind her.

Everyone is staring at their booth, and as Ashleigh and Carlos leave, they all focus on Becca Sue. She slides out of the booth and stands up. "Think I'll go get a breath of fresh air."

She takes her time getting to the door, and when she steps out into the warm night air she sees Carlos' truck heading up the oyster shell driveway.

"They were in a hurry."

"Oh, hi, Daddy." She steps to the bench he's sitting on and sits down. "Forgot you were out here."

"Just seeing to ol' Jameson, but I better get back inside or that waitress will plum forget about me." He stands up, and hands her a flask. "This here's Jameson's, we was a-sharing."

"Daddy, you were supposed to be sobering him up, not giving him more."

"Now, darling, you know better than that." With a wink and tip of a non-existent hat, he opens the door and lets a blast of air conditioning and light out. Then as the door falls shut, the noise and the light both fade.

The smell of the marsh is powerful. She listens to the lapping of water against the big concrete pylons around the bar. Frogs sing and, when they get going, drown out the karaoke music completely. Along with the soft light from a half-lit neon moon, strings of Christmas lights along the roof add a honky-tonk glow to the place.

"Where'd your dad go?" Jameson asks.

"Inside. He left a friend in there waiting."

He sits down. "He did mention her a couple times. I don't need a babysitter, you know. I'm not that drunk. Promise I won't fall into the marsh and drown."

"Naw, it's better out here. Kinda peaceful. Apparently, I've got some figuring out to do. Surprise, surprise, my life is falling apart again. You probably get tired of showing up here in the middle of another god-awful mess. 'Course, that's just my natural state. Well, this time you don't have to worry with coming back here."

"Your daddy was telling me what happened tonight. Sounds

like a real scene."

"It was. Guess I'm not going New York after all."

He shrugs soddenly. "Things change."

"Well, according to what you said in there, I don't change. Magnus is just like your brother, remember?" She smiles and jabs her elbow in his side.

He tips up his flask and takes a long drink. "Just my opinion," he almost whispers in a croaky voice. He stands up and steadies himself a bit by holding onto the railing going up the wheelchair ramp. He tucks his closed flask into his pants pocket. Without looking up, he asks, "Can I tell you something?"

She sits back on the bench and looks up into his face. "Okay."

He pulls his hand from his pocket and looks at her. "Bedroom furniture was from me." He steps up to the door, opens it, and escapes inside.

"Bet it's the first time the Ritz has had to send town cars to the Down Under," Kathleen Worth says as they all exit the bar an hour later.

"Not hardly, dear. From what I hear, the patrons of the Ritz enjoy bar-hopping on the seedy side of the island as a regular habit," Roger says. He counts heads and puts people in two cars.

Becca Sue stands up and steps over to him. "Hope I can get a ride."

"Becca Sue, I didn't realize you were still here! I thought you rode home with Ashleigh and that guy of hers."

She walks past him to the car with her momma, daddy, and Jameson already inside. "Nope, had some thinking to do, and thanks for what you said tonight. I did hear you." She starts to get in the car and then stands back up. "You mentioned one time walking on the beach at sunrise. Do you still do that?"

Roger nods. "Most days, and after a night like tonight, I will need to walk this off. I'll be at the pier at 6:30."

She waves and gets in the front seat of the car.

"Ma'am, don't you want to ride in back?" the driver asks just as a loud snore comes from the back seat.

She laughs. "Don't want to disturb their sleep."

55

"You should've seen it. The market," I say out loud, as I hear steps behind me. I parked my car in the early dawn light, and instead of going into the house, walked to the street where my lot meets the next one.

"Maggie loved it," Jameson responds.

"Are she and Cab up? I guess y'all need to get on the road soon."

"Yeah. So, you been to the beach already?"

I look at him, and he looks down. "Your feet. Sand."

I look down, too. My legs are bare, but shiny with sweat and sand. His legs are tanned, and he's wearing those shoes. Those deck shoes like Caleb always wore. Rich boy shoes. "I saw the sunrise and got to talk with Roger. He has plans to build me a house, more like a cabin really, at the end of the lake. Showed me a picture and the piece of land yesterday. He figures people living out here aren't as into the big mansions."

"You think you'll like a cabin better?"

"I do. And there will still be room for the kids to come. It's simpler, but he knew I'd want the kids to have their own rooms. You know, I am their stepmother."

Jameson folds his arms. "Yeah. They're your family."

I can't help but turn to look at him. "You say that like it's nothing." I shrug. "Like it's, I don't know, nothing new."

He smiles. "It's not to me. You listened too much to Caleb and my mother and your own self. Of course, you are part of their family. An important part."

I nod and look back out at the empty lot next to the soon-to-be Backwater Clubhouse. "And you promise to not let your marriage to the new governor distract you from the kids? They'll need an ally against their Grandmother Mason."

"Yeah, well, you know I said things were in a mess in Piney, and that's why I came to pick up the kids?"

I tuck some stray hairs from my braid back in place, my first attempt, and it's not staying in place well, and then turn to look at him. With the sun to my back, he is in my shadow, and he's twiddling with his thumbs. "What is it?"

"I broke off the wedding."

"Oh, no! But you and Cecelia had everything planned. Oh, wow, I bet her daddy is pissed."

He rocks on his heels. "Oh, yes he is. Georgia is not a friendly state for me at this time."

"Not to mention your mother."

He grimaces. "Not to mention my mother."

"Have you told the kids?"

"No, we still have to head back since school starts Monday, but I was going to take them to the beach for the night, so I'll tell them when we leave here. That way it's just the three of us."

He turns to face away from the intense sun, and we start walking down the sidewalk.

"So why'd you break it off?"

"Somebody asked me this summer if I ever planned on standing up to my mother."

"Oh," I chuckle. "I believe I remember that conversation."

"Five hours driving home gave me plenty of time to think about that, and so I tried something you told me one time that your grandmother did when making decisions. I tried living as if my mother had no sway on me. Don't tell anyone, but I pretended she'd been in the car crash with Caleb." He makes a scared face and we laugh. "But I knew my career in Atlanta is her choice, not mine. And being with Cecelia was my decision at first, but it's not been my choice for the last year. We both knew it, but we are both too scared of our families. So finally this week, we got the nerve to make the decision to call it all off, and as you can imagine it's a mess. Since she's kind of stuck in Atlanta, with her dad the governor and her running for it next year, I took the blame. I'll be back in Piney for a while."

"Well, the kids will like that. You can help Cab work around his grandmother. And don't worry, you're still one of the golden Mason boys that Piney loves to worship. But sorry to hear things are such a mess for you."

"So, sounds like you're not going to New York."

"Naw, I wrote Magnus a letter and left it for him last night. Told him to give my ticket to Sam. Maybe they can get to know each other."

"So, you'll be here tomorrow when we come to see the market?"

We reach the back gate, and I place my hands on it. "Yeah, I'll be here. There are some good people that think I have something to do here. I'm going to try listening to them for a while. Going to think about, well, about things. Somehow I crossed the state line, but brought my Piney thinking with me."

The sun lifts over the house and floods the lake with sparkles. I take a deep breath and breathe in the air that smells like Florida. Like Backwater, Florida. Like home.

Jameson pushes open the gate and holds it for me. "Can the kids and I take you and your folks out for breakfast?"

My feet stop and my brain spins—*Masons and Cousins, this is not a good idea. What does Jameson want? Hopefully it won't be somewhere fancy. What does Jameson want? Momma and Daddy will want to go where they can smoke. What does Jameson want? What could he possibly want from me?* I shake my head and close my eyes. Piney thinking. Piney thinking.

My head lifts, I look at Jameson, and say, "Yes."

THE END

Hope you enjoyed this first book
in the Florida Book series.
Look for number two in 2018!

CPSIA information can be obtained
at www.ICGtesting.com
Printed in the USA
FFOW03n0854070318
45411598-46111FF